LEAVES IN A RIVER

ALSO BY EARL G. LONG

Consolation
Voices from a Drum

LEAVES IN A RIVER

EARL G. LONG

PEEPAL TREE

First published in 2009
by Peepal Tree Press Ltd
17 King's Avenue
Leeds LS6 1QS
England

ISBN13: 9781845230081

ARTS COUNCIL
ENGLAND   Peepal Tree gratefully acknowledges Arts Council support

PROLOGUE

PROLOGUE

On the third of April nineteen sixty-seven, on the morning of his fifty-eighth birthday, Charlo Pardie rose at two o'clock as usual to go and pee, but instead of returning to his bed, he left his home – and abandoned his wife – to go to the house of a prostitute.

His old Austin truck coughed and shuddered in the cold until the third turn of the key, then began to shake from side to side like a dog wagging itself from sleep. The noise had awakened Lucette and in the rear-view mirror, Charlo saw the front door open. He looked over his shoulder at her dark shape in the doorway, outlined by the dim yellow light from the votive lamp. She started down the steps and he kept his eyes on her as he drove off, pulling the truck hard to the right to avoid a breadfruit tree at the side of the short drive to the road. He heard the sound of her voice, but the noise of the engine smothered the words.

Charlo Pardie drove forty miles that night, wearing a pair of khaki shorts, a once-white cotton-knit shirt, and a pair of brown bedroom slippers whose heels were worn down to the inner lining. He knew that by evening the story would be in the mouths and ears of everyone who knew him. They would repeat it and examine it, and offer it to strangers eager to give opinions and to compare it with other senile calamities. He had made this decision because it was compensation for fifty years of hard work, new pains in his body and the quieting of sounds as death prepared its inevitable ambush. There were other reasons, uncomfortable and irrepressible, clawed things trying to climb out of his belly, but he was afraid to sit down and think of them. The other expected acts of a lifetime – marrying, raising three children, caring for them, giving to the poor and earning the respect of others – had all been done.

The sound of the vehicle on the gravel outside her home awakened Ismene L'Aube. She recognized the beat of the engine and the loud clicking of the parking brake. The green hands on her alarm clock indicated three-forty. Ismene waited for the sound of the truck door closing, then got out of bed, found a box of matches and lit the candle in an etched crystal holder on her dresser top. He was coming toward the door when she opened it, his balding head thrust forward as if he were escaping from the faint moonlight.

"Ismene," he said. His voice was tight with the first words of the day.

"Yes, Charlo," she answered, and moved back to let him in. She did not look past him to see whether other windows had opened to the sounds of his arrival.

"I'm staying."

She nodded, and led him into the bedroom.

She lay on her back in the bed, her hands clasped together painfully. She waited for him to speak. He pinched out the candle flame, savoured the brief pain of the hot wax on his fingertips, then got in beside her.

He could feel the tremble of her body through the mattress, and knew she was waiting for him to speak.

"We'll talk later," he said, and rolled over on his side away from her.

Neither enjoyed even the briefest visit from sleep, and they were grateful when the sun made the room uncomfortably bright. The air was rotten with the sharp sour stink of nervous sweat although their only contact had come when Ismene placed one hand over the crook of Charlo's elbow.

"I have some smoked herring. You want that. . . with cucumber. . . and bread. . . coffee?" Ismene asked as she dressed.

"Yes." Charlo sat on the edge of the bed with his head in his hands, then began laughing softly. "I almost fell on my knees and start praying, but I don't think God wants to hear what I have to say. He's probably too busy listening to my wife anyway. Is her good friend, you know."

Ismene tried not to smile and ended up looking as if she were about to cry. "Well, when you get a chance, pray for both of us."

They sat at the table that was large enough for only four chairs. Charlo, one inch more than six feet, was heavy and so hard-muscled that he appeared to be chiselled from mahogany with his edges left unsmoothed. Age had pulled down on his cheeks and the corners of his mouth until he appeared to be perpetually disappointed with life. He ate quietly while his close-set eyes stared hard at the table as if to look through its surface and into a future buried in the dirt under the house. The left corner of his mouth habitually twitched before he spoke, and each time it did, Ismene leaned forward, hoping he was about to say that he had arranged matters so that she had nothing to fear from his family. He did not speak until he had wiped his plate clean with a piece of bread.

"Let me tell you: I know you don't have men coming around here; what you did in town is your business, not my business," Charlo said. "I don't know what I can give you. I don't know what you want. I don't know what a young woman like you wants. I don't even know what I want from you. I just know I have to feel like a man again. You understand? I have to take care of some-body."

He stared hard at her, into her eyes of different colours, the right golden and the left greyish brown, and at her nose bent to the left, and at her full mouth with the upper lip pushed out slightly by her prominent incisors. Even the C-shaped scar on her left cheek was a gentle mark, keeping one's eyes on her face, and making it easier for strangers to find the first words: "What happened?" And these faults, each not beautiful in itself, together had made her customers linger, and sometimes not take all they had paid for, choosing instead to look at her, not understanding why, and not regretting it.

"Yes," Ismene said. Later, she told him that occasionally, one or two of her old clients had stopped by, only briefly, not recognizing the cold, silent woman who answered the door. But that had stopped, too. She would not demand anything from him – not a cent of his money.

Charlo looked back at her without blinking until his eyes watered, waiting for her eyes to light a way to the future for him as he wondered whether he should rush back home and explain to Lucette that he did not know what he was doing: old men do foolish things sometimes. He looked away, out of the window to the road, knew he did not have the fortitude to return home and endure the loneliness of Ismene's absence again.

There was no comfort in the remembrance of his promise to Ismene's father, Bede, that he would take care of her.

The news of Charlo's whereabouts travelled as quickly as a cruel joke along the road to the capital with the bus drivers who saw his truck parked outside Ismene L'Aube's home; and with the transport drivers who brought the produce from his farm and those of his neighbours' to the market vendors. Even without those heralds, the news would have leaped into his wife's ears within a day.

In the early afternoon, Lucette admitted with the most humiliating reluctance to her closest friend and neighbour, Titina, that Charlo had left the house in the early hours of the morning without a word of explanation, and that no one had heard anything from him since. News came in the evening with the bus drivers and their passengers returning from town. Those who'd heard that Charlo's car had been parked outside the house of the prostitute Ismene at Morne Rouge – for an entire day – told Titina first, to learn from her what tone they should give their words. Then they walked quickly to Lucette's house: six men and two women; the children just out of earshot. They came with buttons still undone, belts not fastened, shirts not tucked in, shoes slapping the ground provoking quick bursts of dust. There was anger in the questions. And greater anger in their shame:

"*Ay Bon Dieu*, you think Charlo could do something like that?"

"At his age. . . How can he do that to his family?"

"Now, what's his wife going to do? Tell me."

"How we going to deal with a man like him?"

"You ever see something like that? The assassin, the defiler, the ingrate!"

"The mother ass."

"Well, well, well, I would never, never believe he would do such a thing. Still waters run deep, I'm always saying."

"Yes, my dear."

"*Sacré salaud.*"

"The son-of-a-bitch," Titina said – forgetting the two days that Charlo had spent helping her and her family rebuild their house after Hurricane Janet had shaved its roof off, and sent water into closed boxes and cabinets, and leached colours from their mattresses; he had been satisfied with their thanks.

In Morne Rouge, a man does not desert his wife of a lifetime. If he desires to bathe in more water than can be obtained from his wife's spring, he should seek it away from the village. But he must not leave his side of the bed empty. A man must not do that.

If they had not sensed the great evil that festered in Charlo Pardie's soul, it was because they were good people blinded by their charity and trust in their neighbours.

Lucette sat on the only chair in the kitchen, her arms tight across her chest, moaning softly, and rocking gently back and forth. She had always been thin; now she was too fragile to touch. The rosary that had tethered her to her faith was on the floor, under the heel of her slipper. Her frayed cotton gown, pink with blue irises, hung down over her right shoulder, exposing her breast. Titina adjusted the gown.

The other women stood in a semicircle around her; and the men stood near the door, their hands clasped in front, praying for suggestions; anxious to be useful. They were silent now, hesitant to start on the matter for which they had come. So one of the women started a charcoal fire in the earthenware brazier, and another took the coffee pot outside for water.

When Lucette eventually looked up, the neighbours set upon her with an avalanche of concern, imploring her not to hesitate to ask for anything she needed. She remained silent, unable to find a word louder than the storm of pain in her chest. As each woman silently thanked God that Lucette's misfortune had not fallen on her, they swore to do more than she would ask for. The men assured her that she could expect as much from them as she would from her sons. But who would inform her daughter in America?

Titina positioned herself directly before the afflicted woman, clasped her lowered hands as if in supplication, and offered herself as a wide-eyed and open-mouthed vessel into which Lucette could pour her grief.

Lucette Pardie was aware of her mouth moving, and the plaintive voice of someone inside her describing to the ground her discovery that her husband, father of three, and grandfather of two, had abandoned her and his home for the bed of a prostitute. She – who could never find the absolution to enter heaven – had repaid the gift of shelter, clothes, and food, to take an old man – old enough to be her father – away from his wife, three children, and two grandchildren, his home, and farm. "Is me that gave that girl the clothes and panties she walked away from here with. I taught her to bake, and cook, and sew. I sent her to church, gave her the fifty cents to put in the plate. Gave her everything. In return, is shame she shame me and my family, destroys my home, rubs her ca-ca all over my face. Because of all I did for her? How can I understand a thing like that? How can anyone explain a thing like that? How can that snake of a woman look into a mirror?"

She implored the aid of the three hundred and sixty-five saints listed on the calendar in her living room, and condemned the unnameable prostitute to the million tortures of hell. She beat the ground with her feet, beat her breasts with her fists until Titina, with the help of another woman, held her arms and pleaded with her to let God pass His judgment on the sinners. "God will punish them, you'll see."

The grief sat on her shoulders like a collar of stone, pushing her body into the ground, blocking her ears to the neighbours' entreaties, telling her to go to her bed. Her bed? Her bed? The same bed that the nameless husband had slept in. The same bed that the nameless prostitute had slept in when her body had been torched by the fevers of pneumonia and measles. That viper had stolen the husband of the very woman who had rubbed her back and chest with camphor and eucalyptus oil, and fed her soup one teaspoon at a time.

Then her children would hear the news. And where in her life were the words to answer their questions? She wished she had the strength to tear her heart out of her chest with her nails.

Oh, our Lucette.

PART ONE

CHAPTER 1

Three days after Ismene's birth, Bede L'Aube saw his wife turn ashen and melt away from a fire inside her. The *gardeur's* poultices and incantations did not lower her fever – not even the sacred images, cut from prayer books, that he burned in a saucer, and whose ashes he buried in Bede's yard. He did those things because they expected him to. He wished he had the courage to tell the crowd around him what he was thinking: Are you all too stupid to see that I cannot raise the woman from the dead; that I do not believe what I am doing; that all I know better than you is the smell of death? Ask me to find the best place in your yards to bury an afterbirth, or to find a good name for your child; ask me to identify the neighbour who is painting your name with the filth of gossip. But do not ask me to lift the mountain of death from the chest of a dying woman.

When they saw him refuse Bede's money, the neighbours brought a bamboo pole, tied the ends of the sheet on which the dying woman lay to make a hammock, and rushed her to the village health-centre. New shoulders took the load when a carrier flagged, soft voices calling urgently: "Let's go… faster… let's go."

"Take care. . . take care."

The doctor arrived from the city two hours after the nurse telephoned. He wrote on the death certificate that the patient had died of puerperal sepsis. Bede asked him what that meant.

"It's an infection," the doctor said.

"Who gave my wife an infection?" Bede asked.

"Nobody. . . it comes after some births."

Bede L'Aube said nothing when his sister came and took the baby away – without a word; and he remained dry-eyed and silent for a week. He took the food the neighbours brought him and nodded his thanks. Then one day, he climbed the hill that overlooked his garden of carrots, sweet potatoes, cabbages, yams, tomatoes, thorns and rocks. He wondered why fate should have emptied its hundred garbage carts of misfortune on a man who owned no more than a shingled house and four acres of precipice and quicksand shared with two species of snakes. What was the infection that nobody had given his wife, and which had killed her? He thought of that until his mind went silent and he could think of nothing except to look into a red fog with no sounds or shapes. Nobody. Nothing. Then he cried – sharp childlike squeals and roars that rattled his body. He ignored the tears, and mucus from his nose that soaked his shirt and pants. He cursed every doctor, priest, nurse, politician, saint, medicine and prayer that he could recall. He screamed obscenities, even cursing the grackles and finches for their unsympathetic singing. He cursed himself for forgetting how much he loved his wife before she died. He cursed the world for what it would do to his daughter.

Eventually, he returned home with his chest hurting so severely that the effort of breathing was agony. The next day, he thanked his neighbours for their care and went to visit his baby. His sister had already baptized the baby and named her Ismene. Bede said the name aloud three times and nodded his satisfaction.

"She's a very nice baby, so I found a special name for her," Thomasina said.

"Yes, it's a nice name," Bede agreed, and looked into the baby's eyes as if asking for her suggestions on how he was going to raise her.

"Bede," his sister said, "you can't take care of a baby – most of all, not a little girl. I'm keeping her with me."

"But what about your family? You have your own children to take care of."

"You know how to take care of a child, Bede . . . a little girl?"

"If I have to . . . "

"Give me peace, Bede. Who will look after her when you're in your vegetables? Answer me that. And who will explain it to her when her bleeding begins? Her friends at school?"

"About money for her. . ." Bede said.

"We'll talk about that later." Thomasina looked at the baby's eyes of gold and grey: hot and cold, bad and good, weak and strong, loud and quiet, hard and soft. "This little girl – she will make us laugh a little. . . and cry a lot," she said.

Bede visited his daughter every Sunday. Came with a box of vegetables and salted meat for his sister's family, and a bag of sweets for Ismene. Sat on the front steps asking the same questions he'd asked at every previous visit; and reassured his daughter that she could come back to live with him as soon as she had finished school; though perhaps she would do so well at school that she would want to work in an office or a store in the city.

Ismene always nodded in agreement. Yes, yes, and yes, to everything. She never explained exactly what she wanted and her father never asked. He would add his nods to hers, and always remembered to say: "And you can buy nice new dresses from the stores."

She would nod, and remain silent for several minutes, imagining herself in new dresses of yellow, or orange, or red, or sky-blue. . . surrounded by strangers telling her how nice she looked.

In her eleventh year, Ismene allowed her twelve-year-old cousin to explore her body in exchange for twenty-five cents and the favour of touching the agonizing lump in his pants. But when he asked her to do it again the next day, she demanded fifty cents and would not allow him the slightest contact. It took him two weeks to accumulate that sum with small withdrawals from his father's pocket. One day he showed her a dollar, and she offered to add a kiss.

The aunt found the can in which Ismene kept her savings.

"Where you got that money, Ismene? You stole it?" Thomasina asked.

Ismene refused to say and when her uncle said someone had been stealing change from his pocket, Thomasina whipped her with a switch broken from a tamarind tree, threatening not to stop until Ismene confessed.

After three whippings, Ismene told. "Primus gave me the money."

Primus denied any knowledge of the matter until his father's use of the whip made confession less painful. But he did not say why he had given the money to Ismene. Thomasina gave the money to her husband. Each child plotted revenge on the other.

Whenever they managed to be alone, Ismene would lift her dress and lower her panties to show Primus what he would never ever touch again – unless he could pay. The cost then would be two dollars. Primus threatened to tell the other boys in the village what kind of girl she was. Eventually, Primus confided to a friend – after making him swear three times on a cross, and with the expectation of immediate death if he broke his word – that Ismene would let them play with her body if they paid her two dollars.

Ismene met them on Sunday afternoon when the heat had sent the dogs to sleep, and made the adults less observant. They crept under some guava bushes and Ismene let them touch her small breasts and insert an inch of their fingers between her legs, but when the other boy took his pants off and tried to climb over her, she pushed him off and pulled back on her clothes. The boy refused to give her the money.

Ismene asked twice for the two dollars, and when the boys laughed and turned away, she threw herself upon the back of Primus's friend and wrapped her arms around his neck, screaming for her money. The boy threw her off and tried to run away. She grabbed him by one leg, and when he could not dislodge her, he picked up a rock and smashed her in the face, cutting open her left cheek. Primus panicked when he saw the blood pouring down her face and ran home to call his parents. Others came too, hearing Thomasina's screams that Ismene had been killed. Her aunt and uncle took her to the health-centre to be bandaged, promising to punish her when she was well enough to take a beating. The two boys were whipped until their backs and limbs were covered with purple welts.

Secrets are like children who promise not to wander too far off; or like new toys that cannot be enjoyed until a friend can see them. Secrets must be told with great reluctance to ease the pain of releasing them, and secrets must be told for vengeance. Primus's friend told another friend what had happened with Ismene, and Thomasina found out after the village became too small to hold such a secret: her niece, only eleven years old, was a prostitute.

"I don't believe it myself," the neighbour said, "but so many people are talking about it. . . But I can't see Ismene doing something like that. People just like to talk . . . I don't know why people say things like that. . . and you know how children are. Anyway, I'm telling you because I'm your friend. You understand?"

"Yes, I understand" Thomasina said, and walked home with her friend from the village shop where they'd met. There was not much else to say, and no time to return greetings, or to see who was talking to whom, or to ask about a sick relative. She sat in her kitchen waiting for Primus and Ismene to come home from school, hoping they would stop and play and not arrive before her husband did.

The children came home early, saw her face, said their greetings softly and moved away when they saw the two pots on the hearth with the meat and vegetables still cold because she had forgotten to light the fire. They ate late that night, and went to bed after doing the last things of the day: Ismene washing the dishes, and Primus chopping coconut meat and breaking open a termite's nest for the yard chickens. The husband stayed out in the dark, working by the light of a kerosene lantern, making repairs to the cage that held two fighting cocks.

The next morning, Ismene woke early and was dressed even before Thomasina had put a kettle on for coffee. The aunt looked at the Sunday dress that she wore and waited for an explanation. "I want to go back to my father," Ismene said.

"What you talking about, little girl?" Thomasina asked.

"I know what people are saying about me. I don't want to stay around here."

"Your father can't take care of you. . ."

"I can take care of myself. I can cook and wash."

"Well, you should ask you father first."

"I want to go home," Ismene said.

Thomasina contemplated the little pillar of obstinacy, and did not remind her that her home was with them. "Go and put on your school uniform, and go to school. On Saturday, we'll go and see your father."

Primus watched in terror as Thomasina packed his cousin's clothes. There was the same cold pain around his navel that came when his mother cut a finger or when his father had to dig deep in his foot to remove a thorn or splinter. But this pain was far worse: so large that it left no room for breath; and so heavy that his legs trembled under the strain. He and his father accompanied Ismene and Thomasina to the bus stop, helped them with the cardboard box containing Ismene's clothes, then waved at an immense cloud of diesel smoke until the bus turned the corner. They walked home without saying much.

The rumours had already travelled the five miles to Bede's village, but when Thomasina and Ismene found him in his garden, he did not hesitate to greet Ismene as he always did. He washed his hands with water from a large bottle, placed his hands under her arms and lifted her into the air, laughing and complaining that she had grown far too heavy for him to lift any more.

"She wants to come back and stay with you," Thomasina said.

"Good," he answered, "we'll see how we're going to manage. God will provide."

"Yes, God is good," Thomasina said. And very seldom understandable, she thought.

Ismene did not care if her father whipped her for leaving Thomasina's home. At least as her own father he had the right to do so. She was sure that before the pain was gone, he would find some way of persuading her to forgive him: he would give her the money for something she wanted, or take her to the city. And his guilt would last long enough for her to belong in his house again. She could wash his clothes and clean the house and boil the vegetables – until he taught her to cook meat and fish.

Then he would want her to forgive him for ever letting his sister take her away.

She had not prepared anything to say to her father. She would look down at the ground when he spoke, and nod or shake her head when he expected her to.

But Bede stared at Ismene and grinned, as if Thomasina had brought him a gift he did not deserve. "I'm glad you're home, Ti-Ismene," he said, adding the prefix of affection to her name.

The following Monday, Bede walked her to the village school, talked outside with the headmistress, and asked that she be sent home directly after school. Her new classmates did not see in Ismene's face the apprehension of a newcomer, so when they called her Cat Eyes, it was not within reach of her ears. They had the rumours: let her forget her place and they would chase her back with them; beat her with them; silence her with them.

The boys told detailed stories of what they had done with her, and boasted that they had refused to pay. The girls swore – while making the sign of the cross – that they had seen grown men go into her home when her father had gone to take his vegetables to the marketing depot; had seen her lock the door and shut the windows. What do you think she was doing in there? The neighbours let their children play with Ismene, but tried not to let them out of sight, or out of earshot.

The following January she was twelve years old – too old to return to school. Her former fellow students moved on to more convenient targets for honing their skills in slander and calumny.

But Nico was different. He followed her to the vegetable garden on Saturday mornings when she brought Bede his lunch. Did silly things to make her laugh. Saved to buy her sweets. Agreed with her opinions on the workings of the world and the supernatural, especially the sources of the noises heard only at night.

One day she took his face in her hands and kissed him hard on the lips. When she let him go, he fell to the ground gasping for breath. He begged her to do it again but she would not let him near her for weeks. Then when he had given up and had gone back to making her laugh, she took his hand and put it between her legs. He was so happy that he began to cry, and so embarrassed by his excitement that he could not walk. She made him sit next to her with their shoulders touching. He was fourteen years old and at that moment could not think of anything better that life had to offer.

One Sunday afternoon, when Bede had eaten enough to protect his stomach from the burn of white rum, he joined his friends at the village bar to share vital opinions on the state of world affairs. Nico, who kept their house under close observation, saw him leave and was soon at the back door. Ismene was sitting on the back step scouring the pots with a pad of coconut fibre and ashes. He climbed onto the low branch of an avocado tree and they smiled at each other.

"Your father is at the rum shop," he said.

"And he's going to stay there the whole afternoon," she added.

"But he could change his mind, and come back early," Nico said, hoping he was wrong.

She rinsed the pots and looked directly at Nico as if trying to decide what to do with him. "Let's go inside," she said. She led him into the bedroom, and lay on the bed; she let him remove her shirt and suck on her breasts. She kept her eyes on the shingled ceiling and only glanced at him occasionally when his biting made her wince, or his nails scratched her skin. She let him put his hands under her skirt, but when he tried to get under her panties, she pushed his hand away. He struggled with her until she threw him off the bed.

"Go home now," Ismene said.

He was crying in frustration and anger. "You let the other boys do it for money and you won't even let me touch you."

"Which boys?"

"All the big boys in Morne Rouge. All of them have done it with you. And they don't even like you." He was almost shouting now.

"Go home. And don't put you foot around this place again," she said.

"You're just a nasty whore," he cried, and ran to the road, but there was more defeat than vindictiveness in his voice.

Bede came home after dark, and Ismene heard him walk into the table and curse softly; then she remembered she had forgotten to light the kerosene lamp in the living room. She turned on the flashlight on the floor near her bed, and went to help her father.

"You're sleeping already?" The room was already filled with the stink of cigarettes and rum. His breath stank almost as much as his sweat.

"Couldn't sleep."

"What's wrong *ti-chérie*?" he asked. "I wanted to come home earlier, but you know how people can talk and. . ."

He could tell, even through the hazy focus of his eyes and the yellow light from the lamp that she was not concerned about his lateness and the worn excuse. "What happened?"

"Nico said something I didn't like. . . things people are saying about me, " she answered.

"Nico is a child . . . children say stupid things. You don't have to worry about things children say. Children lie. You didn't do anything bad, here?"

She shook her head.

"Well, don't worry; tomorrow, Nico will be sorry. You'll see." He swayed through the kitchen, came back for the lamp, and went out the back door to the outhouse. She returned to bed.

The pounding on the door woke them at once. "Bede! Bede! Ismene! Is Nico there?" someone was shouting.

Bede went to the door. Nico's parents and a small crowd stood outside. "Nico was here with Ismene this afternoon. He hasn't come home," Nico's mother said. "Don't tell me he's still here. He's inside?"

"No."

"You know where he went, Ismene?"

"No."

"*Mon Dieu*, where did the boy go?"

They set out to search, carrying flashlights, and torches made from bottles filled with kerosene and wicked with cotton rags. Two parties: one heading along the path to the gardens and the river, the other towards the main road; voices calling the boy's name, their shadows leaping along the ground and up into the trees. The village dogs followed, snarling and snapping at each other in their eagerness to be useful, entangling themselves among the searchers' legs; dashing off after every rustle in the dark, every scuttle of a crab, then rushing back when no one followed.

"Nico?"

"Nico!"

"N-i-i-i-c-o-o-o!"

"Ni-co-de-mus!"

"Nicodemus? What kind of name is that?" a voice asked quietly.

"Nico, please answer your mother and father."

23

Voices changed, became tired, became hoarse, then started again.

The dogs found him in a *dachine* marsh, sunken up to his waist in mud stinking of sulphur and putrefaction, holding on to tree roots at the edge of the marsh, but too tired to pull himself out, and too exhausted to speak. It took two men several minutes to dislodge his fingers from their hold. The searchers ran back with him, the women calling their thanks loudly to St. Christopher and St. Joseph; the men exchanging their theories about quicksand and the endurance of children; the dogs begging to find another lost boy.

His parents washed him in water from a barrel. He refused to eat or drink anything, whispering that he wanted to die. His father removed his belt, and that sight persuaded Nico to drink some very sweet tea made from orange leaves.

The neighbours left when it was confirmed that Nico could not provide an explanation until his voice returned. Then they rushed home to claim credit for having discovered the runaway at the bottom of deep crevasses, and boasting of jumping into bottomless quicksands to save his life.

The next day, Nico became ill with fever. So they delayed his punishment for two days until he was well enough to have a confession beaten out of him. At first, he said that Ismene had pushed him into the *dachine*, but after witnesses swore that Ismene had not left her house that afternoon, everyone concluded that his had been the act of a lovesick child, and they shook their heads in wonder at the power of the thirteen-year-old temptress.

The other children stayed away from her, but Bede became more protective, even removing the bones from fish before allowing her to eat it.

She was working with Bede one morning, washing the carrots he'd dug up, when a loud voice, rich and strong as brandy with honey and lime, sent the grackles fleeing in confusion: "Bede! You abuser of all female things! Violator of sheep and goats! Where are you?"

Bede was happily revealing his two remaining front teeth. Ismene was staring toward the voice in alarm.

"Watch your nasty mouth, Charlo," Bede called out, "I have a young lady here with me."

The tall man came into view. "Ah ha! Well I have you now. . ." Charlo Pardie stopped when he saw Ismene. "Ay *Bon Dieu*. I'm sorry, I didn't know. . . that's your daughter, Bede?"

"Yes: Ismene."

"Ah, Ismene. All these years, and I never got the chance to come and see you. I don't have an excuse good enough for you. But your mother left a daughter as beautiful as a vanilla flower. Yes. You have a nice daughter, Bede." He bent over lift her off the ground and to kiss her cheek. "I'm sorry about these things I said to your father. But you know I was only joking."

Ismene liked the tall, sharp man with the balding head, and voice that was strong even when he whispered, and the way he lifted her up so high and so easily off the ground. She was glad when he said that he would stay for dinner. They let her sit in the room while they spoke, exchanged jokes, spoke of the man Bede had bought his land from – who was so obstinate that he did not believe his wife when she told him that termites had almost eaten away the outhouse; so he went in to show her, sat heavily on the bench and fell in.

"His wife was so happy, she almost stopped us coming to help him out," Bede said. "Never knew ca-ca could stink so much."

Before he left, Charlo Pardie took two five-dollar notes from his wallet, and handed them to Ismene. "That's for *you*. . . not for you and your father."

Ismene held the money at arm's length. She had never owned more than three dollars. Wondered what one could do with so much money. When Pardie left, her hand was still outstretched. Bede took the notes from her. "I'll put it in the bible for you. You can do what you want with it."

Charlo came back one month later – with his son; said he was going to the city and invited them to come. Bede shook his head, then seeing the disappointment in Ismene's eyes, asked whether she wanted to go. She almost fainted from the weight of her joy, and found herself unable to speak until she had washed and changed. She took five dollars from her account in the bible.

She sat between Cord and Charlo.

"We have strange eyes, you and me," Cord said.

Ismene looked at his green eyes. "You have eyes like a cat," she replied.

The sight of the city was a jarring as the light from a photographic flash: Bright red roofs, cream and white walls; pink, cream, blue buildings; rutted grey streets – straight as rulers. Everything had appeared suddenly from the top of the hill that hid the city until the last vertiginous descent; then into new smells, new noises, new confusions. People walking more quickly, not stopping to speak, rushing between moving cars. A massive cathedral with a bell tower looking down on every other building and nearby park. It was too much to see at once. Ismene's eyes burned – she had not blinked for several minutes. Best of all were the ladies with pressed hair, dressed in yellow, orange, red and sky-blue.

She had never seen so many faces, so many people in clean clothes – as if everyone were rushing to church or to a party. Everyone wearing shoes. When she saw some beggars the sight made her frown for spoiling her picture. Then, the main street: divided along the centre, and almost wider than her village; on either side, large store windows with clothes, furniture and appliances newer and shinier than anything she had seen except in books and magazines. She glanced at Cord and Charlo, and did not understand their lack of interest in the things around them.

Charlo bought her ice cream that was smooth as butter, not gritty with ice crystals, and bitter with almond flavouring, as the ones made by hand at village bazaars and fêtes. He held her hand when they went to the largest store in the city, where Cord affected boredom with the crowds and the noise. She sat very still when they went to an office with an electric fan hanging from the ceiling, and was overjoyed when a lady behind a typewriter told Charlo he had a very beautiful daughter, that both his children had wonderful eyes. And Charlo did not correct her.

On the way home, she recalled the faces, smells, colours, sights, sounds of the city, and made herself miserable with the embarrassment of returning to her village of shingled huts and dirt paths.

That night, she went to bed aflame with her decision to elect

Cord to the position of boyfriend, wishing there was a friend in the village to help her suffer the unbearable agony of that exquisite secret that encircled her heart like a hoop of thorns.

Before he left, Charlo had taken Bede aside and said to his childhood friend, "How are you going to take care of Ismene? Let her come to live with us. I will adopt her. You can't manage with a fourteen-year-old girl alone in the hills with you . . . unless you get another wife – and that's another problem for the girl."

Bede L'Aube shook his head, "I don't have long to go with this diabetes. When I'm gone, she will join your family . . . I've told my sister that. I need somebody to help me. I can't manage alone."

Bede never mentioned Charlo's suggestion to Ismene, afraid that she would leave before he died.

He had gone to the clinic for confirmation of what he already knew.

"So you can't feel pain when you cut your feet, and you're always thirsty and passing a lot of water?" the nurse asked.

"Yes. So, I have 'sweet pee'?" he replied.

"Yes, Mr. Bede. I think you have diabetes. But let the doctor see you when he comes Saturday morning."

"So what is he going to tell me that I don't know?" Bede asked.

"How to take care of yourself."

"They don't have a cure for it, the sweet pee?"

"No, Mr. Bede," the nurse said.

"Ah. Every time I come here, it's to hear something bad. And it's more bad things the doctor is going to tell me. I have a lot of work to do on Saturdays. . ."

He paused to look more carefully and decided her plainness was infinitely more beautiful than his celibacy. He began searching for the best words for beginning the dance of seduction, then remembered how tired and impecunious he was. He comforted himself with the thought that he could avoid the nuisance of rejection by ending the visit. "You have something I can use when I get cut?" he asked.

The nurse nodded, went into the tiny dispensary, and returned with a dark-brown vial. "Here's some sulpha powder. Wash the cut before putting the powder, and cover it."

He paid for the powder, and was almost out of the door, when the nurse said: "You're not a bad-looking man, Mr. Bede. I'm sure you can find a mattress in the village."

"You knew what was I was thinking?" Bede L'Aube asked.

"You men," she said. "It was all over your face. But I already have a man. And it's not your diabetes. That bastard of mine is headache enough. Walk well, take care of yourself."

"Stay well," he answered. He would try harder next time. And if she said no, he'd wait for a later time.

Bede L'Aube decided that he had sufficient time to prepare for his daughter's future. A smart, pretty girl like that was sure to marry before she was twenty. Wait until Charlo's two boys became interested. He would prefer Constantine, but she would probably want Cord, the younger and flashier one, the one whom she would have to drag out of other bedrooms – women prefer fire to feathers in their beds.

Enough time. All he had to do was to stop drinking so much, take better care of the cuts on his legs and arms: every night, he would wash them in clean water, and cover them with medication. More than enough time. People didn't fall down dead of diabetes.

Death would have to wait until he had built more raised beds for carrots and cabbages. In the evenings, Ismene could help with the weeding and watering. Then some beds for lettuce near the house. Maybe a small pen for pigs – enough bananas and breadfruit for them. Give Ismene some chickens.

The moment a man told his body it wasn't well, it went and got weak. No time for that; too much to do: Pardon me Monsignor Death, if you are lonely for a soul, find another to keep you company – I'm too busy; too . . . too busy. Ah!

He should take his daughter to town, maybe go to the cinema. They would have to sit in the pit because he couldn't afford tickets for seats in the circle, and buy peanuts and soft drinks for both of them. Make sure that no young man touched her leg.

He would wear the shirt with pink and sky-blue stripes . . . and his brown pants. At the end of the month, he could afford to buy sufficient cloth for two dresses for her. The ones she had come back with were too tight – showed too much of her legs and breasts. The child was growing so fast. And looking more and more like her mother, but with one eye golden like his wife and the other grey like his.

The contemplation of a visit to the city put him into that state of pleasantness which obliges thoughts of a woman. He regretted that his neighbour Carmen – with skin as smooth as a tomato – could not visit his bed, which she said, still bore the impression of his dead wife's body. Carmen had said he could come to her home when her husband was away with the government work crew, applying boiling tar to the grey scab of a road that skirted the coast. "He's always too tired to do his business when he comes home, smelling of pitch. . . and my oyster is just drying up and wasting," she complained to Bede.

He hesitated to defile the house of a friend – especially one with a bible on a table near the bed. So they tried the shelter of trees near his vegetable gardens. But their sweat, and his toes digging into the ground for purchase, attracted thirteen species of biting insects obeying entomological imperatives to suck blood, bite into skin, explore crevices and contours, and to seek other forms of recreation on the sweating, reeking bodies. In addition, Bede did not enjoy the sensation of wind blowing cold across his naked backside, and Carmen began to imagine that the object entering her body was a snake.

"Never me, again," Carmen said after this meeting, and pushed him off. It took Bede two months to forgive the world for that frustration.

One morning, Bede waited until Ismene had taken their laundry to the river bank, a mile and a half away, where the villagers whitened the rocks with soap, gossip, scandal, and news. He went to Carmen's house through its back garden; knocked on her kitchen door.

"You alone?" he asked.

"Bede?" Carmen asked, already breathless.

They were almost naked when he followed her into the bedroom.

He covered the bible with the lid of a pan, and touched the horseshoe nailed above the bedroom door for good luck.

She lay on a straw mat near the bed and Bede crawled over her, turning his back on the cold, fixed stares from the sacred images on the walls. When they were done, he thanked Carmen fervently for her nourishment of his body's hungers, and reminded her to look for the box of vegetables he would leave near her back door.

"Felt like a long time since you did anything?" Carmen asked.

"So long, I'm surprised I remembered what to do," he answered.

"At least, one part of you remembered," Carmen said.

"It was good," Bede said.

The next visitor was Lucette Pardie and the older son, Constantine, a week before Christmas. They took Ismene to shop in the city, and Lucette bought her a white and a plaid dress that she thought sensible, but which Ismene would not have chosen. Constantine kept her ears filled all day with wondrous facts about hurricanes and earthquakes, while Lucette interrupted at intervals with appeals to "Leave the child alone".

The hesitation of the villagers toward Ismene diminished with each visit from the Pardies. It was difficult to satisfy one's curiosity if questions could not be asked directly, so neighbours dropped by unexpectedly to leave breadfruit, pumpkins, green bananas and other things that they had in excess, while finding reasons to delay until the right questions could be asked. They usually came when she was trapped at the hearth, unable to move far from their observations and enquiries.

One day, she was peeling vegetables for a soup of salted codfish with dumplings, yam, pumpkin, and potatoes, when Carmen rushed into the kitchen to throw her arms around Ismene as if to shield her from an oncoming blow. A few seconds later, the trembling Ismene saw four men running down the dirt road to her home carrying the body of her father on their shoulders.

A neighbour's child, using a shortcut through Bede's garden, had found him lying across a bed of carrots with his face in the dirt, and his fingers dug into the soil.

This was how people in Morne Rouge died: suddenly, violently, alone; from falling rocks and trees, mudslides, machete cuts, drowning, ignored illnesses. But to Ismene, who has seen other bodies – bleeding, broken, stiff – being carried in hammocks through the village to the health centre or the police station, Bede's death was unfair and deliberate. He had promised to take care of her because she had already lost her mother. She stood near the coffin that Thomasina had paid for, her eyes so swollen that she could no longer see the features of her father's face, aware of the sounds around her – as at a great distance – voices protesting Bede L'Aube's death, as if their unimportance to the world had earned them another injustice – only the women survived to old age. Ismene could smell the rum and cigarettes of the crowd around the house, and slowly became aware of the pressure on her right hand. She looked up into Carmen's face. There were other women crying, but Ismene understood that her father had betrayed Carmen, too.

A priest came and filled the house with his prayers and incense. Six men lifted the coffin off the two chairs that supported it and squeezed through the door. Ismene followed, holding Carmen's hand. Thomasina and her family were beside and behind her. Ismene saw the coffin lowered into the hole behind the village chapel and closed her eyes when two men dug into the pile of dirt with shovels. She smelled the sweat and felt the heat of someone close to her. She opened her eyes and squinted until she could recognize the face of her father's friend.

"Your father wanted you to live with us. . . if anything happened to him. He told your Auntie Thomasina. You can come with us tonight, if you want," Charlo Pardie said. "I'll come back later in the week to find somebody to take care of the house for you."

The mourners – the entire village, and more – brought rum, coffee and stories for the wake; they filled the house with smells, noise and smoke and bruised her shoulders and face with their comfort. Someone began to read a passage of comfort from the bible to Ismene, but fell asleep after the first verse. Several pocketed small items that Bede did not need, and that Ismene would not use. Those still able to walk upright helped their staggering fathers and neighbours home.

CHAPTER 2

Charlo and Lucette did not wait for the end of the wake, wanting to get back to Mandelie before nightfall. Carmen promised to look after the house until he returned.

Lucette had brought a suitcase held together with string, and into this they packed everything Ismene owned. On the way back to Charlo's farm, they rode an old bus that did not even approach the speed limit of thirty miles an hour. Charlo had not driven his own truck, because he was obligated to share in the company and the eulogies of other mourners from Mandelie who had known Bede L'Aube.

After thirty minutes, Ismene became nauseated from the heat and the exhaust fumes that enveloped them. Charlo sensed her discomfort and took a small orange from the pocket of his jacket; he cut it down the middle and offered her a portion.

"Just keep smelling on it. You'll feel better," he said. He was pleased when she rested her head on his shoulder, and he tried not to move with the swaying of the bus.

Lucette frowned slightly, dissatisfied with a young woman who could not put up with such a small discomfort.

At Morne Rouge, the sun set over the horizon of the Caribbean Sea, but at Mandelie, on the eastern coast, the sun went down behind the hills to the west, and when they arrived at the village, the sun had disappeared but there was still sufficient light for her to see the houses and shops on either side of the road that curved like an irregular S through the village.

First, a small shop with two doors at the front and no windows, and behind the counter, a lady with both hands and left cheek startlingly white from unconcealed vitiligo. Then small houses shingled and bleached to silver by the sun and rain, and veined with brown termite pathways. A rum-shop sitting on rocks, with crates of empty bottles stacked in its crawlspace; over its door "Rabot's Bar" was written in red letters on a dirty yellow sign.

She saw the stone church with a wooden school at its side, and a dirt yard with six boys playing cricket. A circle of girls were clapping hands and she heard some words of a song: "One and twenty, two and twenty, three and four and five and twenty. . . "

The bus slowed suddenly, and the driver said: "That dog. . . one of these days, one of these days. . . *sacré chien*."

Ismene turned to follow the other heads looking to the right. She saw an old dog, white with a black head and tail, limp slowly to the side of the road, touching the road delicately with the tip of its left hind leg.

"Always waits until something is coming to decide to cross the road," someone said.

"Must be twenty years old, that old thing."

"Wonder who gives it food?"

"Never known a dog to stink like that. Look at the flies on it."

"Time for it to die."

"Yes . . . time."

Ismene thought that some day she should bring a piece of meat for the village's other refugee.

Then a second curve in the road, around a boulder too massive for the road builders, and an immense mamey-apple tree. Underneath sat two men slamming domino tiles and ignoring the loud counsel of seven advisors.

On the opposite side of the road, Ismene could see a slope covered with scrub and occasional patches of grass leading to the sea. The Atlantic was flecked with white dashes, rougher than the sea at Morne Rouge.

In the crook of the third bend was a cream house with brown trim and a balcony, flowers at the front and a breadfruit tree marking the entrance to a short driveway. Ismene was hoping this was Charlo Pardie's home, when he nodded toward the house and said, "Home."

Constantine and Cord, the two children who remained at home, were waiting at the roadside for their parents and news of the funeral. The second child, Marie-Josette, had married a cook on the military base the Americans had built on the island. Six years ago, she had left with him when the United States Air Force forgot why they had built the installation, and recalled their personnel.

Constantine welcomed Ismene with polite caution, and took her suitcase.

"Ismene will be living with us," Charlo said in response to the raised eyebrows.

"Good," Lucette said, "now let's get in the house before night comes."

They allowed Ismene two days to complete her mourning, and on the third day, when she woke with her eyes dry, Lucette began claiming recompense for the orphan's care. "You have to go with Mr. Charlo to get the milk. He's leaving in a little while."

Charlo greeted her with a small, guilty smile. "I'm sorry you didn't get a longer rest, but we have so much work to do. The cows are in the pasture down by the sea, and the truck can't go there."

She walked behind him, seldom able to keep up, but he never asked her to hurry; waiting patiently for her to catch up, then forgetting and leaving her behind again. He spoke to her only once: "Try and remember the road, you'll have to go back alone to take the milk to Ma Lucette. I have to stay to move the animals."

Then, when she could smell the iodine of the ocean and hear the waves hissing for quiet, Charlo turned to the right, and they followed a smaller path that led to a pasture surrounded by logwood and coconut trees. There was an unpainted hut in the centre of the pasture. It was covered with shingles that the sun and salt had weathered to dirty white and grey, and its roof of corrugated iron was red from rust. It was supported by logwood stilts and at one corner by a rock that had been too heavy to move. A faint sulphurous smell came from a swamp behind the trees at the opposite end of the pasture, and it reminded her of the stink of the mud in her father's *dachine* patch. She felt a sting in her eyes and busied herself brushing dirt from her skirt. The three cows and two calves in the clearing lifted their heads to glance at the visitors, then went back to their grazing.

Charlo indicated the hut with his chin. "This was our first house . . . Constantine was born here. But the mosquitoes! Biting like fire. We had to burn *citronelle* at night to chase them away. And when it rained? Ah!" He shook his head.

She smiled in sympathy; a comforting smile that allowed him to say more, but he could not think of anything that would interest a sixteen-year-old girl. He had not said much even to his own daughter, Marie-Josette. Lucette had done most of the talking. After an old man has asked about a girl's health, and the health of her parents, and how she is doing at school, he must find things to busy himself with. So he asked Ismene to collect a pailful of water from a nearby stream.

After he had washed the udder of one of the cows, he collected the first milk into a white enamelled cup, and handed it to her. "Here, and take a piece of bread from my sack, you need some breakfast."

She sat on the rough bench that served as the front step of the hut, and had just finished eating, and was still tired from the walk to the pasture, when he told her it was time to get back. He helped her make a small crown of leaves for her head to support the milk can. As she turned to leave, he pointed to some black berries near the path, "Pick some *bois grié* on your way back; they're good for you."

Ismene looked at the purple-black fruit, and turned back to him, "You eat them first."

He was surprised and annoyed. "You used to talk back to your father?"

"He never told me to eat something he didn't eat first."

"I see we're going to have trouble with that one," he said under his breath, and went to the berry tree and ate some of the fruit – more than he wanted to; he had never liked them; they reminded him of the war, when there was never enough to eat, and breakfast was sometimes just a handful of berries – if one found a hidden tree.

"A lot of birds, like the *grives*, like them," Charlo said, "makes them poop purple."

Ismene ignored the joke. The thought made her want to spit. "I don't want any *bois grié*," she said, and turned away.

"Walk well," he said, as he stood flanked by a cow and her calf watching as Ismene walked away.

"Stay well," she answered, without looking back.

He watched until she turned left along the main path. She held her hands away from her body like a tightrope walker, her feet gliding over the dewed grass to keep her worn plastic shoes from slipping off. The pail of milk remained perfectly balanced on her head. She seemed to be dancing over the ground.

Charlo was left more angry at himself than at her, concerned that he had not been quick enough with a warning to her that Lucette would not forgive sauciness in her home.

In less than two days, everyone at Mandelie knew that Charlo and Lucette had adopted Bede L'Aube's daughter – from Morne Rouge.

"Sixteen years old."

"You should see her eyes – different colours."

"Must be bewitched."

"You should see her walk – as if she's dancing."

"Hear she has a tongue in her head."

"I asked her who her mother was. She said I wouldn't know her mother. Rude."

"Boys can't leave her alone – always asking to help her carry something."

"Charlo and his boys are going to have to keep an eye on her."

"Lucette has already warned her not to bring trouble inside their house."

"You spoken to her yet?"

"No, not yet, but she's a nice girl."

"Yes . . . a nice girl."

Constantine appointed himself Ismene's primary guardian. His first warning was to Cord: "Don't let me catch you and Ismene up to anything. I know you eighteen-year-olds. Can't see a dress without wanting to jump inside it."

"I'm not even interested in Ismene," Cord lied. "She's not nice enough for me anyway."

"Well, don't let me catch the two of you together. And don't even let Ma see you too close to her. And she's a nice girl."

"Well, don't let me catch the two of *you* together," Cord retorted.

"Fool," Constantine said, then turned to wondering how much interest Ismene had in world geography. He had never forgotten the names of the eight states of Australia and, in the eleven years since leaving school at ten, had diligently added to his store of knowledge of national capitals and territories. At the age of five, he had been transported by the recounting of Nelson's defeat of the French at the "Rattle of Ore Trafain" – the voice of an older student carrying the story across the room of the school. It was not until three years later that he learned that the British Admiral's victory had been at the Battle of Trafalgar. He hoarded these bits of history as relentlessly as Ma Lucette kept safety pins, buttons and bits of cloth.

He learned from the labels on boxes and cans, knew which brands of cocoa imparted strength and vigour, and which biscuits aided digestion. He was able to tell Lucette with confidence that she should use "hot, not boiling milk" for preparing Cord's malted beverage. He could draw with great fidelity the trademark thistle on the empty can of Scottish candies that Lucette kept on her kitchen cabinet. He knew the workings and components of internal combustion engines just as intimately: knew the location of every bolt, washer, and bearing; knew every sound of a sick engine; could improve on the functioning of every valve and carburettor. Other men smelled of sweat; Constantine smelled of grease and fuel – warm, reliable smells. Little boys came to him to learn how to make slingshots from strips cut from the inner tubes of car tires, and the Y-shaped branches of white-cedar trees, or to have him cut wheels for their toy trucks from wooden bobbins begged from the seamstress.

Like the machines he befriended, he was lean and hard, with sharp corners like his father, and tall: six feet, four inches. Every thing sharp: nose, lips, eyes and ears; and fingers long and thin like the tails of boa constrictors. And busy, always busy, too busy to stop and listen to the voices that came when his hands stopped moving.

So, while Constantine held Ismene's ears with stories from the second world war: how a lone defender at the lighthouse, armed only with an Enfield rifle, had held at bay a German U-boat that had surfaced in the harbour, Ismene's eyes sought Cord's attention. But Cord's eyes met hers only when his gaze swept past her to other things. His awareness of her presence became an unremitting itch, but his parents and Constantine formed a protective cordon around their ward, so Cord pretended disinterest, and waited. There was nothing pure about his intentions for her; he wanted to get to her before one of the other village boys did and humiliated him with the boast. This preoccupation diminished his interest in other girls, and increased their interest in him.

Cord's body did not have the sharpnesses and angles of his family. His face had a softness that was almost feminine, as if a forming hand had rounded his eyes, nose, and mouth to excess; then in compensation had given him green eyes, like pieces of an old wine bottle held up to the light: green eyes in a dark brown face, beneath eyebrows that stretched in an unbroken line from temple to temple. But strong. At eighteen, he could lift the back corner of their small truck while Constantine changed a wheel. He was already six feet tall, but with broader shoulders and larger hands than his brother.

Charlo had sent him to school in the city, though after he had done well enough for possible employment in the Department of Agriculture, or as a teacher, or an insurance agent, he went back to the farm at Mandelie – to the quiet, and to the places and things that were his – where the women loved him because he could speak well and had green eyes, and where the men envied him because he could calculate percentages and understood the placement of decimals.

Lucette cared for them all according to old unbreakable rules: Charlo got the head of the large fish at dinner, and on Sundays he would have the largest portion of the chicken breast or the largest marrowbone when there was beef. The boys got the next best portions, and she and Marie-Josette would eat what was left. Sometimes, the women cooked another meal for themselves, after the men had eaten, complaining loudly of the gluttony and selfishness of those who ate like pigs, and would never think of offering to help with washing the dishes.

When Lucette was five years old, she had seen a neighbour come to the doorway of the one-room school where her father was the principal, and signal frantically to him. Her father went outside to speak, came back shortly and whispered to another teacher. Took his hat and left. The teacher he had spoken to tried to stop Lucette, but she bit the woman's hand and escaped.

Her father heard her cries and called, "Go back, Lucette. Go back to school." He did not stop for her, walking as quickly as he could, occasionally breaking into a short run. Lucette followed him home. There were people in the yard, blocking the doorway, and throughout the house. Two women were on their hands and knees wiping up drops of blood on the floor with wet rags. The water in a bucket and basin nearby was already pink. They made way for Lucette's father. They tried to hold Lucette back, but she bit and scratched her way through.

The nurse from the village clinic was mopping her mother's face with a damp cloth. The bed was soaked with blood. Her mother turned her head at the sound of Lucette's screams. Tried to smile, winced. Closed her eyes.

Lucette heard her father ask, "What are we going to do?"

"Pray," the nurse said, "I sent for the doctor, but it will take him a long time to get here. It's in God's hands. I've done everything I can."

Lucette backed out of her parents' room and went to her room to pray. When her father went to her room, she was kneeling at her bed, saying aloud the prayers he had taught her. She refused to eat the supper one of the neighbours brought. When her father looked in on her again, she was asleep. Still kneeling, with her head on the bed. He lifted her into bed.

Next morning, she was back on the floor with her head on the bed. She still refused to eat, but drank some water sweetened with honey, and flavoured with lime juice. Later in the morning, her father lifted her off the floor, carried her to her mother's side, and said, "See what your prayers did; Maman is going to get well."

Her mother looked at her and was strong enough this time to smile. By the end of the week, her mother was well enough to shout at her.

No one explained the reason for her mother's illness, and it was not until after Constantine's birth that her mother confided that she had had a miscarriage.

From that day, Lucette allowed nothing to challenge her faith in the power of prayer. She was convinced that good weather and crops were answers to her prayers, and drought and disease were punishment for Charlo's weaker faith – he was so obstinate. Eventually, she was forced to pray enough for her husband, daughter and two sons. For that task, she armed herself with rosaries, amulets, medals, pamphlets, statuettes of saints, and images of Christ in every room: His pierced, bleeding heart encircled by thorns and surmounted by flames.

She went to mass every Sunday, and always put a coin in the offertory plate. She gave five dollars at Christmas, and three dollars on New Year's Day and on Easter Sunday. For protection against malefaction and accident, she kept a rosary of black beads and a silver cross in her pocket or within easy reach.

Charlo had courted her in the company of two chaperones to show his seriousness of purpose. He was intimidated by the tall slender daughter of the schoolmaster, with a face shaped like an inverted tear drop. She reminded him of a picture of one of the saints in the church who kept their eyes heavenward and did not care where they placed their feet. He was very surprised that she agreed to marry him without waiting to know more about him. But Lucette was a practical woman: she would inherit five acres of hillside from her family; Charlo already owned thirty acres in a well-watered valley, and a pasture near the sea with milk cows.

After the birth of Cord, she felt that she had satisfied all her needs for pleasures of the flesh, and took no further interest in Charlo's prodding and wrenching of her limbs and crevices. After a year of her indifference, he relinquished her to her prayers, and let her grumbling about the neighbours and the prices in the stores send him to sleep. She cared for her family and expected no more of life. Charlo gave her the things she asked for.

She wanted her garden clean: no weeds, no dead flowers, no fallen leaves. The house had to be protected at all times from dust, mud and spiders and centipedes; all bed sheets were to be tucked in when the men had left for work; no dirty dishes were to rest on the kitchen counter. She had to ignore Cord when he whispered: "This woman don't have time to get dirty."

These were the rules for her body, too. She was relieved when the monthly bleeding stopped, and dryness made intimacy painful. She expected Charlo to understand that sweating, grunting and dirtying the bed were things for young people. Old people spoke to each other, then went to sleep.

CHAPTER 3

The pleasure was almost too much for the heart and bank account to endure: in August, the folk festival of La Rose and Ismene's twenty-first birthday on the same day.

Charlo's side of the family belonged to the rival La Marguerite Society, but like everybody else, he conveniently switched allegiances for the occasion – just as members of La Rose would become Marguerites in October.

The previous Christmas, Charlo had travelled, in the company of a bottle of whiskey and one of gin, to the house of Ellit Melchoir and obtained his sworn agreement to provide the music for the La Rose and birthday celebrations at Charlo's home. Charlo was one of the many witnesses who had provided character references for Ellit when the latter was accused of attempted patricide. Fours years ago, Ellit might have succeeded in stoning his father to death if he had not inherited his father's poor eyesight, and if the afternoon had not been so hot.

During the trial, Ellit admitted calmly, with no attempt at regret, that he had lain in ambush behind a dirt wall across the road from his father's house for an hour and a half with a pile of seven fist-sized rocks. The heat of the afternoon made him sleepy, and his near-sightedness prevented him from determining his father's position with accuracy. Also, he had not compensated for the unexpected speed with which the seventy-year-old man had moved out of range. So the fusillade of stones had been less threatening to Justin Melchoir than the sight of his son hurling curses and boulders.

From the witness box, Ellit's eyes never left the judge's face, because that was the only face that he could see clearly. When Ellit rose to speak in his defence, he poured his words into the judge's eyes, nose, mouth and ears. The judge looked uncomfortably around the court, hoping he could lead Ellit's gaze away and spare him from looking back at the defendant's severe squint. Ellit's lawyer had cleverly decided to escape his client's eyes by staring down at the floor with an expression of such overwhelming sorrow that some in court swore he was crying. He had already spent several hours alone in his office with Ellit, and had lost the fortitude to return the latter's gaze.

Ellit explained that he had worked all of his life on his father's estate, but had been disinherited because, as his father said, "If it's violin you want to play, play violin. You're not getting an inch of my land."

The judge listened sympathetically to all, tried not to smile, and put Ellit on probation for one year. The neighbours ensured that Ellit, with his small band of five players armed with shak-shak, banjo, violin, cuatro, and guitar, was kept too busy to hurl any more rocks.

So, in the communities around Mandelie, people asked anxiously where Ellit would be playing on the weekend, and busloads of villagers sought him out along the thin grey roads that disappeared quickly around trees and hills and were rougher than a dog's nose. Ellit was in demand. Ugly: head too large, nose like a lump of putty thrown at his face, chest sunken. Ugly. But when he played, the women whispered, "Oh, Lord," and the men said, "Christ."

Cosmos joined his band for the celebrations at Charlo Pardie's house. The best saxophone player in the hills had once applied for work with a road crew, but when asked what his skills were, Cosmos volunteered with careless honesty that he played the saxophone sometimes at Christmas for masquerade bands. The foreman's laughter had sent him to Ellit for sympathy and occasional employment. He accepted clothes and food from his customers in lieu of payment and was content.

The preparations for La Rose began. The honour guards prepared their military-style uniforms, paraded on the school playground, shouted arcane orders, poked each other in the face and body with wooden weapons, sweated, cursed, and quarrelled to the point of contentment. The elected king and queen added to the ribbons, sashes, medallions, tassels, mirrors, and chains that adorned their regalia. Shoes were waxed, then polished to brilliance with spit. Pleats and flounces were added to skirts, bodices, and sleeves until the wearers resembled caravels under pink, white, and red sails. Black suits were brought out for airing: jackets shiny from wear and ironing; trousers with small belt loops one inch below the waistline; legs that waved to every breeze; and narrow cuffed bottoms that stopped suddenly at the ankles to hold back accordions of cloth.

On the thirtieth of the month, the villagers of Mandelie assembled in and around the church in numbers that prompted the priest to suggest that mass should not be used as a prelude to bacchanals.

The congregation smiled contritely, then went immediately after mass to the school yard for the coronation of the king and queen of La Rose. The honoured couple protested their surprise and gratification loudly and tearfully, despite the large amount of money both had spent during the past year to secure the outcome. Then everybody moved to the grounds around the Pardie's home. Children were sent to find chairs for the older people, then sent running back for iced water. Ismene appeared in a red satin dress tight about the chest and hips and flaring about her legs, and immediately encountered offers of fidelity and marriage. Constantine frowned protectively; Cord strutted, handsome and nonchalant, attentive and flirting, hot with jealousy.

Lucette was in the kitchen, dressed in many layers of pink lace and ribbons, her thin arms conducting the preparation and transport of food. Too much confusion, too much noise, too many suggestions, too much happiness for her to bear alone.

"Where is the thyme?"

"Not enough salt in the beef stew. I smell burning. Put a little more water in the rice; I don't know what made me buy that rice; tastes like cardboard."

"Somebody pass a bigger spoon. . . Soup's sticking to the bottom of the pot. Too much fire."

"Titina thinks she can make soup. . . and fry chicken better than anybody."

"When you heard me say that. . ."

"Enough. People are getting drunk out there in the yard. Time to start eating. You all can talk later."

"I never said I could make soup better than anybody."

"Titina, stir the soup."

"Just because I can cook better than her, she has to say things like that."

"Titina, look at what you're doing. Forget what she said."

"You never hear me saying things about people."

"Titina, give me peace."

"I'm not saying anything."

Two women at every pot. Men forbidden to enter the kitchen. Children waiting at the door and peering through the window, waiting to catch a mother's eye, and a taste.

Charlo sat in the shade of the breadfruit tree at the entrance to his driveway, strategically placed for intercepting greetings and congratulations.

One of the guests, recently arrived from the cane fields of Florida, came dressed in black, with a horizontal band of red sequins across the shoulders of his shirt, a vertical band of red and yellow sequins down the left front, and red sequined stripes down the sides of his trousers. One old man looked open-mouthed at the spectacle for a minute and cautioned, "Mind somebody doesn't throw water on you."

"Why?"

"You look like you caught on fire."

The returnee said something under his breath and moved on to practice his American accent and call the women "Baby" .

Another guest – somebody's aunt returning from London for a visit, determined that the audience should not mistake her for a local – came wearing gloves, a fur hat, a black woollen coat, and speaking in an accent refined to a state of incomprehensibility. Her fur hat drove the excitable opossum-hunting dogs into a whirlpool of frustration, enraged by the refusal of the lady to set them on such easy prey.

The Pardie's yard became a confusion of smells and words: smells from the kitchen of garlic and hot oil, hisses from frying pans; the ring of bottles against glass rims; recitations from ill-remembered poems by Wordsworth and Tennyson; steadfast arguments on the fates of Tokyo Rose and the Wandering Jew; the perfidy of France's Marshall Pétain during the war; the age of

England's Queen Elizabeth II at her coronation; the nature of an aircraft part that fell on the village from an American military plane heading for its wartime base in the south of the island (the base named for an air-force captain who had never visited the island, and neglected to visit even after the honour). Everyone talking, everyone forgetting to listen.

At sunset, the violin tested the crowd with a few notes and finding a warm reception, invited the other instruments to join in. The kerosene and Coleman lamps came on, and the older dancers, unhampered by shyness, hurried to the space cleared for dancing. Vive La Rose.

Ismene's eyes searched for Cord. He diligently ignored her. Late into the night, she took him by the elbow, "Dance with me, it's my birthday." She pressed against him until she could feel his discomfort digging into her belly. And when she could hear his breath hissing in her ears, and feel his heart beating against her chest, she whispered, "Let's go to my room. Don't let anybody see you."

He walked toward the outhouse, out of the lights, circled around the house to her bedroom. She sat on the bed and removed her shoes, let him take her dress off, then her underclothes. She had to help him unbutton his shirt, and to untie the laces of his shoes. She opened her arms and legs to him. Too hurried, too anxious, too much rum. And a barrier. "You're still a virgin. . . "

"You thought I was a prostitute too?"

"No, but people. . . "

"Yes, I know what people say about me."

He sat on the bed staring at her body: black against the white sheet, polished by fine sweat, gold-tinted from the light of the small oil lamp. He struggled for a good thing to say, not needing to touch her now, hurting from this new thing caught in his throat and burning his eyes. "Ismene," he said, "Ah, Ti-Ismene my little sweetheart." A long sigh of regret and relief. "We better get back before they notice both of us missing."

She called him back before he left the room, "Your shirt . . . it's inside out." And stood on tiptoe to reach his mouth.

They were calling for Ismene when he got back to the celebrations. "Cord. Seen Ismene?"

"No. Must be in the house."

"Ismene!"

During a break in the music, when the musicians stopped for breath and gin, Ellit came to sit near Cord. "You know, my friend, after all these years of playing, I can tell who leaves the dance floor with whom."

"What are you talking about, Ellit?" Cord asked.

"Eh-eh. What I am talking about is you and Ismene. Listen to me Cord. Marry Ismene. You hear me? That is all I have to tell you."

"But she's like my sister."

"You and Ismene like each other too much, and everybody knows she is not your sister. Anyway, you've heard what I had to say. Now, let me wet the mouth."

Later, on his way back to play, Ellit beckoned to Cord, "The only thing is, what are you going to do with those little ready-to-open legs you mess around with down by the beach and under the bananas?"

Others heard his laughter through the noise.

"But what are Ellit and Cord laughing about?"

"Must be something nasty – you know these men."

"But, yes."

"Vive La Rose!"

"Blow, Cosmos, blow!"

"Vive La Rose!"

"Hit me with music!"

In September, while arguments raged over who had the most enjoyment at the La Rose fêtes, who drank the most, who did what with whom, and who had the worst hangover, Constantine fell in love. Fell in love with the girl at the parts store who sold him a distributor kit for Charlo's truck, and who listened intently to his latest discovery of the role played by Captain Bligh of the *Bounty* in bringing breadfruit to the Antilles. When he paused for breath, she got him dead centre, right between the eyes, left him stunned and speechless: told him that the descendants of the mutineers on the *Bounty* still lived on an island in the Pacific. Constantine riposted that Captain Cook had been killed and eaten in Tahiti. She surrendered – smiling. Vanquished.

The following Sunday, Constantine drove to the city to visit Mounira Charpentier's parents. They all sat in the cramped sitting room, trapped in Morris chairs with burgundy-coloured velvet cushions, studying the repetition of geometric shapes on the linoleum, and listening to the father discuss in the most profound tones how fond Mounira was of condensed milk diluted with fruit-flavoured sodas.

Mr. Charpentier was tall and slender with a surprisingly large belly pushing against a shirt that was bought to fit his neck size. He filled the room with the smells of smoked mackerel and codfish, salted pork and aged cheddar cheese – all from his small corner grocery that allowed in only six customers at once. Mounira was a miniature of her mother: short, round, and pretty, with delicate ankles – and with her mother's enthusiasm for the preparation and consumption of foods of high caloric value.

Constantine was happy. The parents were satisfied. For several nights afterwards, Constantine heard no voices.

This new circumstance removed one layer of surveillance from Cord and Ismene. But now, as the sole possessor of Ismene's virtue, Cord felt no urgency to get to her, and he put her aside like a good suit to be kept for the right moment.

Ismene waited too, certain that Cord would not abandon her, certain that he would want to claim her virginity properly.

Lucette sensed the change between the two and frowned; told her suspicions to Charlo, who smiled and shrugged. So Lucette sent the neighbours' children to help Ismene when she went to the river to do the laundry at the Stream of Breasts – named for the village women who often sat, only in their panties, on the rocks in the shallow river to wash their clothes. And when she let Ismene travel alone to the city or to the pasture to bring back milk, it was after assuring herself that Cord was busy elsewhere.

She was not going to lose her son to the affection of a country girl of uncertain morals. She wanted a girl from the city, educated at the girl's high school, with good qualities beaten and prayed into her by the nuns.

But still, she loved this girl who had almost become a daughter. Loved her loud country laugh. Loved her obstinacy. Loved her when she stood alone in the kitchen kneading bread

48

in the large wooden tray, her face shining with the joy of making loaves that had no equal in Mandelie. Bread that perfumed their house on Friday evenings when she baked. Made the village children hurry to find indispensable things to do near the oven. Made the men coming back from their plots stop for a smoke. Made the women coming back from the river, balancing buckets of water on their heads, remember things they just had to say to her before hurrying on to prepare supper.

Late, in the quiet dark, when only the fireflies and stars were visible against the trees and sky, and the resinous smell of the scorched *ti-baume* broom came from the oven after Constantine or Cord or Charlo had swept the wood ashes away, Ismene would place the loaves in the glowing belly of the oven. The children would forget the punishments and injuries of the week, and crowd around her, searching for the special things – "There! There! See them?" – the small plaited loaves she made for them, to be opened when still too hot to eat, and seasoned with salty oleomargarine, but not so much as to hide the bread's own flavour; and there were the blunt spindles of bread to be broken for wiping sauces; to be opened for cuddling lumps of black blood-pudding or codfish fritters; to envelop fried fish – heads and all.

On a rainy Friday afternoon, while Ismene was shaping loaves from a pile of dough, and Lucette was replacing shirt buttons, they heard the radio announcer warn that a storm with extremely heavy rains was approaching, bringing with it the probability of flooding low-lying areas.

"I better go down to the pasture and warn Charlo," Lucette said, "he must be still watering the animals. The boys won't be down from the garden for another two hours. And they themselves won't know how bad it's going to be."

As she prepared to leave, Ismene looked at the slate-grey clouds, heavier and lower than she had ever seen before, and said, "I think I had better go instead . . . I can run faster than you."

She found Charlo standing at the stream that emptied into the swamp, waiting for the cows to finish drinking.

"What you doing here?"

"Bad storm and flooding, they said on the radio. Ma Lucette sent me to tell you to get home right away. The boys are still up in the hills."

"Help me with the calves. Let's get them up on the high ground."

They were on their way back down to the pasture when the rain began, heavy and black, driving hard into the earth. Lightning cracked like sharp anger, and wide pressing thunder shook the ground and the air.

"Run!" Charlo cried, and they raced for the hut.

"Sorry you had to get stuck here. This will go on for a while but we'll be OK," Charlo said inside the hut, when he had regained his breath.

"But our clothes – we're soaked," Ismene said, already shaking from fright and the cold.

"You'll probably catch cold, unless you want to take your clothes off and put on the sheet there." He nodded toward an old dirty sheet on the cot in the corner.

Ismene glanced at the sheet, "Don't think so."

"Well, your body's heat will dry them."

Some time later, he pushed a window open against the wind. "Trouble," he said, and moved to one side to let her see.

"Ay, *Bon Dieu*," she said quietly, and went to sit on the cot, shaking her hands as if to dry them of invisible water. "Mr. Charlo, what are we going to do?"

"Wait and pray."

Charlo found a knothole in a board that he looked through to check on the progress of the storm. Opening the window let in too much rain. He watched the level of the brown water rise to cover the grass and then up to the leaves of the lantana bushes. Even when night came, the lightning was bright and frequent enough to let him see clearly to the end of the path from the hut. The water in the field was not too deep to wade through, and the water was not moving too quickly, but the path up the hill had become a channel of roaring, hissing water. To the west were the cliffs, but these were impossible to climb in the dark and wet. To their east was the sea; the swamp blocked passage to the south. He hoped no one would try to get to them. Alone, he would have been worried; with Ismene trapped here with him, he was terrified. He opened the door carefully to see how close the water had come to the floor; it had covered the step and was only six inches from the door sill.

He looked out over the pasture and thought he saw a bundle of cloth floating slowly past. A few seconds later, the lightning lit up the water, long enough to see it was a body floating face-down.

Ismene heard him gasp, and came over quickly, "What is it?" she asked, her voice breaking in alarm.

Charlo did not answer, and she looked over his shoulder. "No-no-no!" she said, "Mr. Charlo, that's a dead person."

"Yes," he answered. "Don't know who it is. . . couldn't see a face."

"Mr. Charlo?" she said.

"Yes?"

"You think we're going to drown here?"

"No, I don't think the water can come higher. It can get to the sea."

He did not tell her that if the water rose another few inches, it would float the house away – perhaps to the sea.

"And I didn't even have time to bake the bread," she said.

"When we get back, we'll have dumplings for days," Charlo joked, relieved that she could think of something other than the storm and the body.

They had no means of telling the time, but Charlo estimated it was about nine o'clock when he suggested they try and get some sleep. It was too difficult making conversation above the rolling explosions of thunder.

They prepared a sleeping place in a corner near the door, away from most of the leaks in the roof. He took some rags from the small cot in the corner. It had been a year since anyone had slept there, but the rags still smelled of sleep. Probably Constantine and Cord had used the cot for needs more urgent than sleep; these thoughts made him uneasy.

He hoped she would not be uncomfortable with him in the same room. He suggested they keep on their clothes. "I'll sleep on the floor," he said.

51

But the blue flashes, blinding even through the cracks in the walls, the hammering of rain on the tin roof, and the noise of the storm made it impossible to drift into sleep.

"Mr. Charlo? You're sleeping? I'm so afraid, I can't breathe. I can even hear my heart beat. Let me sleep on the floor with you. I keep seeing that dead body floating around the house."

"I won't let anything happen to you, Ismene," he said. He pitched his voice low, and hoped he sounded brave.

His arm was trapped between their thighs, and when he tried to pull it away she moved closer, and he let it stay until his fingers tingled painfully. When he pulled his hand over his leg, she moved closer, pressing her hip against him. He thought she was dreaming when she threw her leg over him. He tried to roll away, but she put her arm over his chest and would not let go. He slowed his breathing and tried to will his hardness to go down. She climbed on top of him.

"No," he said, and tried to push her off.

She held him more tightly, and buried her face in his neck, shaking her head when he pushed against her.

He was in agony from her weight on his pelvis. Reached down to ease himself. She shifted her weight to one side and reached down to take him in her hand, caressed him softly with her thumb then moved her encircling hand gently up and down. He was trembling now, wanting her to stop, but wanting to prolong the pleasure for a few more seconds.

Slowly, she unbuttoned his shirt, pausing for several seconds at each button, as if waiting to stop his protesting hand. He lifted his shoulders as she peeled off the shirt. She undid his belt and unbuttoned his pants. Another long pause, so long that he assumed it was over and was regretting it, then she took him again in her hand, and this time he did not want her to stop, hoping he would come to a release before they went any further. She stopped to pull his pants off, then removed her clothes. She lay back down on him and held his shoulders to pull herself up to place her face in the crook of his neck again. He felt stiff hair brush against his navel as she suddenly moved down, a quick, sharp pain, and the indescribable wetness and warmth told him that his life had changed forever. He lay motionless. His memory flew to his first sexual experience and to his last secret hurried affair when the terror of discovery had made it so joyously intense. He never wanted to wake up from this dream where the silent shouts in his mind exulted in the best sin of his life and he felt a gladness in his new body and his breathing grew louder than the storm. He tried to grasp the entirety of his happiness, but his mind leaped from sensation to new sensation, to new smells and tastes and sounds. A finger probing, a hand holding tight, the tip of a tongue against an ear, a lip sliding down a cheek, her salt in his mouth, muscles tightening around him.

Soft quick words from her: "Oh. . . Oh. . . Oh. . ."

He caressed her back with the tips of his fingers, afraid that his rough hands would scratch her skin. Her body had the smoothness of wet dough, and his fingers found no imperfection except a small bump in the hollow between her shoulders. One finger circled it.

"Mole," she whispered.

He explored her body as far as his hands could reach, being careful not to stay too long in the private places, to show his respect. He played with the fine hair on the nape of her neck with one hand, cupped her bottom with the other and caressed her as if to make her skin even smoother. Took her face in his hands and kissed her forehead. Wanted desperately to speak: to tell her that he would give her baskets of gold chains and forests of mahogany and balata; fill her hands with banknotes; buy her stores of dresses; sit forever looking at her face. He searched for words to tell her how happy he was. His eyes burned, he choked on insufficient words. No need to tell her. . .

Her movements were slow and gentle as if she were patiently teaching him to dance. He tried to think of the fire in the skies and of the thunder shaking the world around them, afraid to lose control and call out, pushing with his pride against the force that was hurling him toward a precipice. He was falling. Not yet. . . not yet. . . please. . . please. . . please. . .

A moan started in his belly, pushed up through his chest and roared out of his mouth, sighing as it exhausted his lungs. She began shuddering and he felt her fingers dig into his flesh as she screamed louder and louder, until he didn't know whether she was laughing or crying. Was so alarmed that he asked what was wrong. He felt her body rock as she shook her head.

Then she was laughing: little hisses, as if happy to rediscover the ability to breathe. And she lay on him until they had stopped gasping. Some time later, she rolled off, and they fell asleep. He awoke again because the noise from the storm had lessened, and he felt for her. She took his hand and put it on her breasts. He placed one leg over her thigh, and she opened her legs for him. This time she moved very slowly, as if to ensure that his body would remember hers.

Not a word.

Next morning, when he opened a window to let in some light, she avoided his eyes.

Not a word.

He saw the crusted blood on her legs and on some of the rags, and on himself too. They wiped the blood off with wet rags, and Ismene rinsed them clean through the window. She avoided his eyes.

Only then did he think of Lucette.

CHAPTER 4

Constantine and Cord were ten miles from the village when the storm broke. "This is the mama of storms," Constantine said, "we'd better leave the coffee and try and get back before the river floods."

"No sir, I spent the whole morning collecting coffee and I'm not going to leave it here," Cord replied.

They had been working on the plot of coffee that the family owned in the hills overlooking Mandelie, and Cord was spreading the berries on the ground to dry when Constantine pointed to the clouds building up in the east. Cord continued to rake the coffee while Constantine hurried to put tools and pots away in the small shed.

Then, "Oh, shit!" as the rain came down hard, and Cord tried to rake all the berries into a pile. "Cons, bring me a tarpaulin – this rain is going to wash everything away."

"Think we can make it?" Constantine asked.

"Let's get our tails out of here," Cord shouted.

The Austin truck whined in second gear as Constantine let it roll down the road, steering from memory because the rain was too much for the wipers.

The bridge was built low with no guard rails so that flood water could wash over it, and it had disappeared beneath a sheet of brown water. Constantine braked too hard, and the truck slid to the edge of the water. "We're in Shit Street," he said. "Can't go back . . . not even a four-wheel drive could climb the hill now. You want to stay here? If things get really bad, we can get back up the hill on foot. But we're going to lose the truck."

"We're going across," Cord said.

"You're crazy? I can't see the bridge."

55

"I'm going to walk across. I can feel with a stick for the edge of the bridge and guide you across."

"Well, we'd better do it before I have time to think about it," Constantine said. He was not aware that he was praying until Cord stood at the other side of the water and pointed to what he gauged was the centre of the weir. Constantine put the truck into first gear and drove slowly into the water, his foot on the clutch pedal to prevent the engine stalling; he was barely able to hold back the urge to press hard on the accelerator.

The truck came slowly out of the water and Cord climbed aboard. "I can't believe we did something that stupid," he said.

Constantine nodded, too shaken to speak.

It took them an hour and forty-five minutes to drive the remaining six miles back to Mandelie. Ma Lucette was sitting in her bedroom, so paralysed with fear that she stared at them for several seconds as if confronted by the disembodied remains of her family. "Your father and Ismene . . . they're down in the pasture. I don't know what to do. Ismene went to tell him about the storm. But they haven't come back. Three hours ago. *Mon Dieu . . . Mon Dieu . . . Mon Dieu.*"

"They must be sheltering in the hut. They'll be OK," Constantine said, but his smile of reassurance did not reach his eyes.

"Think we should go and meet them?" Cord asked.

"In the dark? And in this lightning? That's too dangerous. We'll have to wait till morning. Papa and Ismene will be all right, Mama," Constantine said. "We better get out of these clothes," he said to Cord.

The rain did not let up until noon the following day.

One hour after the storm began, Cosmos had become alarmed and decided to leave the small shack he had built on the top of the cliffs overlooking Charlo's pasture, and which he shared with his saxophone. He put the instrument into a blue plastic bag that had come from the banana wrapping station, and headed for Rabot's rum shop. He was always welcome to sleep on a mattress of jute sacks behind the counter when the weather was more than his roof could deflect.

The drain on the right side of the path was already overflowing with a torrent that was cutting into the embankment, and in one spot the red clay had been washed away to expose an outcropping of greyish-white clay. Even in the dim light, Cosmos could see the sparks of yellow that blazed when lightning flashed. He waded into the water, holding onto an overhanging branch. He dug a small, brassy nugget out of the clay and fought his way back out of the water, washed his find and put it deep into his pocket. He ran most of the way to the rum shop.

"Rabot! Rabot! It's me, Cosmos." He banged on the back door of the small shop – which Rabot would never leave until convinced that lateness and severe acts of God would deny him another customer.

Rabot came to the door. "Cosmos? Eh-eh. But you'll drown in this rain. Come inside, quick."

"Let me leave my sax here for a little while, I have something to do. It's all right if I sleep in the shop?"

Rabot nodded. "What do you have to do in weather like this?"

Cosmos handed him the saxophone. "I'll be back right away." And he was running back to the exposure of white clay before Rabot could say any more.

He had managed to dig out about two ounces of golden crystals when his arm holding the root began to tire. He braced his left leg against the bank and pushed hard. He right foot landed on the sodden clay at the edge of the racing water, slipped, and he fell back striking his head on a rock. His unconscious body rolled slowly down the hill, and into the current. The water took him down towards the sea, and his pockets emptied themselves of their treasure of fool's gold.

In the middle of the afternoon the rain had lessened to a steady drizzle, and Charlo opened the door and stepped out. "Am going to get some *bois grié* . . . My stomach is hurting too much. I'll see if I can get some guavas for you."

As soon as he was at the edge of the field, Ismene got out and hastened to the back of the hut where she stood ankle deep in muddy water to relieve her bladder. On her way back, she could see Charlo standing motionless against a tree doing the same.

57

In the act of peeing he was more vulnerable, and in the safety of their distance she could look at him with less apprehension. She had not expected them to survive the storm, and was unprepared for the embarrassment of their survival.

She began cleaning up the interior of the hut, ensuring that there were no bloody rags left unwashed. The burning between her legs made her wince. She was hungry and hurting – and they still had to start the long walk uphill through mud and debris.

Charlo brought back three half-ripe guavas and a handful of black berries. He handed her the guavas and she took two, and some berries.

"I thought you didn't eat *bois grié,*" he said.

For the first time that day she looked directly at him, and her eyes crinkled and her lips pursed as she tried not to laugh. "But I wasn't hungry enough then."

"Poor thing," he said, "you must be so tired. Don't worry, we'll make it back OK to the house."

When they had finished eating, he said, "I wanted you to eat something before I told you this . . ."

"Mr. Charlo. . ." she said in panic.

"Wait, wait. It's not what you think. I have to go and find the body that washed through here last night. It must have got caught in the logwood trees near the shore. We can't go and leave it there. And if I find it, I am going to have to bring it back to the hut – then find some people to help me carry it back."

She nodded, and Charlo saw her face pale, and her breathing quicken.

He took a machete from the hut, and waded through the ankle-deep water to the eastern edge of the field, and as he had expected, found the body trapped in the low thorny branches of a logwood tree. His stomach heaved as he recognized the face of his friend, although the skin was now grey and wrinkled and covered with small white cuts. Charlo slung the corpse over his shoulders and returned to the hut. "Ismene!" he shouted when he was close enough, "It's Cosmos."

She helped him wash the mud off the body and pulled away bits of twigs and leaves from the torn clothes. She gritted her teeth trying not to vomit, and her eyes watered from the effort.

Charlo looked at her concerned, then grateful. "Thanks, Ismene," he said.

They closed the door to the hut and set off immediately for the road. Halfway up the hill, the road had slipped completely away leaving a vertical gash in the earth. "We'll have to go back and try and cut our way out around the landslide," Charlo said. "I hope people from the village are looking for us. It's going to take me a long time to do that alone."

"I can help you . . . " Ismene began.

"Yes. And you won't be able to bake bread for weeks after. And right now, all I can think of is hot bread and butter and cocoa. Two, three, four loaves. Oh God, I'm hungry."

She grinned, and this time met his eyes.

It was near evening when they heard the voices: "Papa! Ismene! Charlo!" It was Constantine, Cord and a group of others.

Then the sound of machetes against *baton balai*, the hard upright shrubs used for broom handles.

"Here! Here!" they answered.

Cord pushed his way through the remaining undergrowth. For a few seconds they all looked at each other in awkward too-much-to-say silence. Then Charlo said, *"Merci, Mon Dieu."* He told them about Cosmos. Two men went on to the hut and asked that others be sent to fetch a bamboo pole and a hammock to carry the body back.

Cord would have carried Ismene all the way to the house on his back if she had let him. Instead, he cut her a highway through the bush, continually asking whether she was well. "Were you afraid? Did you have anything to eat? We were so scared. I would have been so scared. Mama is almost mad with worrying – she must have used up almost two rosaries." Later, he would tell her about Constantine's and his reckless dash across the swollen river.

"Too tired to talk, Cord. You don't know how it's nice to hear your voice again," she managed to say. She held his hand tightly all the way home.

Lucette was standing outside the door of the cream-coloured house with brown trim, her hands tight around a rosary. When she saw them all – Charlo, Constantine, Cord, Ismene, and the others, the tears came, hot burning and good. Then she went into the kitchen to begin cooking: soup – with pumpkin, onions, thyme, potatoes, carrots and beef, with large marrow bones for Charlo. The bread was not as good as Ismene's, but no one mentioned it.

"But what was Cosmos doing out in the storm?"

"Rabot said he brought the saxophone to the rum shop, and took off. Didn't say where he was going. Poor *diable*. Anyway, he must be blowing sax in heaven."

"Yes, but we're never going to hear music like that again."

"No. Nobody will blow sax like Cosmos again. Poor *diable*."

"What a thing! What a thing!"

"What's Rabot going to do with the saxophone?"

"He said he's going to hang it in the shop. He can't sell it – Cosmos was his friend."

Lucette searched the faces of Charlo and Ismene, looking for the things left unsaid. Listening for their silences. "So, did you sleep at all? How high did the water get? Water must have come through the roof. What did you do, Ismene?"

"Pray. A lot," Ismene said.

"That's all we could do," Charlo said, "but in all that thunder, I don't know if God heard us."

The boys laughed; Lucette frowned.

"You all almost died and you're making jokes about it?" She shook her head.

But that night, she held Charlo tightly in bed, asking him to make love to her – and then again, after their breathing had settled, but he pleaded exhaustion. She kept her hands on him.

By morning, Lucette had decided that Cord should marry Ismene. Something had happened to change her, and if Cord did not act quickly, he would lose her. Lucette assumed it was the result of a night of terror. No. . . nothing else could have happened.

At breakfast, when the boys were outside discussing the storm with the neighbours, and Ismene was collecting clothes for washing, she moved close to Charlo, "I think it's time for Cord and Ismene to get married."

Charlo turned his head so quickly that she heard his neck snap. "Cord? Ismene? But I thought you didn't . . ."

"Well, what're they going to do? I tell you I won't be surprised to see her belly start growing in a few months."

Charlo felt the blood drain from his face. His chest burned. "I suppose you're right. But what do you want me to do? Go and tell them to marry?"

"No. Just leave them alone from now on. Look at your face – you look as if I'd just told you she was pregnant."

Charlo shrugged, and shook his head. The thick strong coffee had become tasteless.

He went out to see what damage the storm had caused, to tell of his own adventure, and about Cosmos.

More news came from other parts of the island as traffic began to move again. Travellers said they had seen cars buried in mud up to their roofs; had seen children diving off the roofs of their homes; had seen fishermen rowing boats miles inland from the sea. The government-owned radio station played sombre music all day. The hourly news reports told of the escape of nine prisoners from the jail who swam over the gate in the prison wall. And later, how seven had returned in a stolen canoe after they saw the devastation caused by the storm. The next day, the country learned that twenty people had been killed by drowning and by landslides.

The villagers of Mandelie loudly and passionately recollected the signs they had seen in the sky and the peculiar behaviour of their animals, and their regret at not having paid these sufficient attention. The priest was pleased with the increased attendance at mass, and for a month he provided his congregation with dramatic serialized instalments of the story of the Great Flood. He detailed, to the last cubit, the building of Noah's Ark – which he likened to his small wooden church, although no one had sought shelter there during the more recent deluge.

Several children found the outcropping of white clay with the brassy nuggets. Word went around the village that there was gold to be found on the road that led down to the sea. Furious arguments erupted over ownership of the land, and this had already led to some pushing and threats before the agricultural extension officer announced that the nuggets were iron pyrites with no more value than the clay in which they were embedded.

As proof, he smashed some pyrites with a rock to show their brittleness. "Gold doesn't break," he pointed out. His later observation was even more convincing: "If there was gold at Mandelie, you think no one would have found it before?"

Charlo took advantage of all of these distractions to visit Uselle, the woman who had relieved him of the burden of his virginity when he was fourteen. He told Lucette that he was going to see what damage the storm had caused around Mandelie.

He stopped wherever there was a group of people examining storm damage; exchanged courtesies; gave thoughtful opinions.

There was no one at Uselle's house but he parked nearby and blew on the horn.

"I'm coming. Who's the person?"

Uselle came from a neighbour's house carrying a baby he assumed was a grandchild. She walked as if she owned the ground; magnificent legs, but with the contours of her calves now scalloped with varicose veins, and her lower lip still pouting disappointment. She was the best dancer at Mandelie, with strong arms that pulled a man close, and legs that pushed so hard against him, that afterwards, shaken and elated, he wondered whether he had been inside her. She never betrayed a confidence, never told who had fathered her four children: yellow, red, brown and black – although the village knew from the children's faces.

"Still making children?" he teased.

"You don't remember when you gave me this one?" she answered. "What are you doing around here, Charlo?"

"Just looking at what the storm did. Cosmos drowned, you know . . . found his body on my pasture. Nobody knows what happened. . . Whose baby?"

"My son's little boy. Six months."

"Ah. And where's Rafe? His foot better yet?"

"He must be out stealing again. Left this morning; said he was going to dig out some yams and tannias. But you know him."

Charlo nodded ruefully. Rafe had sneaked out one night to a neighbour's farm to steal yet more of his bananas, and had got his leg stuck in a booby trap. His cries awakened the neighbour who pretended he did not recognize Rafe in the darkness and had beaten him severely enough to break a toe on his other foot. When he stopped from exhaustion, and expressed his great surprise at finding Rafe in his garden, he apologized with tearful remorse and offered to carry him to the Health Centre. Rafe begged to be allowed to walk home. He did not wish for further conversation.

"What else has he been getting himself into these days?" Charlo asked, not anxious to get to the matter for which he had come.

"Well, you know after the *Fête la Rose* he had such a bad hangover he said he was going to leave drinking alone . . . and he was going to preach. He found some old bible and every Sunday used to go over to the cockfights and talk rubbish. People didn't mind, until he got vexed because nobody was listening. One morning, he called them thieves; they ignored him. He called them all adulterers; they agreed. He called them fornicators; they smiled. Then he went and called them *boyaux de caca*. Charlo, such a tra-la-la broke out. They beat his ass. Luckily some women went and dragged him away from the crowd. He didn't look too good when he came home. Now, he says he doesn't believe in God."

"Why did you marry him, Uselle?" Charlo asked.

"After all of you had finished screwing me, who else would want me?"

"That's not true," Charlo said, wanting to change the subject. For a few minutes they looked at each other in silence, both thinking of the night when his parents were away at a funeral and two older friends had implored Uselle to introduce their virgin friend to the greatest of pleasures. After his friends had presented Charlo's case to Uselle, she agreed to meet him in his bedroom. She was lying on the bed when his friends pushed him into the room. He got in and lay next to her. She helped him undress, made him lie on her and raised her dress. She guided him – and he set to with all the enthusiasm, ignorance, and determination of thirteen years and six months. He assumed from her moans that she was enjoying his frenzy and he was still lost in enjoyment when his friends decided to come into the room. Uselle got off the bed, dressed and left. She had not said a single word throughout the entire episode.

Three days later she saw him and called to him. He did not answer because his throat was constricted with embarrassment, and he had become too weak to raise his arm. But that was long ago, and maturity had eroded old discomforts. These days, he found refuge in her occasional advice.

"So you have a problem, my friend?" she asked.

"Well. . . life is a little more complicated," he said.

"Don't tell me you're playing with Ti-Ismene?" she said, laughing – and stopped when she saw his face turn gray. She thought he was about to faint. "I was only joking," she said quickly.

"What made you say that?" he asked.

"I'm sorry, I just thought of the most impossible thing you could do," Uselle said.

Charlo breathed deeply. "Uselle," he said, so softly that she barely heard him, "it is Ismene."

Uselle looked away, then at the ground. When she looked him in the eye it was not for long.

Her voice was hoarse when she spoke, "That's not good, Charlo."

He nodded, then told her all that had happened the night of the storm.

"But she was afraid, Charlo. The poor thing thought both of you were going to die. And she wanted you to hold her."

"You're sure?"

"Of course. What did you think . . . that she suddenly fell in love with you? I hope you haven't said anything about it."

"No. And now Lucette wants Cord and her to hurry up and get married. What to do, Uselle?"

"Nothing."

"Nothing?"

"Just forget it. It was an accident. You know what would happen to your whole family and Ismene if that got out? I've already forgotten what you told me."

"But what if Ismene says no . . . because of what happened?"

"Tell me, if you were in Ismene's place, you'd do something like that? You think Lucette knows everything you've done? When you asked her to marry you, you told her all the nastiness you did before? You told her it was me who showed you where to put your miserable thing? Eh? Tell me that." And Uselle began fanning her face with a piece of cardboard as if the words had made her unbearably hot.

"You have a good head on you, you know," he said. "Please don't even think again about what I just told you." A long pause, then he rose. "Good, I had better be on the road again. Let me leave a little something with you. And something for the baby." He handed her a one-dollar and two five-dollar bills.

Uselle smiled her thanks, and put the folded notes into her blouse. On his way home, he remembered the time many years later, when he had spoken with Uselle at a school fair. In drunken good humour – and Lucette at home – he bought her two drinks, danced with her. "How about giving me the little thing again?" he said into her ear.

"All these years, you never had time for me. Always looking ashamed when you saw me. And now you want to roll in bed with me? At my age, Charlo? When all I have left is one pubic hair for a crab louse to take a swing from? Just shut up and dance, man."

"But it was good though," he remembered.

"And the best you ever had," she said.

"Yes. Even now," he agreed.

He laughed out loud and felt better until he reached the outskirts of Mandelie where he could see the ocean and the bright green of the pasture and the miniature animals. The hut. And Ismene – dancing slowly over the wet grass.

CHAPTER 5

The soil at Mandelie is fat and deep: alluvium washed down from the hillsides, mixed with ancient volcanic ash. In some places, a strong man can push his machete down as far as its grip and not touch a rock. The soil is black and crumbles like the curds of sour milk. And it holds the rain well, so that even in the dry season, the succulent and brittle water grass continues to stretch its blanket over the ground and decorate itself with tiny blue flowers.

There was Pardie blood in Charlo's land, pushed deep into it by rain, sprinkled along its four corners from the wrist of Charlo's Uncle Bone. Red hair, red skin, luminous as if his flesh were on fire. They called him "*Fourmi Rouge*" as a child, but not to his face when he grew to six feet, six inches.

Every woman at Mandelie and beyond loved him until, alone with him, they heard his voices: bellowing that shook the bed; plaintive cries of kittens crying for milk; strangers' voices saying incomprehensible things. Sometimes, two voices at once.

One Tuesday morning he walked through the village naked, brandishing a newly sharpened machete, shouting the name of a long dead neighbour, warning him to stay away from Pardie land, daring him to come out and fight face-to-face like a man. Stopped under a mango tree, swept his blade across the face of a large flat rock so fast and hard that sparks cascaded from the steel. Parents hurried their children indoors and stayed near their houses until evening when Bone sat down at the base of the tree, leaned his back against it and fell asleep. In the dark, Charlo's father crept up to him and called quietly, "Brother, it's time to go inside."

Bone awoke dazed, wondering who had stolen his clothes. A neighbour brought him a pair of trousers. Bone left, apologizing to all, trying to remember the cause of his predicament and shame. At home, he asked himself over and over, "What happened to me?"

One week later, he attacked a plantain tree, sliced through the ten-inch stem with one blow, then hacked it to pieces, screaming curses at the tree, and warning its family to stay away from him and his land.

But after he set fire to a neighbour's house, the people of Mandelie decided to take him under restraint to the capital and ask the authorities to incarcerate him. He evaded the men coming with ropes and sticks. Lost himself in the hill forest for two days. They found his body lying at the edge of his land beneath an immortelle tree that served as a boundary marker.

His left wrist was slit but there was little blood on the ground near the wound. Someone noticed the trail of blood leading away from his body, and they followed it – along the boundaries of his estate. He had reclaimed ownership: walked the four corners of his land. Marked the land with his blood.

Charlo first overheard parts of the story when he was thirteen, at dinner, so intent on the last flecks of flesh from the bones of a fried grouper that the adults thought he could not hear them: how Bone had joked and quarrelled with his voices, how he had chased the priest and *gardeur* who tried to exorcize him. Charlo remembered that their laughter at the table had been light and painful.

"Such a nice person when he was well."

"The children used to follow him all the way home when he came from the garden; used to collect *pommes d'amour* for us."

"Yes. And when that was out of season, used to give us bread soaked in honey. . . always tasted better than when you did it yourself."

"Yes."

"And turtle eggs. You remember the turtle eggs he used to go and collect at night? Used to go alone. Not afraid of anything, that man."

"Poor *diable*."

"Why Bone?"

Shaken heads. Shrugged shoulders.

But when Charlo asked about his Uncle Bone, they did not remember much. Said he died young. . . died in an accident. They became impatient; found things for Charlo to do. But others told him about Bone.

After the death of his parents and two sisters and a brother from malaria, Charlo was the only surviving Pardie at Mandelie. He inherited Bone's ten acres. He never told his children about Bone. The older villagers, anxious to donate their memories, had made that unnecessary.

For years, Bone's land lay fallow, and the undisturbed soil grew more fertile. After Charlo cleared it for planting, his crops flourished with no need for fertilizer. The inevitable rumour was that Bone's blood had enriched the soil, but that perhaps the food was poisoned by the dead man's troubled soul. Charlo, though, had no problem selling his vegetables in the capital; he did not bother his customers with details of his family's history.

He used that acreage for planting his most profitable crops: white yams, mango, cashews, melongene, cabbage, tomatoes, and carrots. Cord and Constantine were not afraid of working that land, but it was difficult getting help from other villagers, except for Vanius and his companion Maude. No one could dig holes deeper and faster and in a straighter line than Vanius, but he could never plant anything at the right time and place. He would have starved if his neighbours had not paid to use his other skills. Maude came to weed and cook. She was ten years older than Vanius and the village drunk, but he had taken her into his small house when no one else had any more use for her.

Vanius had come to Rabot's rum shop one Sunday evening, when Maude, with no money left to pay for cheap white rum, was offering the promise of untold ecstasies to any man who would buy her a shot. He took her gently by the arm. When she tried to fight him, he tied her arms and legs with sisal cord and carried her off on his shoulders. The children followed her curses, threats, and exposed thighs all the way to Vanius's hut. When she calmed down three hours later, he loosened her bonds, but did not untie her until the next morning. She awoke cursing him. He made her brush her teeth with powdered charcoal, and brought her a pail of water and a sliver of carbolic soap to wash herself. Afterwards, dressed in his clothes – shirt down to her knees, and pants rolled up to her calves – she staggered to the lean-to kitchen. She cleaned his pots, and made him the best salted pigtail soup he had ever tasted. She never went back to the rum shop. Drank only at Easter, Christmas and New Year's Day. Drank only whiskey – with her small finger stiffened in impeccable decorum.

There were no preliminaries before Charlo's group began their work: Maude cleared away the ashes from her hearth made of three rocks, and left to collect dry sticks and water. The men began their assault upon the soil, working to the rhythm of a work song.

"Jean-Pierre Roulleau. . . *Poussez!*" Pushing forks deep into the earth with their feet.

"Jean-Pierre Roulleau. . . *Tournez!*" Turning over heavy clumps of black soil ribboned with frantic earthworms.

"Jean-Pierre Roulleau. . . *Fouillez!*" Burying weeds and dry leaves, working them back into the soil.

Meantime, Maude put chopped vegetables and dried salted pork into a tureen half filled with a sauce of coconut milk, onions, garlic, pepper, thyme, and sharp-flavoured, salty oleomargarine.

When the men stopped singing, Maude called out, "Who's taking me to the Carnival *jour ouvert* parade? Vanius is too old to handle a hot young thing like me now." She sat on the ground laughing – the joke too good for her legs to support.

"Sorry," Constantine replied, "I'm stuck with Mounira . . . but I would prefer to go with you."

"How about you, Cord?" Maude said.

"Well. . ." Cord began, trying quickly to think of something more outrageous.

"Why don't you take Ismene?" Charlo said.

"Take Ismene?" Cord and Constantine said in unison.

"What's wrong with her?" Charlo answered.

Carnival one week away. Cord pretended to be joking when he asked Ma Lucette whether he could take Ismene to the city with him for the *jour ouvert* parade from midnight to dawn.

Lucette said, "Yes, I know she will enjoy herself."

Charlo said, "Go on, enjoy yourselves," and looked at Lucette for approval. She nodded.

Cord hesitated, uncomfortable at getting what he had asked for so easily. He went into the kitchen where Ismene was washing dishes. "Ismene, you want to go to *jour ouvert* next weekend?"

"Don't make jokes," she said, slightly irritated.

"I'm not joking, I asked Ma Lucette and Papa. Both said yes."

"Poor devils, they must be getting old," she said. "For true?"

"Yes. Yes."

"Of course, I want to go. What about Constantine?"

"We're all going in the truck. But we probably won't see him after we get there. He'll be busy working on Mounira. . . grinding her valves."

"Nasty," she said. Then, "You're really serious?"

"Yes, little sweet."

She finished washing up quickly, looking anxiously at her nails as if to ensure that immersion in the soapy water had not done irreversible damage.

At two o'clock in the morning of the Monday before Ash Wednesday, they packed the half-ton truck: four at the front, seven at the back. Rear springs pressed almost flat, front lifted so high that the front wheels lost traction with every bump. Cord drove, Constantine cautioned: "Watch for the next corner – bad hole there. Keep it in second gear. Easy. . . easy on the brakes."

"Shut up Cons! Let me drive."

"OK . . . all right. And then he'll say I didn't warn him."

Ismene was pressed hard between Cord and Ellit; her upper arms ached and burned, but she would have sat as close to Cord if she had been alone with him. She was determined that before the two days of Carnival were over, she and Cord would have exhausted each other. Rubbed her legs against his, whispered little indecencies into his ear, touched him surreptitiously and giggled at the pain she provoked.

Constantine and Ellit argued greatly about nothing.

The sounds of steel bands warming up came to meet them on the last great bend overlooking the capital. But the *jour ouvert* parades were late starting. The entire town was in an uproar over the selection of the Calypso King: the judges' choice at the competition had not been the popular one and several members of the audience had climbed up on the stage, taken the crown from the official winner, and placed it on the head of the taxi driver whose song, "Bobby", the entire audience was already humming.

The bands were paralysed, unable to decide which calypso was the road-march tune, but by four o'clock, the sounds of "Bobby" overwhelmed everything else, and the unofficial Calypso King rode triumphantly on the back of a flatbed truck screaming his song through the town.

Cord parked the truck near the police station for safety. Constantine set off to meet Mounira, and the others left hurriedly after reassurances that they would not be left behind.

"Leaving at eight o'clock sharp," Cord warned.

Cord and Ismene danced in the parade for an hour. He pressed hard against her, touched every part of her. She moved behind him, put her arms under his shirt and around his waist, put her fingers down his pants. His composure lasted only five minutes. Turned and shouted into her ear, "Let's get back to the truck and go somewhere fast. I can't take it any more. Oh Lord."

They sped to the beach near the airport, where the sea-grape trees suggested canopied privacy. But every space was taken. After half an hour of driving back and forth, and spurred by the lightening sky, Cord pulled into a driveway that led to a small unpainted wooden house set on cinder blocks. He unbuttoned Ismene's shirt, and was fumbling with the clasp of her brassiere, when a brown and yellow mongrel shot out from the crawl space of the house and announced their presence to the entire quarter. A window opened in the house and an old face of indeterminate sex looked out. "Stop your damn' barking, you stupid. . ." then the face looked at the truck with bemusement that turned quickly to anger. "Get the hell out of my yard, you *salauds*. Police! Police! Help!"

Cord drove back to the police station, banging his fists against the steering wheel, and cursing the insatiable fornicators of the city who left no quick hideaways for others.

Ismene kept her hands between his legs and licked at the salt of dried sweat on his neck, "We'll do it tomorrow night," she said.

They joined another line of tired, sweating revellers shuffling after three men banging on a rusted brake drum, an empty rum bottle, and a steel-band drum.

Constantine and Mounira were following a parade going past the city library when Mounira tugged at his arm. "Think we

71

better stop here. Another band's coming from the boulevard and I don't want us in the middle of the clash."

They moved to the sidewalk "Want to go back to the truck or want to watch?" Constantine asked.

"Watch? You crazy?" she said. "And get a bottle or a stone in the head? No, sir. Let's pitch out of here."

"OK, madam. Let's wait until they just meet, then we're gone."

The combined noises of the approaching bands became drowned out the voices of people around them, except one familiar voice. It was clear, and it was worried – about him. "Watch that woman you're with. She's trouble, man." This time there was a face. He didn't recognize it, but it was concerned, and he knew the voice.

"Mounira?" Constantine asked. He had to shout.

"Yes," it answered.

"Yes," Mounira answered too. "What is it?"

"Not you," he said.

Mounira looked at him, puzzled. "So, what're we doing?"

The voice grew more urgent: "I'm warning you, man. Get away from that woman. She's going to get you in the middle of that mélée when the bands clash, and it's your ass going to get killed. Run, man. Run. She ain't your friend."

Mounira turned to him, "Think we better get..." She stopped, and her hand went to her mouth. She hardly recognized the face contorted with hate and contempt. She stepped back. Constantine turned and ran towards the boulevard. She ran after him.

He turned towards her. "Bitch," he said, before he disappeared into the crowd. Out of the noise the voice was guiding him, Noise, noise, too much noise. Hurting his ears and squeezing his head and chest. He saw the face again, saw its concern for him. He followed it. It was afraid of the noise, too. He ran until he found himself at the eastern edge of the city. It was quiet, just two stray dogs under a street lamp tearing at fish guts. He was safe. The voice and the face had gone, but they had saved him. Time to go home.

By seven o'clock the next morning, it was too warm to dance, and Cord and Ismene returned to the truck. Several of their friends were already asleep in the back, and the others turned up within half an hour, but not Constantine. They waited two hours more, making lewd jokes about Constantine and his girlfriend, then Cord drove to Mounira's home. Mrs Charpentier opened the door immediately. She had not seen Mounira since Constantine had come for her earlier. "They're not going to like that at her work . . . Mounira is never late for work," she warned.

Cord drove around the city, asked at the police station and at the hospital. "I'm going to take you all back to Mandelie and come back and look for Cons. Something bad's happened to him. Cons doesn't do things like that."

He checked back again at the Charpentiers with Ismene. Mounira was in, shaking and crying uncontrollably.

"Mounira, where's Cons? What happened?"

"I don't know. I had my hand around his waist, and we were dancing. And suddenly, he told me to take my hand away. I thought he was joking, but you should have seen his face . . . as if he hated me. I've never seen Constantine look like that. Pushed me away, called me a bitch. Then he ran away from me. What did I do to Constantine? *Mon Dieu*, what did I do?"

"Constantine did that?" Cord asked, wanting to understand too. Mounira looked up at him, and Cord's fear stopped his breath. He felt his body grow cold as if he had been dipped naked into a barrel of ice, and his knees buckled. He picked himself up and gasped loudly through his mouth as he turned away and almost ran for the truck. He was remembering the stories of Bone. Grand Uncle Bone, *Fourmi Rouge* and his voices.

Ismene ran after him, terrified. "Cord, Cord, please, what's wrong?"

"I don't know, but I'm going to go and find Cons. You all had better take a bus back to Mandelie."

The others refused to leave him and they drove through every street again. Maude saw Constantine first. She banged excitedly on the rear window of the truck. They saw him walking slowly up the road that led out of town. Cord pulled up next to him.

"Cons, we've been looking all over town for you. What's wrong?"

Constantine looked at them blankly for a few seconds, then his expression relaxed as if in sudden recognition. "Eh! Where have you all been? I was beginning to walk home. Thought you had left me behind." The right side of his face, his collar and shoulder were lined with a dark stream of blood. He touched his cheek. "Don't know what happened. . . Somebody must have hit me on the head . . . or something. Don't remember. Anyway, I was going to walk home when I couldn't find you all."

"Walk home?" Ellit asked

"Of course. . . It's not that far," he said.

They made room for him in front. Ismene sat close to Cord with her cheek on his shoulder. Her tears soaked through his sleeve and were running down his arm.

A few miles before Mandelie, Constantine's expression and voice returned to normal. "Danced so much this morning, I can't even remember bringing Mounira home. God, I'm tired. Anyway, Mounira had a good time. I was thinking of going back tomorrow . . . watch the bands go through town. Anybody going back?"

"Too tired," they all said.

"Enjoyed myself enough."

"Had a good time, too."

"Yeah, best *jour ouvert* I can remember."

Charlo and Lucette came outside at the sound of the truck. Both looked angry and worried. "It's five o'clock in the afternoon. Where the hell have you all been? What the hell is going on? Constantine, how could you let this happen?" Charlo was shouting. Then he saw the blood on Constantine's face and shirt. Saw Ismene's swollen eyes and the tears.

"Cord? What's going on?" he asked, quietly.

Cord stood close to his father, "Somebody hit Cons on the head with a bottle. He can't remember anything. . . Pa, Cons is injured very bad. . . he's not the same."

They saw Charlo's face turn gaunt and ashen; he looked a much older man as he turned away and entered the house. Lucette followed him trembling, her hands searching quickly for her rosary. Her tears came fast.

CHAPTER 6

Charlo fell asleep just as the cocks began crowing. Then, a morning of ringing ears, red and unfocused eyes, burning scalp, shaking hands dropping cups and spoons.

Lucette was already making breakfast, a Saturday morning breakfast of cassava porridge on a Tuesday morning, made specially for Constantine with large sticks of cinnamon, grated nutmeg, and cloves. Enough spice to make it bitter – just as Constantine liked it. She cut the cassava cake into small regular cubes, concentrating on cutting the pieces precisely, not permitting herself time to think of other things.

Cord and Ismene came into the kitchen together.

"Morning, Ma."

"Morning, Ma Lucette."

"Morning, Cord. Morning, Ismene."

They looked at each other – found nothing worth the effort of saying.

Charlo sat across the table from Constantine. He loved his first son as much as Lucette loved Cord – her baby. He remembered how he had forced himself to be patient outside their bedroom waiting for his son's first cries: how he took the basin covered with a towel from the midwife, and did not even attempt to peep into the room and see the baby. Walked slowly to the yard to bury the afterbirth at the foot of the breadfruit tree, giving the nurse time to wipe the baby clean and to powder it, so that it looked and smelled as a baby should. Smiled at the thought of telling Constantine one day that his blood was in the breadfruits they ate.

He had forgotten to kiss Lucette, and wondered why the nurse kept digging her elbow into his ribs. Both women said the baby looked like him: long and thin. To him it looked pink and wrinkled, frowning and a little ugly – looked like all other babies for the moment.

Lucette had looked at his face and wondered whether Charlo would ever allow her to breast-feed the baby.

He had loved Constantine so much that he could not punish him for the usual tantrums and rudenesses of infancy, found it easier to turn away so that Constantine would not see him smile, while Lucette threatened to flay the child. But when Charlo was away, it was Lucette who taught him to read; borrowed books from her father, especially those with pictures of heroic men about to sacrifice their lives for duty and love.

At four years old, Constantine appointed himself as Cord's guardian and teacher. Went into a frenzy when a yellow-jacket stung Cord on the leg. Set about killing every wasp in Mandelie with a wooden shingle. Protected Cord until Cord grew stronger and took over Constantine's fights. When two older boys made fun of Constantine's recitation of historical events, Cord threatened to make them "kiss Cons's ass." The boys laughed, and threw Constantine to the ground. Five minutes later, they wished they had paid greater deference to Constantine's hindquarters – especially after he pulled Cord and a cricket bat away from them. Later in the day, the boys' parents came to complain to Charlo and Lucette. Charlo called his two twigs of sons. "You're telling me these two skeletons beat up your two boys? These two thin little boys? Eh-eh!"

The parents frowned, and left to whip their sons for lying.

But when Constantine took the gramophone to pieces, Charlo promised Lucette he would whip him if he did not put it back together in thirty minutes – and just as he had found it. One hour later, Charlo took off his belt and went to find Constantine. Put the belt back on when he heard "No Hiding Behind The Door". The reassembled gramophone was on the kitchen table, and Constantine was cleaning a stack of seventy-eights with a kerosene-dampened rag. Charlo pretended not to be surprised.

Charlo became Constantine's first and only hero, and not just because Charlo was the first inhabitant of Mandelie to own a vehicle. When their first truck died, Charlo let him dismantle it before they sold the parts. Constantine studied the engine carefully every afternoon after school, until dark, for two weeks. Then he took it apart, needing help only with the heavy parts. Could tell them what every component's function was.

When he was sixteen, his father took him one Saturday morning to the service bay of the truck dealer. "You think you could use my boy here? He can fix anything. Good mechanic already."

The dealer laughed, called his chief mechanic. "Let's see what your master engineer can do."

Charlo left to finish his business. When he returned, the chief mechanic asked, "Why'd you take so long to bring this boy here? He adjusted the valve clearance, and changed the cover gasket on an engine in less than twenty minutes. The best I can get one of our mechanics to do that is one whole damn' hour. So you're leaving him with us?"

They looked at Constantine. He shook his head. "We have enough to do at Mandelie," he said.

The chief mechanic looked as if he had just lost his final chance at fatherhood. "If you change your mind . . ." he said, shook hands with Constantine – and forgot to shake Charlo's.

"Ice cream?" Charlo asked Constantine as they left. They went to the cafeteria of the largest store in town. He did not eat any, but sat and watched Constantine. Laughed and said over and over, "Fixed the car in less than twenty minutes. You ever seen something like that? Ah."

In return, Constantine measured everything's worth by the amount of approval it received from Charlo. He spent the first money he made – from repairing an engine at Mandelie – on a family portrait. He insisted that they dress in their best clothes, and they drove down to town on a Sunday morning after mass. The photographer wanted to have Charlo sit and Lucette and the others stand around him. Cord pointed out that his mother was too tired to stand. She sat – Charlo behind her and the boys at her side – on a throne made of her men. Constantine had a copy made for the room he shared with Cord. Charlo never tired of looking at the portrait. Showed it to every guest. Said it was Constantine's gift, bought with his first earnings. Shook his head at the wonder of it.

Constantine sent Cord to bed every night with stories of King

Arthur's knights, and selected tales from *The Arabian Nights*. When Ismene came to live with them, Cord gained some reprieve although he found it more difficult to fall asleep. Over a few weeks, Ismene learned that whales were not fish but mammals; and that the kangaroos of Australia could not move their hind limbs individually.

The story of Constantine's illness went through the village immediately: a secret to be kept only from babies. Cord looked carefully into every face, ready to challenge any suspicion that his brother was not well.

Ismene cried almost continuously for three days, until Constantine asked her whether Cord had done something to hurt her. "He's not too big for me to beat his backside," he promised. Ismene laughed and said she could whip Cord any time. They enjoyed that one for a long time, with Constantine saying, "Yes, just bite his knees... stamp on his toes, and grab him where he won't forget."

In return, Cord promised to whip Ismene with something other than his hands.

On Ash Wednesday morning, Lucette and Ismene dressed for church, and to his mother's distress, Constantine insisted on going with them. Neither of her sons had attended that service since childhood. She did not want him trapped in a church of stares and whispers, but did not know how to dissuade him. She looked to Charlo for help.

"I'm going to need help with the bananas," Charlo said, "we've already missed two days because of Carnival."

"You all go ahead, I'll catch up with you," Constantine said. There was a distance in his voice, and Lucette hesitated, searching for some obligation to keep her at home. Then she sighed and started for the church. Constantine took Ismene's hand, and walked slightly behind her, letting her lead him.

In the church, he sat stiffly, eyes fixed on the altar; kneeling or standing only when Lucette nudged him. Occasionally one of the worshippers turned to glance at Constantine and whisper, and Ismene returned each gaze, scowling, begging for a challenge – to be answered after the mass.

After the service, Constantine changed and set off to help the others repair their neglect of the bananas.

At noon, Cord arrived to ask what had happened to Constantine because he had not joined them.

"He left here – over three hours ago," Lucette said, holding on to the edge of a table for support. She called out, "Ismene! Did you see where Cons went? He didn't go down to the bananas."

"No." Ismene hurried out of the house and down the road.

"Where are you going?" Lucette called after her.

"Going to look for him," she called back, her voice breaking with panic.

"Stay here with Ma," Cord said, "I'll go and look for him."

Ismene shook her head. "I can't stay here and wait. . . I can't take it."

Cord went with her. The village found out quickly that Constantine had disappeared, despite Cord's attempt to appear unconcerned. Word spread quickly, and others joined in the search.

A fisherman returning from the bay told them that he had left Constantine sitting on an upturned canoe on the beach. "Yes, we spoke for a while. Constantine complained about a bad headache, and how he had forgotten why he came down to the bay." The fisherman said he'd replied that these things come with age, but he'd kept an eye on Constantine. . . he'd heard about his injury. At times Constantine seemed to be gesticulating and speaking angrily to someone, but he was too far away to hear what Constantine said. "The boy is not well." he said. He shook his head.

They met Constantine halfway along the road to the beach. "Where are you all going?" he asked.

"We were waiting for you down by the bananas," Cord said.

"Oh yes. I forgot. Let's go."

The others stayed back, let Cord and Constantine hurry ahead, wondered quietly how such a thing could have happened to Cons.

That evening, an overwhelming tiredness came over Constantine, and Lucette had to remind him several times to eat before his food got cold. He went to bed early. Charlo asked whether they should write to Marie-Josette in New York; tell her that Constantine had had a nervous breakdown.

"What can she do?" Cord asked.

"But it's his sister," Lucette said.

"Look, all we'll do is make her worry. Then she'll come home and we'll have two problems on our hands," Cord said.

"So what are we going to do?" Charlo asked.

"Let's just leave him alone. I can look after him," Ismene said.

"And if Cons gets out of control, what are you going to do?" Cord asked.

"Constantine is not going to hurt anybody," Ismene said.

The next morning, Constantine seemed his old self, and Maude greeted him with, "What's cooking, honey?"

And Constantine answered, "Chicken and rice, sweetheart."

Mounira came to visit on Saturday afternoon. She had grown thinner, her face was drawn, and she was not wearing make-up. Ismene saw her first, went out to meet her, glad for the chance for news and gossip.

"Constantine, your lady's here," Ismene called out.

"Who?" Constantine answered.

"Mounira," Ismene said.

Constantine and Cord came around the side of the house. Lucette was calling, "Coming, coming."

"How are you Cons?" Mounira said.

Constantine frowned, looking slightly mystified, then his eyes widened in recognition, and he screamed at her, "It's the damn' woman who's been following me around. This is the last time I'm going to let you persecute me and my family. Go away. Leave me alone. I'll kill you if you don't leave me alone!" And he ran to the back of the house.

Cord was the first to recover. He hurried Mounira into Ismene's room and closed the door. Lucette and Ismene had not moved. Charlo came out of the front door.

"What is Constantine shouting about? I heard him in the back cursing."

Constantine returned with a stick. "Where is she? Where is she? I'll make her leave us alone."

"She's gone, Cons," Cord said as calmly as possible, "it's OK now. She ran away. I don't think she'll come back."

Lucette collapsed, and Charlo and Ismene helped her into the house.

"Good," Constantine said, smiling in triumph.

They kept Mounira locked in Ismene's room until the afternoon. When Charlo asked Constantine to accompany him to water the cows, Cord drove Mounira back to town. Ismene went with them.

Mr. and Mrs. Charpentier did not say much; saw hurt beyond comfort in Mounira's eyes. "Drive well," they said to Cord and Ismene.

On the way back, Ismene asked Cord to drive to a small beach that had been isolated when the new highway was built. They drove slowly down the old road whose asphalt surface had worn away to expose the gravel base. "Why do you want to go down there? It'll be dark soon."

"I want to spend a little time alone with you, Cord."

"Always something happening whenever. . ." he began.

"Yes," she said, "but this time, it's just two of us. I want to do it today – all the things your big mouth is always promising to do." She paused, "All of this confusion with Cons is too much. I just want something nice for us, for a change."

They parked behind a screen of pink-flowered *gliricidia* trees, and Ismene took of her dress hurriedly. Cord hesitated. "What's wrong?" she asked.

"Don't know. Don't think I can do it."

"Well, let me see."

She removed his shirt, and opened his pants. But he did not respond. Looked into the distance as she touched him.

"Let's go home," she said, after a few minutes.

"What did I do to you?" she asked when they were almost home.

"Nothing. Nothing at all. It's not you. . . it's Cons. I'm so afraid."

"But I'm afraid too, Cord. Now, what's going to happen to us?"

"I don't know. What if we had a child and the same thing happened to it?"

They drove in silence the rest of the way, Ismene dabbing her eyes with her sleeve.

For the next two weeks, life returned to its same everydays: cultivating, baking, milking, digging, harvesting. . .

"What's cooking, honey?"

"Chicken and rice, sweetheart."

"Jean-Pierre Roulleau. . . *Poussez*."

Charlo visited the priest to ask his advice.

"Mr. Pardie, I can pray for Constantine, that's easy. But I think it would be better for him to see a doctor. That's the harder thing to do."

"Yes, but how are we going to do that? Constantine doesn't know anything's wrong with him. How am I going to make him see a doctor? And I'm afraid of what he might do if he thinks the doctor is trying to find out if something is wrong with his mind."

"Ask the doctor to come see somebody else. Then he can check on Constantine."

Charlo nodded. "It think it's time for Lucette to get sick."

"Yes. . . for the first time since Cord was born."

The men and Maude were working on Bone's land when a boy came running, calling for Mr. Charlo. "Ma Lucette is not feeling well. Ismene said to come quick."

Charlo asked Constantine to come with him. "I'll send and tell you how she is. Don't worry," he said to Cord who had put down his fork, and was coming with them.

"Stay with Ma," Charlo said to Constantine. "I'm going to get the doctor at the Health Centre."

Charlo drove away. He signalled to the head nurse. She saw the agitation in his eyes, hurried through the waiting room. "Eh-eh, Mr. Charlo, I hope it's not too serious."

He explained quickly to the head nurse what the priest had suggested.

"OK. As soon as I can, I'll get the doctor to come to your home. I can tell him what has been happening with Constantine. I hope all this didn't really make Ma Lucette sick."

The doctor sat with Charlo and Lucette in her darkened room for thirty minutes. Constantine was pacing in the front yard when he came out. "Eh, Constantine. How's life treating you?" he asked.

"No problem," Constantine assured him.

They walked to the doctor's car, and Constantine got in. They returned in an hour. "I was asking Constantine to show me where they found 'gold' at Mandelie," the doctor explained to Charlo. He suggested that Constantine should go in to see Lucette, then he spoke quickly to Charlo: "Mr. Pardie, Constantine should go to the mental hospital. He'll go in and out of the changes, but they will come more and more often. And they'll get worse."

"How did that happen to my boy?" Charlo asked.

"You're not alone, my friend. Nobody knows what brings it on. And it's always the good ones. . . always the nicest ones." He opened his hands to Charlo as if for help. Refused payment.

Charlo returned with Constantine to Bone's land in Mandelie. It was land they possessed in the same way that all their neighbours possessed the land. It was the land their foreparents had taken when they had walked off the plantations to claim the forested hills and river banks vested in them by the sharpness of their machetes and their contempt for the French *béchés* with their paper deeds from a King Louis whom no one had ever seen. It was land they possessed by virtue of the blood, afterbirths, and skeletons of all of the Pardies buried there.

"Tiredness," Charlo explained to Maude and Vanius. "The doctor said Constantine is suffering from fatigue."

In his own tiredness and despair, he returned to the harsh comfort of work, forcing his hands into the soil, lifting, turning the sod; wondering what wrong had solicited such a retribution.

Jean-Pierre Roulleau . . .

When they were done, and were returning to the truck, Maude hurried to catch up with Charlo, took his elbow. "Let me take care of him."

"No," Charlo said, "too much for a person. Too much for all of us."

CHAPTER 7

They discussed it when Constantine was working on the car of a friend who had driven all the way from the city – wouldn't let anyone else touch his car. They wanted Ismene to listen to what they had to say; what the priest said; what the doctor said; even what Maude said.

No, not yet. Let us see if he gets worse. Nobody knows. Maybe we can learn to live with it. He hasn't hurt anybody. We can keep an eye on him. There must be a medicine for it. Let us pray. God will provide.

They put it off for a day because they had to discuss it. For a week because they had to repair the roof over the oven. For a month because. . . Two months, four months, eight months.

Constantine followed Ismene to the pasture one morning. They let him go, thinking her company would do him good, someone to whom he could betray more secrets of the universe. He ignored Ismene when she spoke to him, but never took his eyes off her and tripped several times; looked into her eyes even as he rose from the ground brushing dirt from his knees. At the pasture, he did not help her take the animals to drink, or help her tie them in fresh grass. He sat on a rock in the pasture watching her as she worked, and rose to follow when she left for home. Not a word.

When he tried to follow her again two days later, Ismene refused to leave the house. Lucette paid a neighbour's child to go down to the pasture. Constantine did not speak to anyone for more than a week, in retribution.

Then he stopped helping on the farm. Said he had too many vehicles to repair, and didn't want to disappoint his customers. Oiled his tools every night; spread them out in the morning and sat in the shade of the breadfruit tree to wait. When someone drove up, he looked back at the house in triumph, shouted: "See, it's a good thing I waited."

But his customers became nervous with his mutterings about invisible enemies spying on him and following him. They stopped bringing their vehicles.

The children stopped coming too, because there was no more joking and teasing. He never refused to help, but frowned angrily while he cut wheels or repaired broken wooden axles for them. His changing voices sent them running, leaving their toys for older children to retrieve; or they would bring their broken things for Cord to give to Constantine.

Lucette learned to smile patiently when he accused her of putting potions in his coffee to make him hallucinate. He insisted on watching her prepare breakfast; drank only coffee that he made himself. She sought her rosary even more often. Every day she saw a slight improvement, but his relapses wiped these away. She prayed some more and waited for the next improvement.

Maude came by every Sunday evening. More "What's cooking honey?" Then told him a joke that kept him laughing for days: "Sit down Cons, I have some history to tell you. My name is Maude Ficelle. I was born in Mandelie on January sixteenth, nineteen twenty-five. On the morning of August sixth, nineteen fifty-three, I was travelling to the city on the afternoon bus, the *Have Faith*. Fastest bus on the road. When we got to the top of the Island Divide, brakes failed – the party was over for us. Um-hm . . . Yes, Sir. The bus turned over at a bend, and almost all of the passengers were severely hurt. People everywhere, screaming. One man was killed. Another man was sitting on the ground holding his arm which was so badly broken, the bone came out through the skin. He was screaming murder. The dead man opened his eyes and said: 'All you have is a broken arm and you're screaming your ass off, and here I am, dead, and I haven't said a word of complaint!'"

They laughed for half an hour, repeating parts of the joke each liked best. When Maude left, Constantine told Ismene the joke three times; and she laughed just as loudly with each telling. Then he told Cord, who laughed and swore he could never forget it.

Maude came again the following Sunday afternoon, and invited Constantine to help her roast cashew nuts. They left in such good humour that several children followed, giggling at the pair's loud and bawdy song about a man pleading with his lover to writhe beneath him:

> Roullez là bas, roullez.
> Roll down there, roll.
> No, I can't roll.
> Roll, roll, roll,
> Roll down there.
> Roullez là bas.

Maude sent the children scattering throughout the neighbourhood collecting cashew fruits. They bit into the tart astringent flesh, twisted the nuts off their ends, and ran back with hands and pockets filled with grey paisley-shaped nuts that looked like miniature monkey faces.

Maude spread the nuts on the slitted cover of a steel drum. She placed the metal pan over a log fire between four rocks, and let one boy stir the nuts with a long stick. Little tongues of flame licked through the perforations and ignited the oil in the shells of the nuts making each one spit little geysers of steam. When the shells were completely charred, Vanius and Constantine inserted sticks beneath the pan, lifted it off the fire, and poured the burning nuts on the ground. Maude quenched the flames with a shovel of dirt.

After the nuts had cooled, they all sat down to crack the carbonized shells with rocks. The children grabbed and ate as fast as possible, smearing their hands, faces, tongues, and clothes with charcoal.

One of the boys killed a large thrush with his slingshot, and they roasted it, several children sharing drumsticks no larger than their small fingers.

Vanius offered to add to the feast by roasting some dried sardines, but Maude advised against it, warning that the children would keep everyone up later with their murderous farts. Vanius shrugged, and roasted a handful for himself, ignoring Maude's promise to make him sleep in the cooking shed.

Constantine insisted on walking home alone after the children left. Vanius walked with him to the road. "Walk well."

"Sleep well. See you tomorrow."

At ten o'clock, Cord and Charlo drove to Vanius and Maude's to take Constantine home.

"But he left here about four hours ago," Maude said.

Constantine had been nearing his home, could see the lights in his parents' bedroom, when the voice warned him to stay away: "These people aren't going to do you any good – especially Ismene. Watch that one carefully. . . she's not even your sister! Maude's all right, but watch her too. They're all the same. . . just like Mounira. Go down to the beach. Go and clean yourself. Forget those people."

He did not trip once on the path; stepped around the boulders; stepped over the holes. He did not need to look down: it was pitch black, but his feet remembered the path. Saw the outlines of the bushes against the stars. Small things hurried out of his way, swishing through dried *ti baume* and *porier* leaves. Crickets, knocked off branches by his arms, fluttered angrily around him, stopping on his head or arms only to be knocked off again. Once, he heard a nightjar – had not heard one since he was twelve: "*Cent coups de couteau . . . cent coups de couteau*" – threatening the night over and over, but retreating into camouflaged silence when the light came.

He walked across the pasture, heard hermit crabs drag their borrowed whelk shells across the dry grass, and the sudden silence as they stopped to let him pass. He went to the hut and knocked on the door. "Cord? You in there giving it to Ismene?" Laughed, and turned to the beach.

The wind blowing hard from the ocean hissed past his ears, pushed into his shirt, made the legs of his pants flutter. He took his shoes off and stood at the edge of the shore, letting the small waves touch at his toes. Saw quick flashes of green phosphorescence as rolling water surprised clouds of *noctiluca*. He thought he could see through the dark water, to see the white sea urchins grazing on sea grass, tiptoeing on tiny brittle stilts in one direction, then moving back as if they had forgotten what they had set out for.

He looked back toward the village, and saw small yellow flashes from the fireflies, and brighter ones like the flames of torches coming down the path toward the sea.

Several villagers had joined the search party, walking along the village paths calling his name. Eventually, Lucette suggested they go to the hut in the pasture. "Remember that day you shouted at him for opening the clock? And he went and stayed in the hut?"

A party set off for the pasture, lighting the way with torches made from rags and bottles of kerosene. No one was in the hut.

"Let's check on the beach."

"Cons! Cons!"

"Yes. What's wrong?"

"We've been looking everywhere for you. You're OK?"

"Yes, but why're you looking for me? You didn't know I was down by the beach?"

"Sorry," Charlo said, "we forgot."

"I thought you would have kept some cashews for me," Cord said, making himself laugh.

Constantine dug into his pocket. "Here, I almost forgot."

Cord took the handful of nuts and put one in his mouth. But his mouth was too dry to eat it. He put the rest into his pocket.

They took turns watching him after that; had the children spy on him, just happening to pass by wherever he was. He spent more time in his room, sometimes leaving it only to eat and to go to the toilet. He stopped bathing regularly. When the smell became unbearable, Lucette warmed a pail of water and Cord poured the water over him as he soaped and rinsed.

One night, Cord awoke to find himself alone in the bedroom. He went immediately to check the doors. They were closed. Then he heard voices in Ismene's room. He was almost sick with fear as he opened the door slowly. In the soft light of the votive oil lamp, Ismene was kneeling on the bed with her hands joined in supplication to Constantine, tears streaming from her terrified eyes. Constantine stood bent over her, holding a candle near her face.

"Please, God, no. . . Please, God, no!" Cord heard her hoarse pleading.

Then Constantine's voice, rasping, unrecognizable. "Devil. You're the devil. I know what you are. I know what you did to Charlo Pardie. And after him, it will be me. . . then Cord. Then you'll kill my mother. I know you. I know you."

"Cons!" Cord screamed, "Leave Ismene alone!"

Constantine turned and looked at him without recognition. "I'm going to get rid of this devil once and for all. She's already screwed all the village. You and Pa and everybody. Except me. But I'm going to get rid of her now."

Cord, even with his great strength, was unable to get Constantine out of Ismene's room. And he was weakening until Charlo and Lucette, awakened by the noise, came to help. Ismene ran to Lucette's room.

Constantine suddenly seemed to awaken from sleep. "What's going on? I was having this bad dream and I wake up to find everybody piling up on me. I was walking in my sleep?"

"Yes," Cord said, "you could have hurt somebody."

"Sorry. I'm in Ismene's room? Sorry, little sister," Constantine said, and followed Cord to his bed.

Ismene went to lie with Lucette. Charlo put a small mattress on the floor against their bedroom door and lay down. Ismene whimpered uncontrollably. "It's my fault. I know it's my fault."

Lucette put her arm around the trembling girl. "No, *ti-doux-doux*. Nobody's fault."

Cord went to his bed. Constantine was the only one who went back to sleep.

The next morning, Constantine was cheerful, but looked tired. "Didn't sleep well last night," he said, "had all kinds of stupid dreams, but can't remember anything, but it was as if Ismene was in some kind of trouble." He looked at Ismene, "You're OK, *doux-doux*? Look at your eyes, all swelled up."

She nodded. "OK. Seems nobody could sleep last night. Maybe it was the dogs barking."

Cord nodded. "Must be an opossum that was looking for scraps."

"Long time since I've seen one around here," Constantine said. They nodded.

"Long time," Charlo said. Then, "Got to go take the cows to the river. Ismene, come with me. Long time since you did any hard work."

"Want me to help?" Constantine asked.

"No, Cord needs help with weeding around the bananas."

Ismene and Charlo did not speak until they had arrived at the pasture. She spoke first. "Mr Charlo, I can't stay in the house with Cons. I have to go. He's going to kill me."

"We're your family, Ismene, we can't let you go. And go where? Mandelie is your only home."

"I have my father's place in Morne Rouge. The house will have to be fixed, but maybe you can help me."

"And you'll do what, at Morne Rouge? Alone? You'll be safer there alone? And what are you going to do for a living?"

"I can bake bread."

"You don't have an oven."

"Mr Charlo, I can't stay with you all again. It's my fault. It's because of what happened with the two of us."

"How can it be your fault alone. I'm old enough to be your father. I am the one responsible for what happened. I'm the one responsible for you. I'm the one responsible for you until I die, or until you marry. You're my daughter. It is killing me to lose my son. How can I let myself lose a daughter, too?"

"I'm not your daughter, Mr Charlo."

"Ismene, I didn't make you, Lucette didn't make you, you weren't born in my house, but I cannot let you leave us."

"Some day, I have to do something with my life. I can't live in your house all my life."

"I don't know how to let you go, Ismene. I can't even think about it."

"You're making me scared, Mr Charlo. I don't want anything to happen between us again."

"No, Ismene. I will never touch you again. But you're the only happiness in the house."

"I have to go, I know I have to go. If I stay, something bad is bound to happen. I have to go." She looked up at him, at the eyes filled with tears.

"Not now," she said, wiping away her own in the crook of her arm.

Later, in bed that night, Charlo lay on his back and watched the fluorescent hands of the bedside clock march from ten to one o'clock. Lucette turned to face him. "I can't sleep either."

"I was disturbing you? Sorry."

"Charlo, I'm worried about Ismene. I don't know if it's safe for her to stay here with Cons in the house."

"Where're we going to send her?"

"Don't know, but it's either that, or we have to put Cons in the hospital."

"We'll do that if he gets worse and we can't take care of him, but right now. . ."

"Is as if he's jealous of Ismene. As if he thinks you and Ismene have been together."

"How can you say something like that, Lucette. Ismene is like our daughter."

"I know that, I know that's true, but I know what I see in my son's face."

"This is not a thing to talk about. Not about me and Ismene. That's not right," he said, and turned away.

It was not spoken about again, but Ismene felt the coldness from Lucette. No more: *ti-doux-doux* or *ti chérie.* Noted the great care the older woman took not to brush up against her. There was no hostility, but Ismene was no longer her daughter.

Charlo saw the two women grow apart, but did not know what to do. Cord noticed it too.

"What's going on between Ma and Ismene?" he asked his father when they were alone outside one evening.

"Don't know. Constantine's sickness, I think. So much strain on everybody. That will pass."

"I'm afraid for Ismene; she's not eating well."

"This is hard, Cord. I don't know what to do. We can't send Ismene away."

"Nobody is sending Ismene away. This is her home. If she goes, I go too."

"Nobody is going anywhere," Charlo said.

That evening, at dinner, Charlo said to Lucette, Cord and Ismene: "I'm going to town tomorrow to make arrangements for him to go to the hospital."

Lucette travelled with Charlo to the stone fortress overlooking the harbour that housed the psychiatric hospital. Cord promised not to let Ismene out of his sight. Charlo stopped to visit Maude, and to ask her to keep Constantine occupied, and explained what had happened. "We're going to the hospital. We can't take care of him any more."

Maude nodded, her eyes desolate. "My Cons," she said.

The hospital superintendent watched them from his window facing the parking lot. Even after ten years working there, his heart broke each time the parents came. Always the good ones. And he was forced to give the same poor comforts. He wished his faith were weak enough to allow him to shake his fist at heaven and curse. Still, he condemned himself to believe – it made it easier to give consolation – and to secure his employment.

The superintendent was smaller than they expected – even thinner than Lucette, Charlo thought. He looked like a plucked bird: bald, long thin nose, hardly any lips, and wearing glasses with rims as thin as wire. But his voice was large and warm; made them feel that he had been waiting all day and was glad that they had arrived at last. They found it easy to speak, told him more than they knew they remembered.

No, it was not their fault; it's in some families more often than usual. But many, many families have to deal with it. No, nothing they could have done to prevent it. No, nothing to cure it. Was that what happened to Bone? Probably. God will provide.

The superintendent could make arrangements for two nurses, men of course, to come and take Constantine if they wished. But they would have to bring a straight-jacket to restrain him. Charlo was adamant. He would not have Constantine dragged away from Mandelie – not like some wild animal. He would bring him, himself.

The superintendent made him sign a long document turning over care of his son to the government; then handed him a small vial of clear liquid. "It's a sedative. Give it to him in some juice or tea. It will keep him calm on the trip."

On the day they drove Constantine to the hospital, everybody from the village came to stand at the roadside, though they'd said nothing to anyone in Mandelie – not even the priest. Charlo drove; Constantine sat between his parents with his head on Lucette's shoulder; Cord sat in the back.

No one waved or said good bye. They stood silently, tears hurrying down their faces – even down the faces of the little boys with their toy trucks with wheels made from wooden bobbins.

Two attendants came to help them take Constantine into the hospital. The older one whispered to Charlo, "Mr. Pardie, maybe you and your family should let us take him to the ward. I really don't think you should go in there."

"But it's hard for us just to leave him here. We can't even say goodbye?"

"Ma Pardie, the patients in there are… This is not like a regular hospital. I would prefer if you didn't come. When you come to visit your son, we'll bring him out to see you. For now, it would be best if he woke up in his ward."

"You'll take care of him?" she asked.

"Don't worry, Ma Pardie. We'll look out for your son. He's your first son?"

Charlo nodded. "When can we come to see him?"

"Well, we prefer visitors to come in the morning. But you can come any time. Just ask for one of us. My name is Fen; he's West. But don't come every day. It will be too hard on your family. You have to take care of yourself too."

Cord insisted on driving back. They were three miles out of the city when he stopped. "We have to go and tell Mounira. I don't want her to find out by accident."

The store owner was surprised to see them all – without Constantine.

"He's very sick. That's why we came to see Mounira," Charlo explained.

The owner let Mounira take off the one hour left to work. They drove her home. Sat with Mrs. Charpentier. Drank some tea, accepted her cakes and asked whether she minded if they took them to eat on the road. Cord and Mounira looked at each other for a long time. Smiled, said little.

"Well, give our regards to Mr. Charpentier. Sorry we couldn't see him, but we couldn't give him news like that in his shop. With all the customers. . ." Charlo said.

"Yes, he'll understand. But I'm glad you stopped by. God will take care of Constantine."

"Yes."

They drove back without stopping to speak with friends in the other villages they drove by, as was their custom whenever they went to the capital. Did not complain about the potholes or the slowness of the road repair crews. Did not even mention the rips in the asphalt caused by a bulldozer that had crossed the road on its toothed tracks. Did not curse the drivers of the buses that shot like wood and iron cannonballs along roads built for more judicious speeds. Did not stop for fish at Praslin where the boat builders brought *gomier* logs for cutting and shaping into rainbow-striped canoes. Said nothing along the way. Forgot to eat Mrs Charpentier's cakes.

"I want to stop and see the priest before we go home," Lucette said.

"You'll drop us off there?" Charlo asked Cord.

Cord nodded. He did not want to be alone. Not yet.

Word went around quickly that the Pardies had returned without Constantine. Several of the older people came to the small presbytery. They had changed into Sunday clothes; the men held their hats in their hands. They waited in the small yard at the front door until the family had finished speaking with the priest. Charlo came out first to greet them.

"We had to put him in hospital," he explained.

"We understand. But he'll be coming back when they cure him? Yes?"

"Perhaps."

"We can go and see him?"

"Yes."

"What's the place like?"

"Like a hospital."

"If you want us to help you. . . you know, with the bananas and the cows. . ."

"Thanks, we'll manage. But it will be hard."

"The children are going to miss him," one said.

"True," the others answered.

The house was closed when they returned. The next door neighbour came out to meet them. "Constantine is all right?" she asked.

"For the time being," Lucette answered. "Where's Ismene?"

"She took the afternoon bus to town. Left the house key with me."

Ismene's room was carefully made up. All of her good clothes were gone. And she had taken the etched crystal candle-holder that Bede had given her for her First Communion.

CHAPTER 8

The smell of excrement and the heat woke Constantine. For a moment, he assumed Cord had farted, then recognized the smell of old shit, like an old abandoned outhouse. He was sweating where his back lay against the rustling plastic mattress-cover under his sheet. He looked around at the dirty white walls of the room, the barred window, and the barred opening in the door. The green paint of the bed frame was blistered with rust, and the mattress was worn and hard. The pillow smelled of roaches and pine disinfectant. There was also the smell of creosote. A small unvarnished table of white pine, and one chair stood under the window. To the right of the table was a dresser with two shelves. The varnish had been scraped off the top of the dresser, and its surface was covered with scratches and gouges.

Constantine lay still, waiting for the nightmare to end. Tried to call out but was too tired even to lift his leg off the bed. So he waited for someone to come. He heard footsteps and men's and women's voices outside his door. Occasionally a strange face would look through the bars in his door. No words, no interest in the eyes.

When the light faded outside, a naked bulb on the ceiling came on. Soon after, a key turned in the door, and an enormous man in a white cotton jersey, white pants, and white canvas shoes came in with a tray. Shining, very black, and completely hairless, with a smile that had not yet lost its innocence to fear. The smile stretched as he put the tray on the table.

"Dinner," he said. "Eggs, bread, cocoa and a banana. Not restaurant stuff but OK. My name is Fen. I'm a male nurse here."

"Where is this place?" Constantine asked.

"Hospital."

"The hospital? What am I doing in the hospital?"

"You got hurt in an accident," Fen said.

"What accident? I didn't have any accident," Constantine said.

"Well, you knocked your head. Lost your memory, it looks like."

"What about my family?"

"Oh, everybody is fine. Just you got hurt. They'll have to keep you here for a while, but you'll be OK. Just rest, and let your body get well." Fen smiled, and helped Constantine sit up.

"Want to eat at the table?"

"No, my stomach is really sick, and I want to pee."

Fen pointed to an opening in the wall next to the bed.

"Let me help you." He lifted Constantine off the bed with little effort. There was a small sink in the alcove with a bar of yellow soap, and a sunken ceramic bowl in the floor. The space smelled of old shit. Fen pointed to an iron rod with a chain hanging from the end. "Pull it when you're finished."

"No toilet paper," Constantine said.

"Sorry, I'll bring some when I come back for the tray," Fen said."

He waited nearby until Constantine was finished, and helped him back to the bed; place the tray on the bed. "If you have any problem, just ask for me or West. That's not his name. His real name is Solatious. But don't ever call him that if you don't want contention and confusion in here. He likes cowboy pictures, so we call him West. He prefers that name. Well, I got to move. See you tomorrow, Mr. Shaka Zulu."

Constantine was sorry when Fen left. He had not had a chance to discuss any of his favourite subjects. He tried to think of some wondrous facts to relate when Fen came again. Perhaps they could talk about earthquakes.

Next day, the man who brought him breakfast was taller, but much thinner than Fen. Did not smile as much as Fen; seemed to be preoccupied with important thoughts.

"Morning, I'm Nurse West. You slept well?"

"No. Couldn't sleep. . . all these people screaming and shouting. . . "

"Good," West said. "Brought your toilet paper." Still busy with his important considerations, he picked up the tray from the night before, with the food still untouched. "Must eat, you know. Anyway, see you later, alligator."

Constantine managed to eat half his breakfast. He sat at the table where the air blowing through the window diluted the smells in the room. He went back to the bed and was looking at the faces and shapes in the stains on the wall when the voice came again, but this time it had shapes and colours: red and blue lines that shifted continuously. New shape with each word – although he could not understand the words – red and blue sounds.

Sometimes, the shapes came off the wall and hung in the air between the bed and the wall. He thought they were clearer against the white of the wall.

He felt better after eating, strong enough to go to the window. The hospital overlooked the harbour and Constantine could see most of the docks despite the leaves of a royal-palm tree to the right. A cargo ship with a red hull and white superstructure was following a pilot launch out to sea. On the other side of the harbour was the lighthouse from which – as he had once related to Ismene – a lone rifleman armed with a point-303 Enfield rifle and two bullets, had repulsed a German u-boat. In the wake that stretched all the way back to the dock, he could see the voice. It danced in the foam, plunged deep to the bottom, taking him to see the clam shells, bottles, two anchors, and an outboard motor sitting in the mud. Its blue lines remained blue against the colour of the water. Then it disappeared; when he returned to his bed, it was on the wall of the room. He listened to it until his contentment sent him to sleep.

Fen shook him awake. "Family here to see you, Mr. Ulysses Grant."

West was waiting in the corridor outside. The walked on either side of him. Hurrying him, not giving him time for more than a quick glance at faces in the barred windows; or to listen to the screams and calls. "Gotta move, man. Can't keep the family waiting." They took him outside to a yard with casuarina trees ablaze with red, yellow and orange blossoms. A ten-foot high wall encircled the yard. His mother, father, and Cord were standing in the shade of a tree. Lucette was holding a small suitcase and Cord had a cardboard box at his feet.

"How are you, *doux-doux*?" Lucette asked.

"OK."

"You're doing OK?" Charlo asked.

"So far." Constantine turned to Cord, "So big man, what's happening?"

"Fine, Cons. Doing fine."

Lucette laid the suitcase at his feet. "Brought you some clothes," she said, "and we brought you a box of food. Maude sent you some *tablettes*. But don't eat too much. . . will upset your stomach. You getting any sleep?"

Constantine nodded. "I was sleeping when you came. Tired – didn't sleep last night. Too hot. . . they have a plastic cover on the mattress."

Charlo looked at Fen. "We'll take care of that, Mr. Pardie," Fen said. He pointed to the bench behind them. "You all sit down and chat. We'll be just over there." And he walked a little distance away with West.

The family sat together for an hour and a half. Fen or West went about other matters, but one of them always remained within earshot, and well within sight.

When Constantine fell silent, the family kept talking – forcing discussions about the land; plans for the crops; what the neighbours had been talking about; asked repeatedly for his reluctant opinions. They purposely kept their eyes away from the other patients in the yard – naked, dirty, or gesturing repetitively: talking to the air, chasing invisible bothers, scratching at the mortar of the walls with remnants of fingernails. They pretended not to hear the curses, threats, indecipherable rants, and the helpless laughter at unspoken jokes – from everywhere but the sky.

Within the walled enclosures are mothers, cousins, brothers, fathers, daughters, aunts, uncles, and saints. Saints? Yes, and lawyers, soldiers, constables, nuns, doctors, carpenters, philosophers, seamstresses, merchants, and priests. But no children – not yet. Not before they have been loved and celebrated; not before they have written good words, or sung good songs, or painted good pictures, or surprised good discoveries. Do you know them, now? Yes, we'd forgotten until we saw their faces again. Try not to look at the body doubled over until laughter brought it to its knees, begging that its unseen companion stop the jokes: joke after joke after joke, each more hilarious than the last. Ignore the entreaty to follow the fellow carrying a small suitcase, hurrying to catch his ship before the island sinks from the weight of its mountains. Nod at the passer-by who has not seen you in many years, and wants to tell you how much he has been persecuted by his neighbours before he escaped them in the middle of the night disguised as a grenadine tree, leaving them to think that he was still lying in bed. Serves them right – assembled outside an empty house shouting threats; let them catch pneumonia in the rain; he's safe here, protected by the President of the States, Sir Winston Churchill, himself. Don't you think he's done the right thing? Nod. Yes. Listen to the wavering tenor of the one hidden behind the post, face more timid than the throat. A beautiful song, but listen well; hear the words. Words? There are plosives, sibilants, trills, labio-nasals – but try and capture a word. Nothing. Evaporating even as you hear it.

Just ahead is an oval rut stamped in the earth, like a moat guarding a patch of stunted grass. It's creator continues to deepen it – at twenty miles a day, unable to find the end of that road, the only escape from this place of strangers. Bare feet calloused like elongated hooves, propelled by calves hard and large as calabashes.

The Pardies stayed close, arm touching arm, until the sun disappeared behind the heads of the royal palms swaying beyond the west wall of the hospital enclosure.

Fen walked over to the family. "We'll have to get him inside now. We have to check everybody before it gets dark."

Constantine started walking towards the gate with them, but Fen and West held his arms gently. He stopped, knowing that they could easily carry him off.

The family stopped at the gate to look back at him and wave. He waved and tried to smile, but his mouth only twitched.

Then Charlo called to Fen: "Mr. Fen, let me ask you something."

Fen left Constantine with West. "Stay here," he said.

"Mr. Fen," Charlo said, "this place is the worst thing I have seen in my life. I don't know if my wife can survive with her son living in a place like this. I am not going to ask you to give my son special treatment, but I am willing to pay you to see that he is comfortable. I'm a farmer, and I know how much food costs in the city."

"I'll take care of Constantine, Mr. Pardie," Fen said, taking the twenty dollars that Charlo handed to him.

The tall red-painted wooden gate closed behind his parents. His guardians watched Constantine stand looking at the gate with his head cocked as if listening to the sound of the engine growing deeper. They saw him turn towards the suitcase and the package his family had left on the bench. But then he stepped on the bench, grabbed a branch of the casuarina tree, pulled himself up and was climbing toward the wall before Fen and West could move. West started climbing the tree, but did not have Constantine's lifetime of practice climbing fruit trees at Mandelie and jumped back to the ground. Fen ran toward the gate followed by several patients and confused nurses shouting at their charges.

Constantine's fall to the ground had knocked him breathless. He sat on the ground for a few seconds, then decided to run through the guava bushes that covered the slope toward the sea. Perhaps he could steal a boat and row back to Mandelie. He heard the voices of his pursuers behind him, but they were running along the road. He slowed down so they would not see the bushes disturbed by his passage.

The slope ended suddenly at the top of a wall. There was a ten-foot drop to the water, and no boats.

A voice to his left said, "It is an ancient mariner, and he cometh from the bush."

Constantine almost fell into the water from surprise.

"Watch it! Better sit down," the voice said.

Constantine moved back from the edge of the wall and sat on the grass at the bottom of the slope.

"Would you perchance have escaped from incarceration in the institution at the top of the hill?"

"Don't understand what you're saying," Constantine said.

"Yes, a not uncommon problem. My name is Wenceslaus

101

John. Wenceslaus as in the Christmas carol. John as in John. The ridiculous and the prosaic. Former teacher of the classics and accomplished pianist. Now, alcoholic vagrant, family shame, and failed fisherman. But tell me, did you come from that place?" And he pointed back up the hill.

"Yes," Constantine said. "They told me it was the hospital. It's the madhouse."

"Used to be a resident . . . Well, still am," John said, "I drove them cr–. Well, they find it advisable to set me at liberty, on occasion. Danger only to myself, they said."

The failed fisherman wore faded denim pants and a green nylon shirt illuminated with red pineapples; both pants and shirt were far too large for him. His hair had not been cut for so long that it hung in felted gray strips. When the wind gusted, it lifted his shirt to show skin like wrinkled grey paper pasted on his ribs. His face was flushed and its puffiness made him look like a purple baby with its face swollen with sleep.

"What's you name, sirrah?" he asked.

"Constantine."

"A noble name – of Latin derivation. I know that name well. Means. . . what it sounds like. And I daresay, probably describes your quest for freedom. Well, let me do a rare good deed: I shall lead you back safely to the place whence you came."

"Back to the hospital?" Constantine asked.

"Why, of course, Sir. Do you contemplate leaping to freedom from this sea wall?"

"I can't go back there."

"How long have you been. . .?" John asked.

"A day. . . two days, I don't remember."

"I see. Well you should be getting about the business of busyness. Are you especially good at anything? Carpentry, painting. . .?"

"I'm a good mechanic," Constantine said.

"Mechanic. Not many opportunities up there."

"I wanted to draw. But there are no pencils or paper here."

"You should ask your family to bring them."

"Yes."

"Landscapes? People perchance?" John asked.

"No, voices," Constantine said.

He told John about the red and blue shapes that spoke to him. Danced on the walls of his room. Showed him what was under the water in the harbour. John let Constantine speak without interruption. Looked into his eyes whenever the latter fell silent, encouraged him to go on, nodded after every statement. When Constantine had no more to say, he stood up. "Let me put these things away, and I shall accompany my master of the abstract and the sublime to his atelier."

Fen saw the pair coming up the slope. He stood waiting. "Well Mr. Charles André Joseph Marie de Gaulle," he said to Constantine. "I see you've been making friends. How are you, Mr. John?"

"Somewhat parched, but I don't suppose you can remedy that situation," he answered. "I believe I can leave my friend Constantine in good hands. Would you mind if I dropped in to see him again. . . when the fish are not biting?"

Fen looked at Constantine. "You mind if he comes to see you?"

"Hope to see you again," Constantine said to his new friend.

Wenceslaus John came close and whispered into his ear. "Draw, my friend. Draw your voices. Draw, draw, draw."

Constantine nodded. "Yes." He held his breath as long as he could, nauseated by the miasma from John's mouth.

"Whew!" said Fen and West.

When Charlo and the others came to visit the second time, Lucette asked: "Want us to bring you anything when we come again?"

Constantine said quickly, "A notebook and some red and blue crayons."

"Paper and crayons?" Charlo asked, confused.

"Quiet," Lucette whispered. "OK, little sweet," she said to Constantine, "we'll get them for you."

Cord came back the next day, with a drawing tablet of white paper and a box of crayons. "They don't sell just red and blue," he explained.

"That's all right," Constantine said. He asked about the truck, reminded Cord to keep an eye on the mileage and to have the oil and filter changed every three months. They let him outside to check the truck's engine. "A little knocking. Will need a tune-up next oil change," he said.

The brothers sat and spoke until West came over to take Constantine back to his room.

One week after their meeting, Fen brought Wenceslaus John to his room. Constantine brought five drawings to show. "I painted these on my wall first. The shapes were too large for the paper. Then I copied them smaller," he explained.

John looked at the paintings for a long time without speaking. The red and blue lines became faces behind thin vertical bars, grew feathers, flew away from the page, came back to pull his eyes deep into the page until he was caught in showers of red and blue rain. He shut his eyes tightly against the vertiginous rush into the shape that rested on his knee. Even then, the images remained; red and blue lights dancing in the darkness behind his closed eyelids. And he heard them – red and blue voices. Saw faces:

Milton lifting his black sleeve to his face against the stink of the drunkard's breath: "When night darkens the streets, then wander forth the sons of Belial, flown with insolence and wine."

Shakespeare's brow arched in surprised disdain: "The fishermen that walk along the beach appear like mice, and yon tall anchoring bark diminished to her cock, her cock a buoy."

Mocking contempt in Donne's eyes: "But I do nothing upon myself, and yet I am mine own Executioner."

And the laughter: jeering and raucous, mocking his useless erudition. Scenes before his eyes: an unwashed, drunken fisherman reeling in blue and red fish that jumped from his hook as he reached for them; laughing as they fell back into the water; rushed back to his unbaited hook. Failure. Scholar. Teacher. Philanderer. Drunk. Vagrant.

Failure.

His head fell back, and he forced his eyes open, unblinking even in the glare of the sky. "Oh God! Oh God!" He began to shake at the understanding what he had seen. Constantine had drawn the pictures of his mind – had drawn his thoughts. That was why the pictures changed constantly. They had become John's nightmares when he looked at them.

Fen and West came to look at the pictures that fell from John's hands. "You're OK, Mr. John?" West asked.

John nodded weakly.

The attendants looked at the pictures, and quickly averted their eyes. They handed them to Constantine.

"Don't know anything about art," Fen said.

"Neither me. Can't draw a thing," West added.

"What do you think?" Constantine asked John.

Wenceslaus searched desperately for something sensible to say, and Constantine asked again, thinking that his visitor had not heard.

"The strangest things I have ever seen. You actually see these shapes?"

Constantine nodded.

"Can you see them now?"

"No, only when I'm alone," Constantine said.

It was two weeks before John visited again. His hair was cut, and he wore a white shirt and khaki pants, still too large, but clean. "My wife advanced me a small sum for purchase of these garments. Next, I'll try and get some proper nourishment at her table," he explained, laughing. "Anyway, my friend, now that I am comfortable, body and scalp not itching, I want to sit quietly and listen to you story. Tell me all."

"Things are not clear in my mind," Constantine said. "Not sure if some things really happened, or if I dreamed them. A lot of things not clear."

"In that case, I'll tell you mine: an interesting wasted life."

Wenceslaus John, Bachelor of Arts, Literature, Cantab., came from a family of scholars and teachers. He married a plain and reserved woman his family happily approved of, but left her for a neighbour who screamed and contorted like a hooked eel in bed, did things to him that would have sickened his wife, and never wore underclothes.

His first and only child was borne by his lover. It lived for three days. Mercifully – because it was born without a brain.

The school authorities expressed no regret when they fired him. When he told his lover that he had been fired, she packed his clothes into a cardboard box and told him, "No money, no love."

105

The rum shops had welcomed him only until his savings ran out, but the brotherhood of town alcoholics continued their generosity – kept him drunk. His former students provided him with cast-off clothes, and hoped silently for his death.

"So here I am. That's my story. Your turn next. Take your time. We can take our time, here."

The Saturday afternoon after he saw Constantine's paintings, John obtained a pass to visit his wife. He sat on a bench in the town square until dark, then walked slowly past the stores, stopping at each display window, looking carefully at every item before moving on, selecting the words he would say to his wife. Then he went to see her. His wife was angry when she answered his knock, and angrier when she saw who it was.

"Half past nine, at night. What the hell is wrong with you? What are you doing here?"

"Constance," he said, "I have met your namesake, and he is life and death, light and dark, madness and reason, sound and colour. I swear I am no longer the misguided man who abandoned our holy sacrament."

"What? Now he's madder than usual – and it's to my house he comes. Shit!" Constance moved to shut the door. This was the first time he'd heard her swear.

He held the door open. "See?" he said, blowing toward her. She winced from the stench but when she could breathe again admitted that she did not smell rum.

"Told you," he said.

She let him in, but insisted that he sleep on a blanket on the kitchen floor. He lay awake as long as he could, savouring the smells of garlic and burnt cooking oil. He marvelled at the quiet of the house; did not even lash out at the moth that crawled over his neck. The next day, she cut off his rancid ropes of hair after he had bathed, and gave him two dollars for the barber. When he returned she gave him some more money for clothes, but said she wasn't ready to have him back in the house until she was convinced that he was prepared to do something useful with his life.

"So," he said to Constantine, "I think I shall go down to my fishing hole and angle a grouper for the wife. Convince her of the joys of sharing a *court bouillon*. There's always the fish market if I don't catch anything. Eh? Ha! Wonder if they would let you come with me to the sea wall?"

Fen agreed to let Constantine go with John down the hill to the water's edge; but accompanied by a trainee nurse. John caught one five-inch soldier fish – all eyes and bones.

Six months later, Charlo and Cord asked the superintendent to let Constantine return to Mandelie with them for a visit. To their surprise, he agreed enthusiastically. He suggested that Constantine stay only three days. Perhaps longer the next time.

They stopped at Praslin to buy sea eggs, pies made from the roe of sea urchins piled into cones around a stick in an empty sea urchin shell. An expensive treat for a special occasion.

Some passengers on the evening bus to Mandelie saw Charlo's truck near the sea-egg vendor's booth. Saw Charlo and Cord. Recognized Constantine.

When the men arrived home, there was a small crowd at Lucette's door.

"What's cooking, honey?" Maude called.

"Chicken and rice, sweetheart," the three men shouted.

Lucette wanted Constantine to remain inside and "rest", but he awoke after the cocks announced their sighting of the faint yellowing of the sky and he was under the hood of the truck as soon as it was bright enough to see clearly. He went in for breakfast only after he was satisfied that the truck's engine was tuned to factory specifications. Later he went with Cord and Charlo to collect dry coconuts for making copra.

By the next evening, he was exhausted from the unaccustomed exertion, although they had not let him do too much. He was unable to rid himself of his unease over the seeming location of familiar sounds and sights: It was as if he was just awakening from sleep and the things around him had not yet come into clear focus. When he spoke, he heard even his own voice coming from a distant source. It reminded him of hearing voices around a corner – before one came upon the speakers. He wanted things to come closer, like the walls of his room at the hospital, so he could touch them. There were no red and blue lines stretching, bending, and spinning – telling him stories, showing him things, taking him places. There was too much green and brown here: things were sharper and harder – not good for red and blue lines. Too much noise: wind blowing loudly through the house at night, and carrying voices, all speaking at once. Occasionally, one voice would rise above the others to threaten him. That voice terrified him because it did not belong to anyone he knew. He wanted to be near Fen at the hospital. Fen was not afraid of anyone or any voice; always knew how to take care of problems. He thought of pushing an ice pick into his ears to deafen himself so that he wouldn't hear any more voices. He pushed his index fingers hard into his ears, but the voices grew louder when he blocked off the sounds of the wind and night creatures.

He was angry that the voices had followed him to Mandelie, and had defiled his parents' home, like unwanted guests. He wished he had brought his crayons and paper. That night, after a supper of tuna fried in a light flour batter, and smothered in a sauce of onions and tomatoes, he said to Charlo, "Pa, I want to go back to the hospital. . . tomorrow. . . or the day after."

"But your family is here," Lucette said.

"Yes, but I still have good friends there: Fen, West and Wenceslaus."

Charlo and Lucette looked at each other. Lucette nodded.

"Yes, all your friends are there," Charlo said.

Oh, our Constantine.

PART TWO

CHAPTER 9

The passengers on the bus had noted Ismene's suitcase, enquired whether she was going on vacation, or to a job in the city, or – and they laughed at that cleverness – whether she was running away from home. She laughed with them. Imagine.

An old man had made room for her on the bench seat. "You prefer to sit by the window?"

She nodded, and he stood to let her slip past. "It's OK," he said, "sometimes looking at the trees when the bus is moving makes me sick."

"I used to get sick every time I got on the bus – when I was a child," she said.

He told her that he was going to the city hospital for a hernia operation; he thought his infirmity was the result of lifting heavy bags of copra on his farm. "No children to help me," he said. "Everybody's gone to the city. They think life is better there. But you don't have friends in that place. If you fell down dead in the street, nobody would ask who your mother or your father was. Just pass by. Go there, you get lost. Nobody cares who you are."

"You're right," Ismene had said. "People go to the city and disappear."

"Disappear," the old man agreed. He looked at the trees rushing past for a second, rested his chin on his chest, and closed his eyes, making everything around him disappear.

When she'd arrived in the capital, Ismene went immediately to the Charpentiers. Told them she felt partly responsible for what had happened to Constantine, and could no longer live with the sadness of what had happened at Mandelie. Mr. Charpentier offered to give her work in his grocery, then caught his wife's eye and let his insistence fade. For a brief moment, he had enjoyed the sensation of squeezing past her behind the small counter.

The next morning, Mounira helped her with make-up, and

she left for the office she had visited with Charlo and Cord years before. The same lady was behind the desk, but she had grown thinner, and wore glasses that looked like black wings. She did not recognize Ismene. Said that there was a position available for a clerk-typist; whispered that she would not take it herself: boring, bad pay. Ismene did not mention that she could not type, but thanked her and asked whether she knew of anything else.

"What're you looking for, sweetheart?" the secretary asked.

"I'm a good cook. . . and I can bake, too," Ismene said.

"A cook? Why're you looking for work in an office, dear? Why don't you try a store or. . . a bakery?"

"I wanted to do something different."

"Young lady, in this city, if you don't know somebody who can help you, you aren't going to get shit. You hear me? Not one shit."

"Well, thanks anyway."

"Good luck, dear," the woman said.

Ismene went to the store where Mounira worked. Asked her about the bakeries in the city. There were three: The largest was in the eastern part of the city, near one of the largest slums, but even the rich people sent their servants there for bread. Half an hour from the store. Take care.

The owner of Metropolis Bakery was too busy to see Ismene. "Mr. Grotte said to come back this afternoon at four o'clock," a counter-clerk said.

"Tell him I'll wait," Ismene said. It was nine-thirty in the morning.

Half an hour later, a fat black man with a perfectly round head, eyes like embers in a hill of charcoal, and dressed in white shirt and pants, came through a back door, opened the small gate to the back of the counter and began collecting money from the cash drawer. The clerk whispered in his ear. He straightened and looked at Ismene.

"You the one said she'd wait till this afternoon?"

"Yes."

"Ah!" he said. "Since you don't have anything better to do, come!"

Ismene followed him into an office that held only a small desk, a chair, and a bench.

He jerked his chin at the bench. "Sit."

He counted the money he had taken from the store, wrapped it in a rubber band, and put it into a biscuit tin on the desk top.

"You can bake bread?" he asked.

"Yes."

"Cakes?"

"Sponge cake, fruit cake, coconut turnovers, rock cake, patties, and butter bread."

"You worked in which bakery before?"

"No, the lady who adopted me taught me."

"Who's that?"

"Lucette Pardie, at Mandelie."

"Don't know her," Grotte said.

Ismene considered telling him that Lucette owned an oven and sold bread too. But then he would want to know why she was asking him for a job. "Just bread for the home," she explained.

"I don't have any women working in the ovens," he said. "If I had anything it would be in the front, selling. Well?"

"If that's what you have. . ." Ismene said.

"I'll give you a chance. One week. Come."

He took her to another room, lifted a white apron from a nail on the wall, and handed it to her. "Thirty dollars a week, if you can do the work. "Monday to Saturday. Half-day on Wednesdays." He looked at an alarm clock on the desk, "And almost three hours gone already."

They went back to the front. He turned to Ismene, "Seventhirty to four."

"Helen," he said to the clerk behind the counter, "show her what to do.".

"Yes, Mr. Grotte," Helen answered. She looked hard at Ismene, "You got a job already?"

"Just for a week. . . I don't know," Ismene said.

And between cakes, bread, and customers, the two women searched each other's pasts and circumstances.

Helen was light-brown, tall, thin and flat-chested – breasts no larger than nipples, big bottomed – a surprise when she turned around, gap-toothed and freckled. Yet every man who carried in bread and cakes from the oven in the back paused to flirt with her.

113

Several of the men who came in to buy did too. Occasionally, they teased Ismene, promising gifts of clothes or jewellery. But always distractedly, as if hesitant to displease Helen.

Before they left for the day, Ismene said, "I've never seen so many men after one woman. You must have a lot of boyfriends."

Helen smiled slowly. "It's what they know I can do."

"Eh?"

"All the men know I can give the best screw in town. But only Mr. Grotte decides who gets it. Only fat and ugly Mr. Grotte. It drives them crazy. The men in the bakery – they want to say they got the boss's woman. Let them get their own bakery first." Her laughter came as a scream.

Ismene looked at her open-mouthed, then desperate for something to say, she asked, "You know some place I can stay?"

The next day, at their lunch break, Ismene collected her things from the Charpentiers and brought them back to the store. After work, she walked uphill with Helen through the slums at the eastern edge of the city, between shacks of weathered grey wood, covered with shingles, flattened tin cans, and irregular geometries of corrugated iron, porous to every noise and smell – and to every rain shower. These pitiful wooden defiances against the wind, rain, termites, and the natural laws of degeneration, clung with wooden pegs to yellow volcanic tuff. Some had tendrils of wire borrowing electricity from a neighbour whose larger connection stole the power from the government's lamppost.

This hillside was a fortress against the rare incursions of city constables anxious not to soil their khaki uniforms in enforcing the laws that gave them employment. After all, many had to return to their homes there when they finished work for the day. And it was their supervisors who owned and rented out the newer houses – the ones with black power lines attached to glass insulators under the eaves, and with a standpipe in the yard. As for the annual threat from the Prime Minister to send in the bulldozers? What else could he say? That he would shortly move his office to the neighbourhood? Let him try. His newest girlfriend (the prettiest and fiercest of his four women, the one whose children were covered with hair as scarlet as Julie mangoes, the one who left scratch marks on his back that only his doctor saw but that the whole town knew about) would be the first to make his shortcomings public, because the bulldozers would have to go through her bedroom with its king-sized mattress to get into the neighbourhood.

The two women walked through small spaces of beaten earth that served as yards, kitchens and thoroughfares; among children with mucous-streaked faces, legs covered with yellow pustules, scalps with white incrustations of ringworm: bare-bottomed little boys, little girls with no more that the remnants of under-wear. They crossed open sewers lined with grey-green moss and populated by blood-red worms waving incessantly at the sun, everywhere, the smells of smoke, cooking, decay, excrement, cologne, talcum powder, fish entrails and heated coconut oil.

A woman's called: "Daniel. *Daniel.* But where is that child?"

Another smaller voice sang: "Oranges and lemons say the bells of St. Clements. . ."

Helen stopped at a house that had once been painted light green with white trim. It sat on four-foot posts, and the space beneath it was crammed with boards, empty margarine and oil cans, boxes of white pine, empty soda and liquor bottles. A small, rat-like, black and white mongrel lay curled up near a pine box. It poked its head toward them and sniffed cautiously. It beat the ground furiously with its tail when Helen said, "Hello, Cinderella."

Helen knocked on the front door, "Virginie, you home?"

"That you, Helen?" a voice answered, "I'm coming."

A short, muscular, light-complexioned woman walked around from the back of the house. Her hair was plaited into thin braids on the right, but had been left combed out on the left. She held a long wooden spoon in one hand. "Come 'round to the back," she said. There was a large enamelled pot on an iron brazier near the back steps of the house. She sat on the last rung of the steps and stirred the thick brown mass in the pot. Warm embrace of cinnamon, cloves, burnt sugar and coconut. The dough of macaroons.

"Virginie makes *tablettes* to sell. The best in town," Helen explained. "Now Virgie," she continued, "My friend Ismene is looking for a place to live. She's working with me. You still have a room?"

"The room's still there. Show it to her."

The floor of the living room was covered with yellow linoleum with a random pattern of red and black squares. A small table in the centre was decorated with two birds made of cow's horn and a vase holding red, white and yellow crepe roses with buds of silver foil. There were four Morris chairs with dull, blackened varnish on the arm rests. No cushions. And a dining table with four, rush-covered chairs near a window to the left of the door.

The room-to-let held a black iron bed with "VONO" printed in gold letters on the side frame. The mattress was uncovered. There was a stand with a wash basin and matching ewer, and a tall dresser in one corner. The breeze coming in through the window carried in the smell of hot coconut oil and spices. From it, they could see over the roofs of the other houses to the city centre and even to the harbour. Helen pointed to a pink and white house a little further down the slope. "My parents' house. I live there."

"Five dollars a week, darling," Virginie said.

"OK," Ismene said. She refused a taste of the finished macaroons. "Thanks. When I come back. . ." She hurried back to the bakery with Helen.

For six months, Grotte never gave Ismene a chance to work in the bakery. Never even let her see the ovens. Never let her pass by without pressing against her, but his protuberant stomach fended off more intimate contact. She did not mention this to Helen.

Nor did she mention the occasional bruises on Helen's face, the slight limp, or the bandaged fingers. However, one Monday morning, when Helen came in with a swollen lip and a sprained wrist, Ismene asked if she had been in a fight.

Helen was amused. "I was wondering when you were going to ask. Yes, of course it's that fat bastard. But it's not to hurt me. I come better when he beats me."

"*What*?"

"You don't know that? A man never hit you when you coming? Makes it sweeter."

Ismene shook her head. "No."

"Well, next time, try it with your boyfriend. By they way, who's your boyfriend?"

"He's in the country," Ismene replied.

"Doesn't come to see you?"

"No, I don't think. . ."

"Then what're you waiting for? All these men in the bakery. I can fix you up."

"No," Ismene said, "no, no, no."

But Helen introduced her to one of the bakers: "Fender, Ismene doesn't have a boyfriend. And she hasn't had an 'um' since she's been in town."

Fender, twenty-five years old, clean shaven and muscular, powdered with enriched flour, smelled of yeast, sweat and bay rum. He shook hands formally with Ismene, and asked whether she had anything around the house that needed fixing. The next day, he brought her a small battery-powered phonograph and three records – calypso, country and western, and Nat King Cole singing in Spanish.

On Friday, after repeated pleas, she agreed to go to the cinema with him. He came to meet her dressed in his red nylon shirt (bought for last Christmas), brown pants pressed to wind-cutting sharpness, and white shoes. She ate the roasted peanuts he bought, let him hold her hand, but did not want his arms around her shoulders. When he walked her back home, she let him kiss her on the lips, but did not open her mouth for his tongue.

He asked if he could come to visit her at home the next evening.

"If you like," she said.

He brought her a package of assorted Danish biscuits. They sat on the back steps until it became too dark to see faces. She let him play with her breasts and put his hands on her knees. One hour later, she opened her mouth for his tongue. Moaned when he put his fingers against her panties. When his breathing became too loud she pushed his hands away, but gently, so that though he did not persist, he did not feel offended. They sat quietly for a few more minutes, until his arousal waned. He kissed her on the cheek and rose to go.

"See you tomorrow," she said.

"You bet." He held his hands to his face so he could smell her on his fingers – all the way home, and in bed.

Occasionally, on Wednesdays, she went to the central bus depot to speak with the driver of the bus that had brought her to the city. He had carried her letter to Charlo. She would ask whether he had seen the Pardies, and whether there was any news of Constantine. The driver mentioned these enquiries to Charlo, brought back the little news that Charlo gave in return. The day before Christmas eve, the driver gave her an envelope from Charlo. It contained one hundred dollars. No message.

She bought Fender a pair of black shoes, and gave Helen and Virginie perfumes. She bought herself a black satin dress that clung to her body.

On Christmas eve night, Ismene, Helen, and Virginie went to the cathedral in the city centre, but had to remain on the pavement outside the main entrance because the church was crowded with parishioners eager to make up for all the masses they had missed during the year – and to compare new clothes.

Afterwards, they went back to Helen's home for the stewed liver, bread and vermouth that Helen's mother had prepared. There was a man sitting in the balcony of the house.

"Who's that?" Ismene asked.

Virginie jumped several inches into the air, screamed, whipped up her skirt, and ran whooping toward the stranger. He rose slowly, his face impassive as if he expected no less of a greeting. He nodded to Helen and Ismene, then peeled Virginie from his chest and shoulders.

Helen explained, "That's Philippe, her boyfriend. Works on the cable ship. They must have just come in. Hello, Philippe. This is Ismene. She works with me. . . stays by Virgie."

Philippe shook hands seriously, bowed, and said, "A delight, madame."

Ismene stifled her giggle.

His hands were as rough as lanyards, and he was compact and hard – like Virginie. He took a box from the balcony, opened it, showing them the bottles of wine, rum, gin and whiskey he had bought duty-free; mentioning with becoming modesty how much money he had saved.

When they had eaten, Philippe suggested that they go to the *Stellar Paradise* nightclub. Ismene hesitated because Fender had promised to visit her. Could they wait another half-hour? Philippe was gracious. Fender arrived fifteen minutes later, smelling like a sandalwood plantation, dressed in a black rayon shirt and trousers, and in the shoes Ismene had bought him.

At the nightclub entrance, Philippe loudly insisted on paying for everybody, but his friend at the door waved them in.

"What's happening, Philippe? Long time no see."

"Struggling man. You know how it is."

"Home for Christmas?"

"Yeah. Stop by for a drink tomorrow. Be looking out for you."

"Sure, man. What's happening, ladies? Feller?"

The walls of the nightclub were of varnished wood that reflected little of the light from three bulbs hanging from the ceiling, under white conical shades. The dancers looked like swaying silhouettes: young women with forbidden boyfriends, husbands with their maids, employers with their secretaries, and brave wives with their lovers. Ismene straddled Fender's right thigh, let his hands roam over her and inadvertently whispered "Cord" in his ear. He pulled her closer, thinking she had said "God."

They left the club after four o'clock, unsteady with drink and exhaustion.

"See you all, later," Virginie said when they were halfway home. "And Ismene, you all can use both beds." She screamed at her joke.

"She's staying with Philippe?" Ismene asked Helen.

"Don't think so. He lives with his mother," Helen answered. "They're probably going down by the wharf. Virgie likes to do it in the open – by the sea, with her sailor."

Ismene and Fender said goodbye to Helen and went in. She slipped her dress over her head, and went to put on the Nat King Cole record. Fender took off his clothes except for his shorts and lay on the bed. Ismene turned off the light, removed her slip, and crawled in beside him. She let him take off her underclothes and waited. Half an hour later, she heard his snores above the music and the words of "*Ay, cosita linda, Mama.*" She went to sleep in Virginie's bed.

Fender woke after ten o'clock. Ismene was already making a breakfast of smoked ham, bread and coffee. "Bad headache," he said, "but I'm ready to try again. Want to come back in the bedroom?" She shook her head. Virginie could come back any time.

They ate breakfast silently. He left in the early afternoon when Virginie arrived – her hair dishevelled, the back of her dress soiled with mud, her perfume exchanged for petroleum distillates, and running as if she had just been given the gift she wanted most.

Grotte invited the bakery staff to his home every Boxing Day for drinks and snacks. Always the same: smoked ham, bread, salted nuts, cheese crackers, shortbread biscuits, liquor and sodas. Always the same brands.

The old stone house, set on the slope of the hill looking north over the city, had a quarter-mile drive lined with royal palms, three acres of fruit trees, and grass. No neighbours within earshot.

The living room was larger than all Virginie's house. Windows reached from floor to ceiling. Old, carefully tended lacquered furniture declared, rich, rich: I may be a fat ugly baker, but I'm rich. I married a woman with class. You can sneer at me, but what do you have?

A portrait of Grotte's late wife stood in frozen disapproval on a large cabinet filled with crystal glasses and decanters. Ismene thought she was the most beautiful woman she had ever seen, but cold, like an expensive porcelain doll. Helen told her later that Mrs. Grotte had died in childbirth, and the baker had never remarried; he could get what he wanted without a licence.

The guests sat stiffly in his expensive chairs, afraid to lean back or touch the arm rests. Laughed loudly at his jokes; repeated them to even louder approbation. Ate and drank modestly. Grotte made a short speech about his satisfaction with their work, but exhorted them to work even harder during the coming year, reminded them that no one was indispensable, not even himself. The staff nodded in agreement. The oldest employee, who swept out the ovens, told again how Mr. Grotte had rescued him from a future of destitution, shook hands with Grotte, and returned to his seat dabbing his eyes.

After the party, Grotte asked Helen and Ismene to stay and

help him clean up. He would drive them home. Ismene caught some looks of surprise, saw the hurt and humiliation in Fender's eyes. She was about to make her excuses and leave, but stopped at the almost imperceptible shake of Helen's head.

When they had finished tidying up, Grotte looked around, nodded in approval and said, "Come."

Down the polished floor of the hallway, past photographs of unsmiling relatives paralysed in high collars and ancient formality, they followed him into a large bedroom with a massive four-poster bed in the centre.

Ismene stopped. "I can't stay here, I have to go home."

Grotte turned his little glints of eyes on her. "You have another job?"

"I can find something else to do," she answered.

"Yes," Grotte said, "be a domestic."

Ismene turned to leave.

Helen took her arm. "Nothing is going to happen to you. We only want you to watch."

"Watch what?" Ismene asked.

"Him and me."

"You're crazy?" She wanted to leave, but found it difficult to move.

"Sit," Grotte said, pointing to the only chair in the room.

He went to sit on the bed while Helen undressed. He got up when Helen went to the bed and lay across it, face down. Grotte removed his belt and stood over her.

The belt came down fast, and Helen screamed. Ismene jumped out of her chair. "Sit down!" Grotte said.

He hit Helen again, but this time she said, "Yes."

After the fifth blow, Helen said, "Now." She opened her legs. Grotte tore his clothes off and threw himself on her back.

Ismene stared in open-mouthed incredulity at the scene, but her fright had waned, and she could not tear her eyes away.

Grotte began hissing through his teeth and suddenly reared back. Helen's body convulsed and she was screaming obscenities into the mattress, tearing at the sheet.

He came off her slowly and lay beside her gasping. Helen rolled away and Grotte sat up. He looked at Ismene, and said, "You."

She took her shoes off and let them undress her. Lay on the bed, face down. Screamed when the belt hit her. Once. She opened her legs.

She cried uncontrollably all the way home. "Cord, Cord."

The next morning at work, Grotte handed her an envelope. She opened it when she went to the toilet. It contained one hundred and fifty dollars.

Fender did not come in to see her during the day. She did not see him over the next two days. Then, on the pretext of going to the toilet, she went towards the bakery, looking out carefully for Grotte. She asked an apprentice to call Fender. He came back to say that Fender was kneading bread, could not come out.

That evening, he came to her home and sat on the steps, his jaw muscles writhing as he ground his teeth.

Virginie came back from selling her confectioneries and noticed the tension. She went in and changed, "Going to the cinema. Don't wait for me. Coming home late."

"So, we're not talking?" Ismene asked.

Fender kept his eyes on the ground. "I know what happened," he said.

"Nothing happened," Ismene said, "I know what you think, but I don't have anything with Mr. Grotte."

"Everybody knows what he does with Helen. Now, he wants something fresh."

"I think you'd better go," Ismene said, and went into the house.

Fender followed her. "Sorry," he said.

She took his hand, and led him into her room. Stood close to him and took his shirt off. Undid his belt. He pushed off his shoes and took his pants off, and his socks. She pulled his shorts down and pushed him onto the bed.

He lay down and watched her undress. She came to lie down next to him and closed her eyes. "Do what you want," she said. He rolled over on her, then paused. "You're just lying there," he said.

She did not respond. Turned away when he tried to kiss her.

"What's wrong?" he asked.

"Nothing."

He shook her shoulders.

"Stop," she said.

He shook her more violently, became enraged and slapped her face. She pushed him off, turned over and buried her face in the pillow. He continued to hit her shoulders and head. "Bitch! You bitch! You let Grotte take you for money, and won't let your boyfriend touch you. A fat ugly shit like Grotte. You dirty, nasty bitch!"

He got off the bed and began dressing. "Bitch, bitch. You can just kiss my ass."

Ismene was crying. She sat up in the bed, rubbing her bruised shoulders. "I want fifty dollars," she said.

"What the hell you talking about?"

"Fifty dollars, or I'll tell Grotte you beat me up ... hit his 'fresh thing'. When he's finished with you, you won't be able to work again."

"Piss on you. Make me pay you fifty dollars! Not even fifty cents," Fender said as he left.

The next afternoon, Helen handed her a paper bag. Inside was an envelope. Ismene did not open it until she got home, but she knew it contained fifty dollars.

Grotte invited her home again with Helen, but the next time she was invited, she found herself alone with him. The next time, there was another man in the bedroom. The stranger sat in the chair while Grotte whipped her. When Grotte was spent, the man got up and left. Not a word exchanged between them. There was seventy-five dollars on the chair.

"Yours," Grotte said. He took his wallet out of his trousers. "Here's another twenty-five."

The next time, Grotte sat in the chair naked while another man, silent like the first, exhausted himself on her. Occasionally, Grotte's visitors wanted to talk with Ismene. Grotte would shrug impatiently. "It's your money," he grumbled, and left them to talk.

One man, about forty years old, did not whip her on his second visit, but sat naked with her on the bed, and began to tell her about his family. Grotte left the room in disgust.

"Why don't you stay home with your wife?" Ismene asked.

"I feel I'm living with my sister," he said. "Once a month is not enough for me. For Christ's sake, I'm still a young man. What's going to happen when I hit fifty?"

Other men slipped jewellery into her hands when Grotte was not looking. One, after he had put on his clothes, took her hands, and said fervently, "I love you." He looked into the black ice of her eyes, her tightened mouth and hurried off. He never came back.

His place was taken by an government minister with a large head barely supported on a frail neck, bald but for two tufts of hair over his ears. He asked her to call him Casanova, and she thought that was an unusual courtesy – her other visitors remained nameless. The minister stayed longer than the others; he was only able to overcome the hesitancy of his mature age by preliminary and impassioned oratory on matters of pending legislation. Ismene listened with convincing interest, nodding her head when he looked at her and raised his brows. She shook her head vigorously when a frown replaced the raised brow. Yet, in those Niagara Falls of words, she occasionally obtained a droplet of useful information, such as the name of a sympathetic police sergeant, or which civil servant would accept fifty dollars to expedite a building permit, or which importer sold flour at a fair wholesale prices – information Grotte would not have shared.

The one who called himself Casanova was grateful that she never smiled at his flapping nakedness as he paced the room in his drawers and socks, arms stirring the air to illustrate a point of national importance. She never expressed impatience with him, knowing that on days when he managed to make his voice heard in the legislature, he was capable of pounding his victory and enthusiasm into her for an acceptable five minutes.

She felt betrayed when he stopped visiting, until she learned from Grotte that he had died of cancer of the stomach. He called her into his office to tell her, and to give her an envelope of heavy ivory-coloured paper. "From the minister," he said. "He asked me to give you this if anything happened to him.

Her hands trembled so strongly, she was unable to tear the thick paper.

"It's not sealed," Grotte said, and took the envelope from her. He lifted the flap, and took out small bundle of dollar notes. He counted them. "Five hundred dollars," he said.

"What's that for?" Ismene asked.

"For not laughing at him," he said. "That's why I sent him to you and not to Helen."

"Poor Mr. Casanova," Ismene said.

"His name was Jardiniere."

One Saturday morning, she stood at a street corner waiting for a car to go past. She recognized the driver as one of Grotte's frequent visitors. The tall one, the handsome one with the trimmed moustache, and the smile like a Christmas card, and the long fingers that promised to go deep. The one with the expensive clothes and the new Morris car. The one who never smelled of cigarette smoke. The one who shouldn't have to pay for a woman. He had never asked for her, or for Helen.

She waved to him.

He glanced at her and looked directly ahead. Nostrils narrowed as if to resist a stink.

On Monday morning, Grotte called her to his office. "These men pay you for one thing. They're not your friends. Understand?"

"Yes, Mr. Grotte."

She also understood that he had told her she was a prostitute. Nothing else. She had two things to do: sell bread during the day, and herself at night. No importance to anybody. If she were to die, who would mourn her? Three, maybe four people who would hurry from the cemetery, say forgiving things about her during the night and, a week later, would not be able to find her grave among the other unmarked mounds in the paupers' end of the cemetery.

Two things to sell: baked goods and good body. She went to the stores and bought a new dress and some expensive perfume, and went to the hairdresser.

In two months, Ismene had one thousand, four hundred and seventy-nine dollars and fifty-three cents in a savings account at a credit union. None of her clients had seen her smile, even out of politeness at their jokes – but they had not come for companionship.

She and Helen quickly realized they were being used alter-

nately: going from the challenge of Ismene's intense self-posses-
sion to Helen's loud wantonness.

The man who had not welcomed her greeting reappeared at
Grotte's house, about a month later. Grotte called her into the
living room. He saw her mouth tighten, and her eyes narrow.
Before she could speak, Grotte's guest said, "I'm sorry."

"It's me who should be sorry," she said, "I forgot my place."

"Please, Ismene. You know how people search for scandal in
this town. I have a wife who is jealous of the rain if it wets me. I
know what I did hurt you. I brought you something to make up
for it." He handed her an envelope.

"Please, Mister, I can't take your money for nothing."

"At least, open it."

"You open it," she replied.

"Take the damn' thing, and take the man upstairs," Grotte said.

In the bedroom, the visitor tore the envelope open, and
removed three one-hundred dollar bills.

"Why are you giving me all that money?" Ismene asked.

"I want you to come and spend a night with me... at my home."

Ismene's nostrils flared. "Please leave me alone, Mister. And
take your money." Her voice almost failed the passage through
the dryness of her throat.

He left the envelope on the bed, and walked away. Ismene put
the envelope under the mattress.

The man was back a week later. She had expected him to return
– for his money, or his money's worth. He sat on the bed next to
her, and put his arms around her shoulder and kissed her neck.
"I still want you to come. . . my wife is going to the States in six
weeks. . . I'm going to be alone for two weeks. I want to make up
for the way I treated you downtown."

"No, Mister. I'm not going to your home. Mr. Grotte does not
want us making friends with the men. . ." she stopped.

"And I'm one of them?"

"Yes."

"I'm Grotte's friend, but I am not one of them. I handle
business for Grotte. . . That's why you see me here. I don't pay to
use his women."

"What are you doing here with me?" she asked.

126

"You're special."

He kissed the nape of her neck, so softly it felt like a powder puff. He stood and pulled her against him, pressed his cheek against the top of her head. She was surprised at how much she enjoyed being held that way. Pressed herself hard against him. He wrapped both arms around her shoulders. "I like your smell . . . like a baby," he said.

She sat on the edge of the bed, pulling him with her. Helped him remove her clothes. When she was naked, he stood over her, still fully clothed, looking at her body, frowning slightly.

She was about to ask what was wrong when he said, "I want to spend a whole night looking at your body . . . That's why I want you to come to my home."

"I'm too afraid to do that, Mister. Why can't you look at me here?"

"Because other men have been in this room, in this bed. I don't want to be thinking of that."

She shook her head, disappointed that he had stopped holding her.

"Listen, Ismene. Come to my home. If you're uncomfortable, I'll take you back at once."

"I'll come," she said. She wanted to be held again, wanted him to kiss her on the neck, nibble on her earlobes, caress her shoulders, press his cheek against hers. He undressed and came to lie next to her. She closed her eyes and waited. When he did not climb over her, she opened her eyes and turned towards him. He was smiling. "I like you . . . You don't have to give me anything for the money. I want you to give it to me when you really want to, not because I pay you."

He ran his index finger from her chin down to her toes. Lifted her right foot, and took her toes to his mouth, ran his lips along them as if playing a harmonica. He saw the fine beads of perspiration on her forehead and between her breasts. He kissed her other foot, then took her toes into his mouth.

He saw her jaws clench hard, and he laughed quietly when her hips erupted from the bed, leaving a damp admission of her excitement on the bed sheet; watched her body twisting as if trying to escape an encirclement of thorn bushes. He discovered new islands on her body to explore with fingertips and tongue; invented new pathways of invasion; listened to her voice battering the air: "Hunh. Hunh. Hunh." When he stopped, her jaws hurt from clenching her teeth. She pulled his hands between her legs; she thought his body glistened like honey in a spoon.

He pulled his hands away. "When we do it at my home, it will be much, much better."

"Don't go," she said. She wanted him to stay until comfort made sleep irresistible, and he could walk away without waking her. She wanted to feel in love without expecting its return. "What is your work?" she asked.

"Customs broker. I get people's things out of the customs; get it to their businesses."

"A good job?"

"Sometimes I make a little money. Depends on who you know at the customs."

"I came from the country. Don't have much school. I had to take what I could when I came to the city. My parents are dead. I don't have any family."

"You know the old lady who sells roasted peanuts and soft drinks near the cinema? Always wears a madras and a large straw hat? That's my mother. Father's dead now. Even if I made a lot of money, I'd still be the son of a peanut seller. I did well at school, and thought that could get me a good job; I wanted to work at the bank. . . but my mother was a peanut seller. They didn't tell me that to my face, but you could see they didn't want my mother coming into their business to see me. Still, it was a rich woman who married me. Maybe she wanted to do something to throw in her parents' faces. Sometimes people do strange things to get away from family.

"Your wife's nice looking?" Ismene asked.

"Let's not talk about my wife. . . Yes, she's nice," he said.

Silence.

"So, you'll come?"

"To your house? Yes." She did not care if Grotte killed her when he found out. This relationship was too rare to let escape. She wouldn't tell Helen about it yet; not until she visited her new friend's home, and knew what his name was. If he wanted, she would become his mistress – exclusively and secretly, of course. Such an enjoyment to contemplate.

The man returned once a week, paid her a hundred dollars each time to scorch her body with his fingers and tongue; never took as much as he had paid for – what she would have given him with screaming enthusiasm and sincerity for free.

Grotte agreed to let him have her for an entire Saturday evening – for two hundred dollars. "And only because you're my friend. Remember. . . don't hit her," he said to the man with the smile as bright as a Christmas card.

The man picked her up half a mile from the bakery, where a massive ceiba tree hid the street lights. Drove three miles to the top of the hill that overlooked the city, through overarching branches of orange and red bougainvillea to a massive cinder-block house, painted white with green trim. Three German shepherds ran to the car and silently escorted them to the attached garage. The dogs sniffed at her, bared their teeth but did not bark.

Inside, there was crystal everywhere: mirrors, picture frames, vases, glasses, figurines – and paintings that she thought were ugly – garish, distorted, rough – in thick, carved, golden frames.

He noticed her bewilderment. "They're expensive. . . the paintings."

"Oh," she replied, thinking that photographs of real people would have looked better.

"They are mine," he said. "Everything else you see here. . . even the house is my wife's. Well, the car is mine. She won't let me buy anything for the house, so I can never forget that she did me a favour marrying me. My father worked for her father until he died." He spoke without rancour, but smiled as if he had finally triumphed in his domestic conflict.

"Where are your children?"

"None. And she says that's my fault, too."

Ismene said nothing, too fascinated by the colours thrown by the glass prisms, and the million little reflections that mimicked every movement. Even the air felt cleaner: no smell of cooking or disinfectants, only the scent of lemons. She followed the man into the bedroom; wished he had let her into the kitchen. She would have been happy to cook dinner for them, and clean up

129

afterwards. He led her through a bedroom as large as her home, and into the bathroom. More crystal, white linens, everything perfumed. She had never seen hot and cold taps before. He turned the shower on and adjusted the temperature. "See if it's warm enough for you."

She stuck her hand into the stream. "Yes..." although it was warmer than she liked. She hesitated.

"Something's wrong?" he asked.

"I have to pee," she replied.

"Go on," he nodded towards the commode, "I want to watch." He pulled over a silk-covered padded stool, and sat down to face her.

She was surprised at how much that excited her. Not like the time a client had asked her to pee over him while he lay in the bathtub. She had refused, even for a hundred dollars more than he paid for expected services.

She opened her legs so that he could see her clearly. She returned his smile, and was breathless when she was done.

"And I'm going to stay and watch you bathe," he said. Ismene undressed and entered the shower. His gaze never left her – intense, as if looking for some part of her that his explorations had missed. When she was done and stepped out of the shower, he licked the droplets of water off her breasts and belly, then he dried her and wrapped her in a large white towel. Then he undressed and showered. She tried not to look at him, but his reflection in the mirrors mocked her. She had never seen him naked before, and he had never allowed her hands below his waist. But she had seen the enormity of his excitement when he played with her body. He was as large as she had suspected.

When he was showered, he put on a white terrycloth robe, took her hand and led her into the bedroom. The luxury frightened her: white and gold everywhere. Everything shone, even the bed covers. It made her shiver. She was beginning to wish she had not come. Then his arms were around her and had lifted her off the ground and onto the bed. He let his robe fall to the floor, and pulled the towel off her.

This time there were none of the usual prolonged explorations. He lay on her and while she was still opening her legs for

130

him, rammed into her, hammering against her body. He took her from the back, sides, standing, kneeling, leaning against the bed, suspended – her arms around his neck and her legs wrapped about his waist. His breath roared. She gasped. He cursed. She shouted execrations fouler than anything she had dared say before. He matched her word for word until her voice failed from shouted curses, prayers, entreaties, and praises. She wanted to cry. He began to whimper, and grabbed her so tightly that she was unable to breathe. She felt a river of heat, a quick pulsing, and his legs folded. He lowered her to the bed, still inside her. She waited for him to roll off her, but he began again, supporting his weight on his elbows. It was more painful, and she was about to plead for a respite when he shuddered and stopped. He was drenched with sweat; his chest heaved as he tried to suck more air into his lungs. She was grateful when he lifted himself off, but the pain of his withdrawal brought a small scream from her. He stood over her and began to laugh quietly. She smiled back. She was happy.

"The bitch," he said.

"What?" she asked. Cold and suddenly terrified, she sat up.

"Not you," he said, "my wife."

"What are you talking about?" she asked.

"My wife," he said again. "When the bitch comes back, she'll be sleeping in the bed where I screwed a whore. On her nice satin sheets, in front of her picture. . . in front of all her expensive art. She'll have to lie in your sweat; put her face in your spit; put her hands in your juice. . ."

Ismene did not hear what else he said. She ran to the bathroom to get her clothes. "I'm going home," she said, when she was almost dressed.

"Don't be stupid," the man said; "the dogs would kill you."

"I don't care, I'm going."

He went to the front door, and opened it a couple of inches. Instantly, two black muzzles poked through, and two pairs of unblinking eyes looked directly at Ismene. She stepped back quickly.

"I'll take you home in a minute," he said. "Let me get dressed."

"Don't know why you're so upset," he said, "What did you expect? That I was going to divorce my wife for you?"

"You didn't have to treat me like that," she said. His words scorched her face like heat from a waiting oven.

"You did what you did for money. And I paid you for more than I took. You know damn's well you wouldn't have come here for nothing."

"I liked you enough to do anything you wanted," she said.

He clicked his tongue impatiently.

"You're right," she said, "I should have known better. Sorry I forgot I'm a whore."

They said nothing on the way back to the dark privacy of the ceiba tree. As she stepped out of the car, he reached into the glove box, removed an unsealed envelope and handed it to her. "Here," he said.

She took the envelope, because taking money in exchange for what she gave had become a reflex: money for bread, money for cakes, money for her body. The thought came to her to fling the money back at him – into his face – but only for a second. Instead she said, "It's not enough."

His face narrowed as if pinched. "I just gave you two hundred dollars."

"That's not enough for what you did," she said.

"Get out of my car."

"No." Her voice was cold, sharp, and clear as the crystal in his home. Dangerous as Grotte's voice. He imagined her confronting him in public, or throwing a rock through his car's windshield.

He reached for his wallet, and gave her all the money it contained. She put that into the envelope without counting it, opened the car door and set off to walk the mile to her home, attended by a late-night audience of stray dogs, feral cats and nonchalant rats.

She should have known. . . should have known. Prostitutes should not believe in fairy tales; there was no comfort that could absorb the agony of this humiliation.

Charbonette, the charcoal seller at the bottom of the hill, would read her face later in the morning on her way to work; would hear the words in her mind however hard she tried to smile over them. Charbonette would want to know why she forgot that a rich man would not risk association with a prostitute for more than the fifteen minutes required for emptying his balls, and getting dressed. The black-powdered fuel vendor, protected from politicians, police, thieves – and vanity – by a tongue as sharp and venomous as the barb of a stingray, and a temper as implacable as a house fire, would tell her – tongue restrained for the naïve country prostitute: "Let me tell you, Ti-Ismene, any man who pays to enter the door between the legs of a woman is not a friend. And whoever takes money for opening that door is not a nun. So take that misery off your face. . . you hear me? I hope you took the money. Business is business."

A month later, her breasts began to hurt with a new tenderness, and when her mornings began with nausea and vomiting, she accepted at once her obligation. She climbed the narrow stairs to the small storeroom above the store at the bakery, squeezed her eyes shut, and flung herself down the stairs. She awoke to Grotte's voice asking what the hell she'd been doing up there, and Helen sponging her face with a wet cloth. She would not let him take her to the hospital, but let him drive her home. She refused to tell him why she had climbed the stairs to the storeroom.

During the night, she was awakened by an cramping urgency. She sat on the chamber pot with her head resting on the bed. Sat there until the cocks began annoying the world with their crowing. After the sun rose, she hurried to the outhouse. Saw the frilled dark-red mass of tissue roll with the movement of blood in the bottom of the chamber pot.

From that moment, she felt a new peace. In the following days, she smiled and joked less with the customers, but was more contented. It was as if she'd found an answer to any doubt she had had about herself. Her duty to herself was to earn sufficient money to buy her independence, even if it meant selling the only thing of value she had. As for her latest source of debasement – forget the prick; it was not her place to tell him that the misfortune of his childlessness was not due to the failure of his balls.

She went to church for the first time since her arrival in the city. She sat on a bench near the entrance, the place reserved for those who never had much to put into the collection basket. It was dark in the corner under the statues of the Archangel Gabriel menacing a black bat-winged devil with a silver spear. At first, the figure of the fallen angel frightened her, then she felt a brief pang of sympathy. There was some comfort in the shadow provided by one of his wings.

She recognized two of her clients returning from receiving communion, their heads bowed in massive piety over clasped hands. She was surprised at the second man: he was one of the best clients, alternating between Helen and herself. Helen called him Mr. Cow because of his habit of moaning loudly in bed.

The mass ended half an hour later.

She smelled Virginie's cooking even before she saw her house. Garlic, onions and coconut oil, with a touch of curry and thyme, braised lamb liver and kidneys. Helen was sitting at the kitchen table with a mug of coffee. Eyes swollen.

"So, what made you go to church this morning? You can't make any money there. You have to give. How much you gave?"

"One dollar," Ismene said.

"Well, I made ninety, last night. Could have made more, but you know the little police major, always starched up? Well, he was in good form last night. I tell you if that man ask me to marry him, I wouldn't say no."

"He's not married?" Virginie asked.

"Nope."

"So, how much you got?"

"Nothing," Helen said, then exploded with laughter. "I gave him back his money."

"You what?" the others asked simultaneously.

"I tell you I gave him back his money. Forty dollars. Every cent."

"Why?" Ismene asked.

"Because he was so damn good. I even gave him another freeness hour. That's why I'm so tired."

"You like him a lot. Eh?" Virginie said.

"At least, he never gave me crabs or clap, or made me pregnant or hit me. Always brings me a little present. I'm sure its things he done steal; you know how the police does steal when they investigating stealing."

"Well, looks like we'll see you in church with him, too," Virginie said.

"Not me, no sir. When I was small, I used to be in church whole day Sunday. Morning, noon and night. Then my father had his stroke and I had to leave school to help my mother with him. She herself never used to work. It wasn't enough money selling in the bakery so I started to make a little on the side from Grotte's friends. Of course, people told my parents and my father put me out of the house. But is me still taking care of them. They don't want to see me but they damn' glad to see the money. Shit. I ain't going to no church. Ask Virginie why she don't go to church, too. And ask her how she got this house."

"You too?" Ismene asked.

Virginie nodded. "Stopped when Philippe started comin' by here. Now, is only one man for me."

"Liar," Helen said.

Virginie grinned, "Well, let's just say he's the chief man. Anyway, girl, I used to pass in church too, five-thirty mass every Sunday morning on my way home from doing what I was doing. Saturday afternoon, I used to go to confession to the same priest. Good looking man, nice and tall. Used to tell him everything I did during the week, in my sexy voice. I know he liked it. Used to make him start breathing hard – like he'd just run around the church block. Every Saturday, same thing, same penance – say the rosary five times. Then one day, don't what know what passed in my head, I told him that if he wanted something from me, he could have it any time."

"You said that? In church?" Ismene asked. "What happened?"

"He didn't say anything for a while. My heart was beating so hard, I thought I was going to faint. And just as I thought he was going to say, yes, he looked straight at me and told me not to come back to him for confession. I was so ashamed, it was like somebody pour ice down my back. I never set foot in there again. I almost ran out of the church. *Eh bien*."

"Girl, I wouldn't go back there either," Helen said.

Virginie poured more water into the skillet. Moved back from the cloud of steam. "One thing, though. Confession didn't do anything for me. I stopped taking men when I got what I wanted. I got my house."

"Except for Philippe," Ismene said.

"Right," Helen said, "and his nephew . . . and anybody with a nice car and a hundred dollars."

"But I never saw anyone come here, except Philippe," Ismene said.

"You didn't hear what I said? Nice new car. She want a ride first; that's where she does do it."

"Shut up, Helen" Virginie said, but she was laughing. "We're joking, but if it wasn't for women like us, a lot of men would leave their wives. Men want screaming and all kinds of nastiness they can't get from their wives. Wives take care of the children and the house. We take care of the men."

Virginie removed the skillet from the small kerosene stove. The others helped with the rice and vegetables. They ate in silence. "What you going to do with the money you're saving?" Helen asked Ismene.

"You know, a small bakery," she answered.

Helen pretended to look disgusted. "Child, I'm still young, and I'm going to enjoy myself. One of these days, I'll start saving." She stared into the distance. "I wanted to be a nurse. I used to have nice soft hands."

"You still have nice hands," Ismene said, then she looked away and continued eating. She did not want any further conversation. They could pretend all they wanted, but the looks and the whispered comments would follow them for the rest of their lives. There would be no redemption with time or money. Helen would never become a nurse. Someday, she herself would get her bakery, but her customers would tell their daughters on the way home: "That woman selling the bread? She used to be a prostitute in town. Some people say she's still one. If you don't study at school, see what will happen to you?" And to their sons: "Don't let me see you anywhere around that woman. Just stay away from her, you hear me?"

Not a thing to do about it. Not a thing. No government or church office where she could pay to restore her reputation. Only one thing to do: get her bakery. No reputation to lose, and too late to stop. She still needed to make more money.

The memory of the statues at church still troubled her: The horned devil, dark-skinned, bony, naked, teeth bared, cringing

136

under the heel of the pink avenger. The archangel in his Roman soldier's tunic, his back adorned with white-feathered wings, pink face impassive and unblemished. She dared not feel any sympathy for the devil, but could not feel any kinship with the celestial being. There was no guardian angel for her. If anything happened to her, only two whores would care.

And Charlo. He would care. He had promised her father to look after her. She imagined sitting next to him on a rock in the cow pasture. Not saying anything, or touching, or looking at each other. Just sitting together. Close enough to smell his sweat and to hear his breathing. Not touching or anything. Just watching the leaves move in the wind, and the grackles whistle. That would be so nice. She was certain he would care.

Grotte allowed Ismene to remain at home for a week after her fall down the stairs. He was waiting when she arrived at the store on her first morning back.

"You feel better? Good."

"Yes. Thanks very much," Ismene replied.

"Well enough to come to my place? A lot of people are asking for you. Look like you have a lot of friends."

"When do you want me to come back?"

"Tonight," Grotte said. "But one thing: from now on nobody must touch you without wearing a condom; OK? There's a box of them on the dresser."

"I never do it without one," she said.

"Then, make sure they know how to use it."

"You show them, Mr. Grotte. They're your friends."

He looked back at her for a long time. Felt the same pang in his belly – of pity and jealousy, and something a little like real desire, that made him want to hit her until she broke and he had to hate her for surrendering. Wondered what it was about her that made him overlook her defiance. If it weren't for the money she made for him, she would probably make him a good mistress – a scorpion for a mistress; he would wake up suddenly from sleep every night to enjoy the surprise of still being alive.

"Don't want anything bad to happen to you. Helen had to go to the doctor the other day. Some shit gave her a bunch of lice.

Made her scratch like hell. I'll kill the prick when I catch up with him. . . A big shot business man, too." He stopped, stared without blinking at her. "And because I don't want you falling down stairs again." He congratulated himself silently on getting the last word.

Ismene's expression did not change. No surprise on her face, she went back to the counter. Grotte's mouth pursed and his eyes narrowed. He had let the scorpion win again.

"I don't like it when you're not there," Helen said, when Ismene joined her. "I'm more afraid. What's going to happen to us, Ismene?"

"I don't know, but I'm saving my money."

"For what?" Helen said.

"You going to do this for the rest of your life? Work for Grotte? What happens when the men don't want to see your old face again?"

"I can still work here in the shop. . . Grotte will take care of me. And anyway, what else I'm going to do? Go teach school?"

"Yes. Go and tell little girls what will happen to them if they don't study."

Helen laughed. "And I can show the little boys what to do."

Ismene waited outside the bakery one evening until Fender came out. He ignored her when she called his name, but she persisted. Held on to his arm and refused to let go. Her voice was urgent: "Fender, I want you to help me do something important."

"Now, you want to use me?"

"No, I'll pay you," she said.

"What? Pay me to do what?"

"Come and see me tonight. Please."

Fender came late, when she already in bed. But she was glad to see him.

She sat with him on the back steps. "I want you to help me build my own oven," Ismene said quickly.

Fender jumped to his feet. "You're crazy?" he almost shouted.

"Fender," she said calmly, "I want to go back to Morne Rouge. I don't want to go on living in the city. Even if you don't help me, I'm going back. But I want to bake bread again. I'm a good baker. Bread and cakes."

Fender looked at her, looked at the ground, the sky; looked at her again. Took a deep breath. "OK. But you'll need about three thousand dollars. Three thousand dollars! Where are you going to get that kind of money?"

"I don't know, but I'll get the money. And I told you I'll pay. You'll help me?"

"Yes," he sighed, and stood up, brushing dirt from the seat of his pants. He did not believe she would find the money, but perhaps her dream would keep her in the city. And when it died, it would be too late for her to leave.

Ismene slipped her hand into his shirt. "Sleep here tonight," she said.

And if she had asked him then and there to build an oven the size of a church, he would have started at once.

She let him labour over her body for two hours while she thought of her oven and the pastries she would fashion. She touched him in the right places when his efforts slowed. When he was done, she said it was good.

He arrived at work red-eyed and tired the next morning, but he sang all day – and even as he left. Eight and a half hours of "*Ay, cosita linda, Mama.*"

PART THREE

CHAPTER 10

Saturday. Lucette always found something to do at the front of the house at four o'clock in the afternoons – when the buses from the city arrived at Mandelie. This time she was searching for weeds in a bed of zinnias and purslanes.

It was important to see who had bought what; who had returned to visit, and who came with news or surprises. She thought that the young woman who got off the green and blue *Safe Passage* looked familiar. The woman turned back to the bus and took a small suitcase from a passenger. She was as pretty as the girls Lucette's imagination had selected for Cord. Well dressed, with delicate ankles – like Mounira. The woman walked up the drive. Lucette rose to meet her.

"Ma Lucette, how are you?" she said.

"Mounira?" Lucette said in astonishment. "I'm so sorry, little sweet . . . I didn't recognize you. But you've got so thin."

"Yes, I know."

"But don't worry. I think you're even prettier," Ma Lucette said quickly.

They held each other for a long time, laughing tears.

"You're not going back tonight?" Lucette asked.

"Well, I don't know if you have room for me. I wanted to stay until tomorrow . . . if it's all right."

"If it's all right! Ah! You haven't even got here and you're talking about going back tomorrow."

"Work on Monday," Mounira said.

"Work on Monday," Lucette agreed, "But Mr. Charlo and Cord will be so glad to see you. We should have come to see you, but it's so hard for us. And we didn't know how to talk to you about. . . "

Mounira took Lucette's hand to interrupt her. "It's OK. Don't think about it," she said.

"So glad to see you again," Lucette repeated.

At sunset, the women heard the sound of the truck and went to the front window. Mounira felt a tightness in her chest as she watched Cord step down from the cab. She saw that his face had lost much of its softness. The lines in his forehead had deepened, and his eyes and lips had narrowed – as if he had looked more closely at life and found deception. He was thinner and resembled Constantine even more.

Charlo's hair was almost all grey, but his step was firm and his eyes angry. Ready to meet the enemy.

The men went around to the kitchen; Lucette and Mounira went to greet them. "Ma. Miss," Cord said to them.

Charlo nodded at Lucette. Looked toward the guest, "Good afternoon, Miss."

Mounira grinned and Cord looked closely at her. "Mounira?"

"Ay, *Mon Dieu*!" Charlo said.

The men took turns lifting her off the floor, soiling her dress with dirt from their arms and clothes; apologized, and squeezed the breath out of her again.

"But look at her."

"So pretty."

"You're well?"

"Yes."

"And your parents. They're well?"

"Yes."

"So how are you?"

Asking again and again as if to ensure that she was not hiding any small secret of ill health from them.

"Staying with us a little while?" Cord asked.

"Just one night," Mounira said.

"Just one night!" Charlo said in disbelief. "But you haven't even arrived."

After supper, Lucette took her to Ismene's old room. "You don't mind sleeping here?" she asked. "Used to be Ismene's room. But you know she left us. Haven't heard a word from her."

Mounira hesitated, nodded. "I'm sorry."

Lucette looked directly at her for a second, and appeared to change her mind about a question that had already pursed her lips. She hurried about the room, rearranging things that had not been touched in a year, dusting clean the furniture, and smoothing the taut bed covers.

A knock on the door, and Cord's voice. "It's me, Cord."

Lucette moved toward the door. "Well good night, little sweet. Sleep well." She left the room, took Cord's elbow and whispered quickly. "Ask her about Ismene."

Cord and Mounira asked about each other's health again, about each other's work, about plans.

"So, got a new boyfriend?" Cord asked.

Mounira shook her head, "Not yet. How about you? Still running women?"

Cord laughed. "Nothing serious." Then the laughter left his face. "Mounira, you didn't ask about Ismene tonight. You know what happened to her?"

Mounira's eyes widened in surprise. She had not anticipated the directness of the question. But she hesitated too long. She nodded. "She came to our house. Told us some of what had happened. Said it was partly her fault. Told us not to tell you where she was if you asked. She stayed with us for four days, then said she'd found a job – wouldn't say what, wouldn't say where. I see her every now and then, but she won't tell me anything about herself. But she looks all right – dresses well."

"I see," Cord said, wishing that he did. "Whenever I go to town, I drive around a bit, hoping to see her. I keep asking the bus drivers. One said he had taken her to Morne Rouge, but had brought her back to town the next day. He knew she wasn't living there. Then Pa got a letter from her: she thanked the family for taking care of her after her father died. She said she was well, and we shouldn't worry about her. But for now, she wanted to take care of herself."

"You miss her, Cord?"

"A lot, and I think Pa and Ma Lucette miss her even more."

"I thought you and she had something going," Mounira said.

"Didn't get very far."

"Why?"

"Sometimes people can be too close," Cord answered. "Anyway, I'd better let you get some sleep. I'm tired myself."

"Wish you could stay," Mounira said. And her mouth dropped open as if in amazement at her own forwardness.

Cord stopped at the door and turned back. "You remember the last time I saw you, at your home, after we had brought Cons to the hospital?"

"Yes, you kept staring at me."

"Well, I was thinking that it would be nice. . . you and me."

She heard his voice break, and saw the frown leave his face. She let him kiss her hard, let his hands go down her back and pull her close, waited until he hardened against her, then pushed him out of the room. "Before we get into trouble," she said.

The next morning at breakfast Mounira ate every fragment of the fried jacks and bread on her plate. Cord nibbled at his food but did not appear concerned at his loss of appetite. Lucette's nose twitched with anticipation at every word and movement, her eyes everywhere. Charlo spoke of the weather, and how glad he was to see Mounira again, and how she should visit more often and bring some of her mother's cakes.

The next morning, Charlo and Cord went to one of their gardens to get vegetables for Mounira to take back, and Mounira stayed with Lucette to talk about the woes of living in the city, to shell pigeon peas, peel vegetables, pick grit out of rice, and season a chicken and a rack of lamb. Lucette repeatedly expressed her regret that Mounira would not have a chance to really enjoy good country cooking for a week. Mounira agreed.

Cord insisted on driving Mounira back. When they left, Lucette said to Charlo, "You saw the way those two were looking at each other?"

Charlo shook his head. Mounira's visit had reopened some of the pain, but he was relieved that she had come. If they had gone to visit her, it would have been to bring news of Constantine. This time they had waited for her to ask, but she had not. Let Cord tell her.

As soon as they had started off for the city, Cord asked Mounira, "What we going to do now?"

"That's what I've been thinking. I'm not sure how our parents would take that. What happens if Constantine gets well."

Cord slowed down and looked at her. "Mounira, Cons doesn't

even know us, he treats us like friends who come and visit now and then. We try and get him to come and stay with us sometimes, but he says, 'next time'. Wants to stay in the hospital and draw. Cons ain't goin' to get better."

"What's he drawing?" she asked.

"Strange red and blue figures. The things give me nightmares. Ma Lucette got sick the first time she saw them. Pa looked at them once and started crying, saying that he understood then that he had lost his son for good. You don't want to see them, I tell you."

"Cons and I used to talk a lot about everything. He never told me he was interested in drawing. Didn't know he could draw," Mounira said.

"Cons used to read a lot. He couldn't draw... I know that. One of the nurses at the hospital told us some man named John encouraged him to draw," Cord said.

"Wenceslaus John?"

"Don't know. You know him?" Cord asked.

"Everybody in town knows him. Won all kinds of scholarships to go abroad and study. Came back to teach. People said he was the brightest person in the country. Then he started drinking. Left his wife for some little girl. Made his life one big mess. Now, you see where he ended up. Never seen such a thing."

"Now, how did Cons get mixed with a man like that?" Cord said, not expecting an answer.

Mounira shrugged. "I was hoping we would talk about better things. This is the first time we ever been together, you know."

After a pause, Cord said, "Well, think of all the things we could do now. We could stop on the way. I know a place. . ."

"Too quick, Mr. Cord," Mounira said, "I don't want to start off being one of your women. You think I don't know about you?"

"Sorry, but let's stop for a while. I don't know when I'll see you again."

They drove to one of the secluded places in the hills that Cord knew well. They spent an hour frustrating themselves. Dishevelled each other's clothes, smeared Mounira's make-up, tore a button from Cord's shirt.

When he dropped her home, he declined her parents' invitation to come in, pointing out the late hour and the long drive back.

"Let us know the next time you'll be coming. I don't have anything to give you to take back," Mrs. Charpentier said.

Mounira walked him back to the truck. "Don't make me wait too long," she said.

"No," he said.

He stopped a mile out of Praslin, near the home of a young widow with whom he slept occasionally. In return, he provided her and her two young sons with vegetables and fruit. The door and windows were already shut, but he could see thin verticals of yellow light through chinks in the door. He stopped and waited for her to come to the door, knowing she would have heard the sound of the truck – he did not want to be standing on her steps if she had a visitor.

He turned the headlights off when she opened the door. She was clutching a thin robe about her. "Cord?" she asked.

"Yes, it's me. Too late?"

"No-no. Was just getting ready to go to bed. You're comin' in?"

He locked the truck and went into the house. "Boys?" he asked.

"In bed."

"So how you doing, Lille?"

"Struggling. How about you? Just had a good time? I can smell perfume on you."

"Cons's girlfriend. I just took her home. Must have got the perfume when I kissed her goodbye."

"Yep," Lille said. "Don't tell me you're doing things with your brother's girlfriend."

"No-no, nothing like that," he said, trying to look surprised and scandalized at the suggestion.

"So, what brought you here tonight?" she asked.

"Hadn't seen you for a long time," he answered.

"It's been a while. Let's go in the room. . . and be quiet. I don't want the little rats comin' to see what's going on." She turned off the light.

They went through their routine of each undressing the other, and he lay diagonally across her – she could not breathe under his weight.

When they had finished making love, she expected him to dress hurriedly, claiming that he didn't want to keep her up too late. But he did not roll off her. In a few minutes he started again. She began shaking and felt an agreeable numbness in her legs. She did not know what she had done to bring him to that state of excitement, but she was pleased with the effect. There was even a third time.

Cord was surprised at himself. His first release left him unsatisfied like a man who, lost in a forest and driven insane by thirst, ignores a spring to look for a stream, and finding that, rushes past to find a river. He thrust harder to discover an answer that must lie deeper. He was aware of his release, but the need became still more urgent. After the third time, the urgency had worsened, as if there was something in him was seeking expression but couldn't find articulation. He paused to regain his breath, then like a long delayed expiration, it came: the despair, frustration, and anger over what had happened to Cons. The unfairness. Nothing had helped: not the masses and the prayers; not the visit to the *gardeurs*; not the doctors. Nobody. Nothing. And what had the Pardies done to hurt anybody? Slept with a couple of women? Then why hadn't it happened to the families of every man who had slept in other beds? And Cons of all people: The one everybody loved, who wouldn't even defend himself at school, who gave and gave and gave until. . . That? What had Charlo done? Hadn't he worked hard enough? And Lucette, who sent more prayers to heaven than all the people of Mandelie put together? That was her reward?

He began clawing on the mattress with his fingers, as if to dig himself into it; then his body began pounding uncontrollably against her, pushing her deep into the bed. He stopped and rolled off her, and lay on his back, picked her up as if she weighed no more than a pillow, and placed her on his stomach. His hands grasped her hips and he lifted and pulled her down on him until she was forced to bury her face in a pillow to stifle her screams. She was gasping, trembling violently, and she hooked her nails deep in the skin on his back. Then his body went rigid and his breathing stopped. She felt him burning inside and around her.

Lille lifted herself off him; patted the bed around them.

"You've soaked my sheet," she said, "and hurt me too. What's happened to you tonight?"

"Don't know. Must have kept too many things inside for too long."

Cord swung his legs to the floor and his knees buckled and he collapsed on the floor.

"Cord! What's wrong?" Lille asked in alarm.

"Ma?" a voice called from another room.

"It's all right, it's me. Go back to bed," she answered.

"You were too much for me," Cord said. "My knees just gave in under me. Too much."

He sat on the floor with his back against the bed. When his breathing had quieted, he pulled himself up, and dressed slowly. "That was the strangest thing," he said.

He took his wallet out, and asked her to turn on the light. Handed her all the money it contained.

"What's that for?" Lille asked.

"You've always been very good to me," he answered.

"Cord, what's happened to you? You're paying me? You used me to get rid of what was troubling you, and now you're paying me? Like some street woman? I thought I was your friend."

"I'm sorry *doux-doux*," he said, "that wasn't the right way to do it. . . but I wasn't taking advantage of you."

She would not take the money from him, but did not object when he placed it on the dresser.

"I am your friend," he said.

Cord was relieved when Lille turned her face away as he tried to kiss her on the cheek. He drove away ashamed of how he had treated her, still unsatisfied, hurting from his activity, still frustrated, angry, and confused.

He did not notice he had taken a wrong turn until the air grew cooler and he saw the tree ferns of the upland forests. It was impossible to turn the truck around on the steep narrow roads. No houses on those steep slopes. He stopped the truck in the middle of the road and wedged two rocks behind the rear wheels. Pulled hard on the parking brake and shifted the gear lever into first. He tried to remain awake until dawn, but fell into intermittent sleep, tortured by dreams of scorpions crawling into the truck. A barking dog awakened him, and he drove further up the hillside until he found a turning space near a woodcutter's shed.

That was the third time he had driven off his route. He could not keep his mind off Constantine. Did not know what to do about Mounira. At the back of every worry was the one that remained like a mountain in the distance. Would his brother's illness come to him too?

There was no comfort in trying to convince himself that there was nothing he could do about the future. He had already decided that at the first hint of darkness approaching his mind, he would walk to the tip of the finger of land that sheltered the bay and throw himself headlong down to the rocks two hundred feet below – where the sharks came at night to search for the bodies of animals that had slipped down the cliff, or other victims of carelessness.

He did not know to confront the changes in Charlo. He looked into one's eyes and nodded – but did not hear a word you said. No one dared to joke or laugh at home. Long silences, eyes quickly averted. Sentences beginning, "You remember. . . ?" then left unfinished. Everyone trying to seize a vague anger and direct it at an even hazier enemy. Guilt over ordinary things like listening to the radio, except for news of the weather. When the batteries died, Cord did not replace them for a week, and no one mentioned it.

They were loading vegetables onto the truck for transport to the city, when Maude – waiting until Cord was out of earshot – said to Charlo, "But what's wrong with Cord these days? He's walking around as if he can't remember which foot is right and which is left."

Charlo grinned; the first time Maude had seen more than a faint smile in almost a year. "Woman," he said.

"Which woman? I haven't seen him with any woman."

"That's why. He's all tangled and twisted and upside down over Mounira. Remember Constantine's old girlfriend?"

"Ay-ay-ay!" Maude cried, "What are you telling me! Well, the dance is over!" She began working faster to hide her confusion and excitement; trying frantically to find some way to bring up the subject with Cord; tripping in her haste; dropping the vegetables.

151

"Take care," Vanius said to her, "you look as if you can't tell your right hand from your left."

Maude did not find an opening until Cord and Charlo were about to drive off, and in desperation she called to Cord: "If you see Mounira in town, say hello for us."

"Mounira?" Cord said hoarsely. "Which Mounira?"

"The one making you zig-zag. The one who was here the other weekend. You think everybody doesn't know what's going on? Look at you face. Can't even speak."

Cord drove away with the truck's engine screaming in second gear. Charlo asked whether he was having a problem finding third gear.

Cord was happy that Charlo did not have much to say. He was preoccupied with fantasies that included rescuing Mounira from rampaging floods, hurricanes, and civil disorder. Taking her to picnics on the beach; dancing for hours with her; flinging her hundred and thirty pounds effortlessly into the air; hearing her plead in his ear: "I want to have your baby." It was a good trip to town.

Charlo kept back a box of yams, tanias and potatoes. "For the Charpentiers," he said.

They stopped to visit Mounira's family before returning home, and found things to talk about until Mounira came home from work. At that point, Cord discovered the power of silence required to deal with the abundance of black fruit cake – with an inch of icing – and lime squash flavoured with banana essence that Mrs. Charpentier hurried to make.

On their way out, Mounira asked when they would be visiting Constantine again. "I want to see him," she said simply.

Charlo nodded. "Yes, that would be a good thing."

Cord found his voice, "Next weekend is Whitsun. Monday is a holiday. How about if we come to town on Saturday morning . . . go and see Cons? We'll pass and meet you. If you want you can come spend the weekend with us. Eh, Pa?"

"Of course," Charlo said. He had derived so much amusement from Cord's agitation over Mounira that he was almost sorry she would be visiting them again.

"Drive well."

"Stay well."

"Give our regards to. . ."

"Yes, give our love, too."

Charlo and Cord asked Lucette about Whitsun. Lucette agreed, but she and Charlo could not come: There was too much to do. Cord should drive alone to town to meet Mounira and to take her to see Constantine. Yes, that would be easier on Mounira if there weren't too many people around. Remember the last time? What a terrible thing for the poor girl. Poor devil. Don't think the worst. By now he must have stopped thinking that way about her. Tell Cord to be sure Fen and West are there. . . for safety. Such a nice girl. Oh God.

Cord stopped three times along the way to pee. His shirt was soaked with sweat, his heartbeat loud in his ears, right shoulder burning from tension.

At the hospital, he explained to Fen how Constantine had attacked Mounira, and asked whether she could remain behind a protective barrier to see Constantine.

"She could stand just outside the gate," Fen suggested. "They could see each other through the bars."

Mounira remained in the truck, and West went to get Constantine. Cord and Fen walked with Constantine to the locked gate. Cord called through the barred window to Mounira.

"Mounira?" Constantine asked.

"Yes. You don't remember Mounira?" Cord replied.

Constantine shook his head.

Mounira walked slowly to the door, her face tight with fear.

"That's Mounira?" Constantine asked. "Nice girl. Your girl-friend?"

Cord shook his head. "No. Just a friend."

"Well I think she would be a nice girlfriend for you. Anyway, how's the truck working?"

"No problem."

"Good. Don't forget to check the brake pads when you rotate the wheels when you change the oil." Constantine glanced at Mounira briefly, his face blank, determined that she should not see the pain

153

in his eyes. Time for her to forget him; time to find somebody else. Time for him to forget too. Maybe she could like Cord.

On the way to Mandelie, Cord and Mounira drove mostly in silence. Occasionally, one would begin a statement then let the words fall quiet and die; or ask a question and not listen for the answer. Until Praslin – when the smell of the ocean insisted on other thoughts. Smells of smoke, wood shavings, fried fish, lantana flowers, dried sardines, animal manure. Sounds of grackles and finches, and bored mongrels begging for trouble; wind rushing through the trees; waves slapping the shore. Mounira placed her hands on his thigh. He wanted to say good things to her in return, but remained silent because he was afraid of saying something that would cause her to remove her hand.

At the house, Lucette looked closely at Mounira's face and said, "You saw Cons."

Mounira nodded. Lucette nodded in return and hurried back to a sudden urgency in the kitchen.

Before they went to bed, Lucette asked whether Mounira wanted to attend the early mass with her and Charlo – at five-thirty. Mounira asked whether she couldn't go at seven o'clock – with Cord. "Yes, make him go to church," Charlo said. "Why should you suffer alone?"

The next morning, Cord waited until the sound of the truck had died and was wondering about waking Mounira, when his door opened and she came in. She stopped just short of his bed and lifting her nightdress up and over her head, let it drop to the floor.

She moved towards him, her face pleading.

"No," Cord said, "stay there."

He rolled off the bed, and crawled on all fours to her. Kissed the toes on her left foot, crawled around and kissed her right heel, then left shin, right calf, left knee, right thigh, left hip, the small of her back, her hard round abdomen, left shoulder, right arm, left breast, the nape of her neck, right earlobe, left corner of her mouth, her forehead. He stood behind her, bent, picked her up and carried her to the bed. She was trembling and whimpering. She moved to the centre of the bed and closed her eyes.

He lay on her, supporting his weight with his elbows, and cradled her head in his hands.

She wrapped her arms around his neck and locked her legs tightly around his waist.

She screamed for the next ten minutes.

When Lucette and Charlo returned, Mounira was in the kitchen swizzling eggnog. Cord was outside washing mud off his rubber boots. Both looked like candidates for beatification.

"Hurry, so you can take Mounira to church," Lucette said.

"Yes, Ma," Cord said.

Lucette waited until Cord and Mounira had driven away. "You saw their faces when we came home; those two been doing something."

"I didn't notice anything, and they're big enough to know what they're doing. I don't know how Cons is going to take it if them two get serious. Nice girl, anyway."

"Yes, but jumping from brother to brother. I'm not sure that's a good thing."

"I'm not getting into the people's business." Charlo rose to leave. "Going across the road." He had seen the look in Cord's eyes; knew what it reflected. It was so good to look at a girl that way; the way he had done when he had tumbled into love with a visiting second cousin when he was thirteen. She had been eleven, then. Her parents had come to visit, and the children were sent to sleep on mattresses in the attic. During the night, in the darkness, the girl had crawled out of her bed and crept in beside him. For hours, she whispered all the mysteries of women into his ear, and let him touch some of those mysteries. Just before dawn, she went back to her mattress, leaving him paralysed with adoration and discovery. For the rest of the day, his eyes followed her everywhere. His appetite abandoned him, and when she left in the evening, he went into the outhouse to cry for half an hour.

The only other time in his life when he had confronted such an assault of love had been on the night when he expected to drown with Ismene. His marriage to Lucette had been a sensible enterprise. He envied Cord and Mounira. They at least would have more than two nights.

CHAPTER 11

In addition to the misfortunes Wenceslaus John had visited upon himself with his choice of women and drink, he also chose the wrong time to seek redemption in the eyes of his wife. Earlier in the month, she had joined the exodus from her neighbourhood to see the *The Ten Commandments*, the greatest cinematic event in the country's history. She sat in rigid mortification for three hours, the back of her neck scorched by the imagined flames from her neighbours' eyes – much as the stone tablets of Moses had been etched by celestial fire when the American-accented voice of God issued His injunction against adultery. It was little relief that she had been the victim of her husband's sin.

Still, the unkempt, wasted man remained her husband, and although she had not expected him to ask for her help until he could no longer walk to the rum shops, she was obliged to help him. But as the headmistress of the girls' elementary school, she was also forced to maintain her reputation as one who brooked no laxity of morals, took no prisoners and was unacquainted with the principles of surrender.

Her requirements for reconciliation were simple and, she thought, probably unachievable: he had to stop drinking completely (he had made some token efforts) and get a job.

He tried. For seven weeks he stayed away from the hospital. Old friends and pupils took him into their offices; but his hands trembled too much to hold a pen, and the symptoms of his sudden withdrawal from alcohol were too disturbing. His employers paid him to stay away, then apologized for not having employment better suited to his intellect.

At night, he slept in the work shed of a cabinet-maker at the south-east corner of the city. The cabinet-maker assumed that his presence would provide an inconvenience for thieves.

John used a pile of four jute bags as a mattress, and in place of a pillow, a pile of wood shavings that also served to abate the fetor of rotting fish guts, dead animals, and sewage from the stream that flowed just ten feet away from the shed. Once, that stream had been a river deep enough to take a fisherman's canoe, but, as trees on the hillside were cut for charcoal and to make room for more shanties, its feeder springs dried up, and now, its greatest depth was no more than six inches. When it rained heavily enough to flush its layer of putrefaction to the sea, he had to walk more carefully than ever to avoid the contents of outhouses from higher upstream.

Some nights, when business was slow, the prostitutes came by to sit quietly, or to listen to him remember the poems he once taught. Especially Sunday nights – when their business seemed inappropriate. Would he mind reciting again the one about the *belle dame?* And his eyes would go far away and his voice took on a dark sonority as he recited Keats's *La Belle Dame sans Merci.* They shivered when he intoned, "' . . . Hath thee in thrall!'" Nodded their heads solemnly when he was finished, waited for him come back among them, and asked:

"What is 'sedge', Mr. John?"

"And 'woebegone'?"

"And 'thrall'?"

Then they would look into the great distances of the night, to look into their memories as little girls in classrooms reciting nursery rhymes and thinking about the crisp uniforms they would one day wear when they were nurses at the health centre, or smelling the new cloth on the shelves behind them in their own shops, or lying back in the comfort of a boyfriend's new car – until the smoke from smouldering cigarettes caused their eyes to water and overpower the smells and colours of tenuous memories. If any of the women heard a familiar poem, she did not mention it, because she did not want to be burdened with the obligation of remembering useless words.

Occasionally, they brought him an undershirt or socks or a belt that someone had forgotten on the floor or under a bed, or made him laugh with their stories of the ambitions and futilities of their customers. Every other night, they cooked a little extra, to supplement what he survived on during the week. None dared offer him the comfort of her body for fear that it would be an affront to the dignity that accompanied him like an starving mongrel (and who knew what diseases lay in ambush within that wretched body).

He gave them the comfort of knowing someone who was surviving a destitution even greater than theirs.

They asked to see one of the paintings he told them about. The ones made by his friend, the mad man. He asked Constantine to lend him one of his drawing tablets; showed it to three of the women. The oldest woman shivered as if confronted by the proximity of her greatest fears. He put the pictures away quickly as the other women rushed to the stream to vomit.

None of them ever mentioned the drawings again.

John lay awake long into the night thinking of the effect the drawings had had on the women. The next morning, he made himself unrecognizably clean and went to the office of a former pupil who owned a large import-export business, and who was a noted art collector.

Pell Merse was sceptical. Would look at the pictures as a favour to his old teacher, but really. . .

The next day, Merse saw the pictures and spent the rest of the day sick from all of the aspirin he took to soothe the worst headache of his life.

When Merse got home that night, his wife refused to believe that he had not suffered some catastrophe. "You just saw some drawings? And that made you so sick, Pell? Look at your face. What kind of pictures could do that?"

"You didn't see them, Myrtle. You've never seen pictures that changed as you look at them. There are damn' eyes looking back at you. . . making you see the things in your mind. I swear I saw myself dying. Made me so sick, I don't think I can eat dinner. Don't think I'll ever eat again."

"Who made those drawings?" Myrtle asked.

"A patient at the mental hospital. Wenceslaus John's friend. John wants to be his agent. . . He thinks he can sell the pictures – and I think the pictures are more valuable than he knows."

"John? That old drunk? You're joking."

"Give him a chance, Myrtle. It was John who stood up in front of my first class at the college and convinced us that we were the smartest people in the world. Maybe if he had worried as much about himself as he worried about us, he wouldn't be out on the streets. I owe him. . . He was my teacher."

"Just don't bring the things here," Myrtle said.

When John saw Merse again, the exporter asked him to talk to Constantine's family.

John learned from West when the Pardies were due to visit, and was at the hospital waiting with Constantine when they came again. Charlo thanked him for the companionship he provided to his son. Fen had informed them of the unusual friendship.

"Have something very important to tell you," John said. "Looks like Constantine Pardie is about to become a famous artist."

"Artist? Don't understand," Charlo said.

"Constantine has been drawing these wonderful pictures and I asked a good friend of mine who knows a lot about art, and he said Constantine can make good money selling them. It's not the money, but Constantine shouldn't let a talent like that waste away."

"So, what are you telling us? Sell them?" Charlo asked. "But what is Constantine going to do with the money? He doesn't need it. We can take care of him. And who's going to buy his drawings?"

"There are collectors for almost everything, Mr. Pardie. . . especially rare things," John answered. "And you never know what can happen with your family. Everybody is apparently in good health, but can you guarantee that for ever? Anyway, you could put the money in a savings account for him. Money does not become obsolete. Who knows? Someday. . ."

Lucette seized upon that thread. "I think it's a good idea. Cord?"

A long pause. "Maybe we can we use some of the money to buy new furniture for Constantine's room?"

Fen nodded.

Cord looked at his father, "If Cons lives longer than all of us. . . perhaps. Let's try it."

Charlo said, "Mr. John, I'm going to talk to a lawyer. I don't want anybody taking advantage of my son. If he sees nothing wrong, I'll agree. But we want everything on paper. And no pressure on Constantine. Never, never ask him to do anything. If he wants to draw, he will draw. If he doesn't, leave him alone. You understand?"

John glanced at the muscles on Cord's arms and the green glass of his eyes. He looked at his own withered arms and nodded. "I've never stolen anything in my life," he said. "Not even what I thought was mine. Most of all, Constantine is my friend – and I think I'm his friend."

The family shook hands with him. "Don't do anything without letting us know, you hear?" Lucette said, and took Constantine's hand to lead him to a bench where they could speak.

"Yes, don't worry. Thank you Madame Pardie, Mr. Pardie, Mr. Cord," John said.

Eleven days later, Wenceslaus John exchanged a large brown paper sac containing twenty of Cord's drawings on heavy paper for a white envelope containing one thousand, two hundred and fifty dollars. "One thousand for the artist; two hundred and fifty commission for you. OK?"

"Right you are, Sir. Thank you." John walked quickly to his wife's home, clutching the envelope in terror in his right pants pocket.

Meantime Pell Merse drove quickly to his office and locked the package of drawings in the bottom drawer of a large filing cabinet. He intended to leave them there for a long time – until their value had increased twentyfold.

John was relieved when Constance took the envelope from his trembling hand and opened it. "Where did you get all that money, Wence? You didn't steal it?" she asked.

He told her. "No, no, no, no. You know I wouldn't steal that kind of money. Not all's mine. One thousand for Constantine, two hundred and fifty for me – commission."

"I don't need your money. Use it to buy yourself some new clothes. You had better start looking respectable."

"You think I can sleep here tonight? Haven't slept in a proper bed for a long time. Hospital mattresses are a special mischief."

160

Constance smiled, "Come inside, Wence."

She left him in the sitting room listening to the radio, and went to the fish market to find a large grouper. She would make him a court bouillon – with hot bread, and cocoa.

That night she helped him take his clothes off – his hands trembled too much to unbutton his pyjama shirt or undo the knot in the cord of the pants. When he lay exhausted on her, she suggested that she lie on him instead. He surrendered his pride to reality.

The next morning, she giggled at the little smile of triumph on his sleeping face. Went into the kitchen to make him an omelette seasoned with ground black pepper, minced onions and garlic. Made him eggnog flavoured with vanilla beans, but added only a teaspoon of Napoleon brandy. She cut a large section from a papaya, scooped out the seeds and sprinkled it with lime juice. Placed the fruit in a saucer and set that in the centre of his plate.

She went into the room to wake him, humming, "Here comes the bride . . ." Shook his shoulder gently. Then sat on the bed and cried.

During the night, the heart of Wenceslaus John had burst from a surfeit of happiness.

CHAPTER 12

It was a year after her miscarriage when Ismene went to Grotte's office. She knocked, and when he did not answer, walked in. He looked up. "Sit."

She stood near the door. "I'm going back to Morne Rouge," she said.

"Eh?"

"I'm going back to Morne Rouge."

"Going back to where? Morne Rouge? You crazy, woman? You don't leave here until I tell you. Nobody walks out on me. If I killed you now, you know the police would blame you for it? Even your friends would say it was your own damn' fault. You know the men you meet at my home? They're the ones running the country: ministers, police, lawyers, doctors, businessmen, and so on and so forth. Important people. And you want me to disappoint them? What if I tell you, no?"

"I'm going. . . You can find other women," she said, and flung her defiance into the two burning coals in his face.

"You know, in all my life, I have been afraid of only two women. My wife and now, you. Not even of my mother. But you, Ismene. . . I had the feeling that if you stayed here, one day you would take my business and my property. Or kill me. Because you're like me. Hard.

"My wife came from a very poor family, but when she looked in the mirror, she knew she didn't want to die poor. She hated poverty like a disease. That's why she married me. And every day I was afraid she would leave me. I used to spy on her, send people to follow her. When she got pregnant, I couldn't sleep because I wanted to be sure the baby was ugly enough to be mine.

"I gave her everything she mentioned. So what happened? She died. The woman died to escape me."

"Sorry," Ismene said.

"If I had the courage, I'd make you marry me, Ti-Ismene."

Ismene's head jerked back as if he had struck her face. It was several seconds before she could speak. "I'd die first." She was angry that he had used the diminutive form of her name.

"No, Ismene. You'd enjoy it. You'd never have anybody tell you what to do again; never have to depend on anybody for anything. Your own car. . . How many women you know have their own car? I know you better than you think . . . because you're just like me."

"Think what you like. I know what I want, and I'm going to get it."

He shrugged. "So, you're going back to the bush. Going to build a bakery. Going to be a big shot at Morne Rouge . . . run the place. Like Grotte in the city," he said. Smiled.

"Who said anything about a bakery?" Ismene said. Her face itched with embarrassment and surprise, and she wanted to sit so that she could breathe again.

"Listen, you think any of my people can do anything without my knowing? Not one, not one of them. But I can't say I'm disappointed. Here." He opened the drawer of his desk and removed a brown manila envelope. "That's for your oven."

"If it's money, I can't take it," Ismene said.

"Why not?"

"I don't want to owe you money."

"I asked you to sign anything?" he asked.

"No."

"It's your money. Commission on sales in the store. Oh, and when you get a man, get a man like you: hard as wood. Not like Fender . . . he's like bread. He's OK . . . but not for you. Too soft." His eyes shifted from her to the door and stayed there – she was dismissed.

As she closed the door behind her, she heard him say, "What to do. . . That woman?"

Helen and Virginie did not take the news well. That evening Ismene endured several hours of pleas, tears, warnings, threats, and more pleas. Helen lost her voice, and Virginie lost a great clump of hair over her right temple from pulling at it in her distress.

The following Saturday morning, Ismene left on the five-thirty bus for Morne Rouge. She was relieved that the passenger next to her was too sleepy to ask where she was going to, and why, and who her mother was.

There is great satisfaction in forgiving: It is an acknowledgment that someone else has committed a greater sin than the forgiver. When the women of Morne Rouge gave their bodies, it was not for money – not immediately. Nevertheless, it was comforting to forgive. They were up early enough to see Ismene arrive, and four children were sent to help carry the boxes and suitcases deposited around her. When she was near her old home, they came out of their houses – to do something or other of course – and were immediately surprised and delighted to see her again.

First the remonstrances: "You could have come to see us now and then. . ."

"All these years and not a word from you."

"Last time I saw you, you were a little bundle of sticks. Now, look at you. . . all nice and dressed up."

"You've come back to stay, Ismene?"

"Yes."

And the men volunteered to help her clear the weeds from the front yard of Bede L'Aube's old house-lot, each hoping to understand the skills she must have learned in the city.

Bede's house had been carried away piecemeal by her Aunt Thomasina and her husband. Only the front and back steps remained, and some stones from the kitchen. The outhouse had become a leaning tower of vines.

Carmen, who had loved Ismene's father many years ago, invited Ismene to stay with her until she could build her own house. Carmen was delighted when her invitation earned her twenty dollars a month in rent.

There followed a month of negotiations, arguments and quarrels – with builders and contractors. Then they began on Ismene's house. Stone and concrete blocks. White with green trim. A balcony the length of the house at the front. Overhanging eaves to keep the house cool. Another room with a counter with a glass top and glass front – for bread and cakes.

Then she went to the city to see her friends and to tell Fender that she was ready to start building her bakery.

When Fender came, he walked around her house, looking at the trees to see which way the wind blew. He chose a site where he said the wind would take the smoke away from the house, but would spread the smell of baking bread along the road. "People can't drive past the smell of hot bread," he told her.

Fender was not Ismene's lover. He slept in another room. Everyone knew that because Carmen had gone to Ismene's house very early in the morning on a very pressing matter and had seen Fender sleeping on a mattress in the living room. They were surprised, but pleased that the men from the city would not begin a pilgrimage of vice to their village.

Fender came Friday nights and left Sunday evenings. He built the oven of brick; plastered it with mortar made from coral collected from the seashore and burned to make quicklime. He built an open shed of corrugated iron over the oven, with an opening for the chimney. The oven was larger than Ismene expected.

Ismene sat on the back steps of her house watching the builders make the finishing touches. "But that thing you built me is as large as a house," she said to Fender.

"Don't worry," Fender said; "the next bakery is six miles away. And people going along the road will stop here for their bread. Buses and cars. And if you bake cakes? Well . . . mama!"

"We'll see," she said, "Now, we have to talk about how much I have for you?"

"One dollar," Fender said.

"What? How do you mean 'one dollar'? You did all that work for nothing?" Her eyes widened. "Grotte paid you. . ."

He nodded.

"Why?" she asked. "I don't want to owe that man anything."

"You didn't sign any paper with him. You don't owe him shit."

"And if he thinks I do?"

"Out here? At Morne Rouge? Grotte can do what he wants in the city. Up here, he doesn't have any friends. And I think he's afraid of what you'd do if he messed with you. Probably cut his balls off. And I think you'd do that."

"No," Ismene said, "I wouldn't cut them off. . . I'd crush them with my hands. And make the fat ugly bastard swallow them."

"Let me tell you something," Fender said. "I'm going to miss you – although I, too, was a little afraid of you. I don't know what you're looking for, but I know it wasn't in the city. The person I feel sorry for is Helen: I think she likes what she's doing for Grotte. At least he takes care of the people who work for him. Or breaks their necks."

"Whose neck he broke?" Ismene asked.

"What they told me was this. . . " And Fender told her what he had picked up over the years at the Metropolis Bakery.

A boy about fourteen years old, just getting his moustache, appeared early one Saturday morning outside the bakery belonging to a Mr. Alexandre, in the east side of town. He sat there until the sun shone directly overhead. He left but came back on Monday morning. One of the bakers called him across and offered him a loaf of bread, asked his name.

"Grotte," the boy said. The workers laughed, assuming it was a nickname – a fitting one.

The boy ate the bread; asked if he could sweep the front of the store. When he was finished he offered to do inside – for another loaf. One week later, he was sweeping the oven, carrying out the garbage, and running errands. A month later, he was taking bread to the shops in large baskets carried on his head. One day, a street vagrant knocked the basket off the boy's head, grabbed two loaves. Grotte calmly walked to the vagrant, broke both his arms, and broke his neck. The police, glad to be rid of another vagrant, decided that Grotte had acted in self-defence.

He never said where he came from or who his parents were. Some of the workers joked that his parents were pigs: he was so ugly – the kind of ugliness you couldn't stop looking at.

Within a year, Grotte was working in the oven; never taking time off. Five years later, he bought the bakery from Mr. Alexandre. Where he got the money, nobody knew. Nobody ever accused Grotte of stealing. He bought the properties near the bakery and built two larger ovens; but kept the old, smaller one – that was for cakes. He never tried to make anybody like him. Never tried to cheat anybody. Never joked with anybody. Most of his employees have never had another job. Only one person ever stole from him. Don't know if Grotte got his money back, but nobody ever saw the thief again – just disappeared. Nobody messed with Grotte.

"Know where some of his money goes? Into the pockets of politicians and the police. So nobody can touch Grotte. You can imagine what he knows about all the big shots. Then he gets all the money back through the women he uses. Sorry, I didn't mean you. . ."

"It's all right," Ismene said.

"But he liked you," Fender said. "He was afraid of you though, wanted you to know who was boss. Word went around the bakery that if anybody touched you, their ass would be split up to their neck. That's why I had to stay on your good side. You know, if you change your mind about me, I'd be glad to do anything you wanted."

He paused and was looking at the ground, when a man's voice called from the front of the house, "Miss Ismene."

"'Miss Ismene'? Who's calling me 'Miss Ismene'?" she answered.

A head appeared around a corner of the house. "Need any help with the baking?"

"You're a baker?" she asked.

"No, but I can do other things." He walked into the yard.

Ismene stared at him, trying to recall the vaguely familiar face. Then she remembered the boy who had almost killed himself because she had not let him put his hands into her panties. "Nico?" she asked tentatively.

"Yes, Miss Ismene."

"Stop calling me 'Miss'," she said. "You not still jumping into quicksands?"

He laughed. "Not since you left Morne Rouge."

"Well, I'll have a lot of work when Fender goes back to town. How are you, Nico?"

"I'm struggling," he said. "Little jobs. . . on the road, my garden. By the way, there's a man and his wife squatting in your father's old garden. . . where they found your father. The man's my distant cousin. Anyway, I told him you were back, and he should ask permission to stay or work on the land."

"What did he say?" Ismene asked.

Nico looked uncomfortable. "Told me to take my ass off the property. And to tell you if you wanted the land, to come and make him leave."

"I see," Ismene said.

Fender rose to leave. "Think about what I said."

"Yes, Fender," she said, "and if you need anything, ask me first."

The next morning, Ismene went to the garden. Saw the changes. There was no one else there yet, so she sat under a cashew tree. About fifteen minutes later, a couple came along the path. They were in their forties; both wore faded torn clothes. Ismene rose. "You're the people using my land?" she asked.

The woman made a small squeal and stopped. The man came closer. "You're Bede's daughter?"

"Yes."

"Well, you left the land lying there useless for over ten years. You didn't expect somebody to use it?"

"Not without my permission. And I noticed somebody moved the boundary markers."

The man scratched his foot with the tip of his machete. "Nobody was using the land."

"It's my land, and I want to use it," she said.

"Make me leave it," he said, and folded his arms. One second later, he was lying on the ground clutching his groin. His mouth formed a silent "O", and he was breathing in small sips, as if the air had become too hot.

Ismene took her right shoe from between his thighs, and picked up the fallen machete. "When you're ready to talk, come to my house. I'll give this back to you then."

A few seconds of elation and relief, then anger that the trespasser had forced her to hit and humiliate him. . . in front of his wife. Even to protect her property. One new enemy.

Later in the morning, Nico's trespassing cousin came to discuss leasing the land from her, and promised to pay for replacing the boundary markers. "I'm glad I've had my children already," he said, "because I don't think I'll be able to have any more."

Ismene gave him six of ten loaves that Fender had brought from town. "Try your thing out tonight. I'll bet it still works," she said.

"Don't make me laugh – it hurts too much."

Nico came to work for Ismene. Never stood too close to her. Would have begged to die for her. He suggested that she invite the parish priest to bless the bakery before they began selling. "But I don't go to church," Ismene said, "and the priest must have heard enough about me."

Nico asked the priest. The priest was hesitant. Nico's parents and several neighbours asked again. Told the priest they did not want dissension in their village, that Ismene was a child of Morne Rouge. And hadn't she given up her previous life? And hadn't she come back home? The priest agreed to bless the bakery at noon the following Sunday.

So, Ismene left it to Nico to negotiate the purchase of fire-wood; to stock the oven, and to sweep it out with *ti-baume* brooms. Later, she let him put the spindles and rolls of dough into the shimmering luminous cavity, and remove the loaves with a long wooden paddle. He insisted on making the paddle himself – said he had to have something of his own making around the bakery.

It was only natural that when Ismene considered getting someone else to help her at the counter, one of Nico's girlfriends came to see her and got the job.

Sometimes when the rush was over, and they sat together talking, Nico wondered to himself whether she was lonely enough to let him stay the night. He never suggested it – her eyes said no. Cold eyes, looking at distant things, unshareable things.

Cold eyes that confused and challenged: not the eyes of a city prostitute as the rumours had assured. Cold, unafraid eyes that forced a person's eyes down; made him look behind her, or to the side. Maybe it was because she did not have time for poor men. But the rich men in big cars who came to her house did not stay long, or even get past her door. They left Morne Rouge looking angry and bewildered; did not even wave back at the children. No men stayed around except the builders and Nico – and Nico slept in his parents' house.

The village women stopped to chat after buying bread and cakes. So, the men stopped too: for bread, to chat, and to look at her. Wondered which of them would dare, or how to begin. The children came to watch her knead the dough and to wait for small plaited loaves spread with margarine or guava jelly. Sometimes, they saw her eyes grow moist. Asked: "You crying, Miss Ismene?"

"No. It's from flour that got in my eyes."

They rushed to help: "Let me do the bread, Miss Ismene."

"No. Me, me. Miss Ismene."

"I can do it. Miss Ismene."

"Go wash your hands."

"OK, Miss Ismene. Let me try."

Two small indentations in the dough: "Oh, but it's hard!"

"You're too weak. My turn, Miss Ismene."

"Aah! It's heavy. You must be strong, Miss Ismene."

I-told-you-so smiles from Ismene: shooing the children away; pushing stiff-armed into the rubbery hill; pulling the edges up and to the centre; then forcing the centre down: a volcano. Pouring salt water into its crater. More flour: the volcano growing from the outside.

Later, the perfume of hot bread. It stopped cars and buses going through Morne Rouge. People bought extra loaves as a precaution, because it was too difficult to eat and not share; or to let the bread grow cold while a neighbour ate. Crisp, hot, perfumed – bread that tasted like no one else's. Better than the loaves made by machine in the city, or from Grotte's bakery. Bread to be eaten the day of purchase, before her sadness made it sour. Maybe it was her sweat. Maybe she cried into the dough. Some said that she baked the bread with the heat of her body. Others said that she spoke to the dough; that she kneaded it with the affection that was meant for a man's parts.

"You think you could spare a little butter, Miss Ismene? Ah. God will bless you, Miss Ismene."

She baked three days a week, rising early every morning to take the bus to the city for supplies, or to make bread and pastries. She was afraid of morning solitude: when loneliness came like a persistent undertaker pursuing her as she busied herself sweeping already clean floors, rearranging ornaments on the dresser or picking dried dough from crevices in the kneading tray.

When she did not have to travel to town, she filled a large flower vase on the shop counter with sprigs of allamanda, ixora and bougainvillea. Arranged and rearranged the flowers for symmetry one day, then irregularity another, or interspersed short-lived hibiscus blossoms along the rim of the vase.

But at night the wind called maledictions through the eaves and spaces around the windows and the darkness was not deep enough to hide menacing shapes near the door or against the curtain – menaces that were betrayed as dresses or blouses left hanging on a nail when morning came. There were nightmares of bodies floating toward her as she stood waist-deep in floods; a tall, thin silent man with pure white eyes who followed relentlessly as she walked along a beach covered with sharp fragments of shells; voices from the mangroves pleading: "Give it to him." Or Grotte's voice coughing: "Come! Sit! Go!" and clawed feet scurrying over her roof – always over her bedroom – something that belonged to the night searching for her. In the morning she told herself it was rats attracted to crumbs from the oven.

At these times, she hugged her pillow and called, "Charlo, Charlo," until sleep came – or until the morning.

She thought and thought about it constantly for a week, then the next time she went to the city she gave the bus driver a note for Charlo – and waited.

She knew immediately who it was when, three days later, truck wheels crushed the gravel outside her house. He was on his way back to Mandelie from the city. She ran out to meet him, her heart beating so hard, she couldn't breathe; stopped an arm's length away, too weak to move. "Mr. Charlo," was all she said.

He put his arms around her and almost had to carry her into the house. She pressed her face against his chest and cried until the front of his shirt was soaked and clinging to his skin. He did not ask how she was, or ask her to stop; held her until she was spent. Gave her his handkerchief to blow her nose. His mouth twitched with all the things he wanted to say.

Then she told him everything, as if she had memorized every

detail – because one day she knew she would have to tell him. She started with the passenger on the bus who was going to the city for an operation.

"Yes," Charlo said, "that must have been Ben – he had a hernia. He died years ago."

She told him about Helen and Grotte, Virginie, Philippe and Fender. About Casanova, about the man with the smile as bright as a Christmas card and his house of crystal. About the money, the bakery; the baker's large Vauxhall car with leather seats so smooth that a passenger would slide from door to door at corners if she did not hold on to an arm rest. She even described the portrait of Grotte's wife. And the men – every one. The injuries and the humiliations. The rare joys – especially with her two friends. She laid out everything unwrapped and unfolded before him – and waited for him to walk away.

He told her about Constantine and his strange pictures, and his friend Wenceslaus John. How Constance's drawings had become even more frightening after John died: how, to look into a drawing was to see yourself dying. About Mandelie. About Lucette.

About Cord and Mounira.

"Cord and Mounira? No!"

"Yes."

He did not tell her how painful her leaving had been. How he hated going to the pasture in the mornings.

Then it was time for him to go. She held his hand. "You'll come back?" she asked.

"If I did, perhaps I wouldn't leave again."

"You'll come back?" she repeated.

"Ask me to come back, Ismene."

"Come back, Charlo," she said.

He kissed her on the scarred cheek, and went to his truck. Looked out of the window as he drove away. Nodded.

CHAPTER 13

Lucette set about to straighten and level her road to heaven. She had found herself more and more often alone, and for longer, with Constantine and Ismene gone. Charlo had to employ two boys from the village to help with the gardens and the animals. It became even lonelier when Cord busied himself with Mounira – although she looked forward to Mounira's visits. And she visited Constantine more often.

On one of her visits, she found Constantine sitting with a woman who looked to her like a teacher. She was dressed in a black cotton dress with purple lace and white buttons. A black leather handbag hung from her arm. Thin, erect and prim. Constantine reflected her posture. He saw Lucette first. He pointed her out to the 'teacher'.

The woman rose and extended her hand. "My name is Constance John. I was Wenceslaus John's wife."

Lucette took her hand. "I remember him well. How have you been?"

Constance shrugged. "Wenceslaus died a happy man because of your son. I remember the night he came back home – you know he had left the house – and said, 'Constance I have found your namesake and he is light and life. . .' I don't remember it all. Some time after my husband's funeral, I came here and asked to see his friend. Constantine has been very nice to me, and I enjoy coming to talk to him."

Lucette looked at Constantine. He nodded, relaxed now that his mother was there – which made the teacher less intimidating.

The two women spoke hesitantly at first, but over the next hour Lucette had satisfied all the questions Constance had about her son. Lucette learned enough about Wenceslaus John to keep her laughing and shaking her head in wonder for weeks.

When Constantine left, the women walked to the bus stop. Of course, if Constance were interested, she could enquire about selling Constantine's pictures again. Constance would discuss the matter with Merse.

On another visit to the city, Lucette insisted on taking Constance with her and Charlo to visit the Charpentiers when she went to discuss preparations for the wedding of Cord and Mounira.

Mr. Charpentier insisted that the wedding be in the city, and the reception at his home.

"I'm prepared to pay for everything – after all, Mounira is our only child."

Mrs. Charpentier nodded cheerfully.

Charlo reminded them with equal cheer that they could expect about one hundred guests, and invitees of the guests, from Mandelie. "It might get a little tight in here," he said, "and then they'll want to dance. I think Cord has already made arrangements with a small band at Mandelie."

Mr. Charpentier agreed immediately that the wedding and ceremony should have a more convenient venue, but he insisted on providing the food. Charlo would pay for the drinks. Mrs. Charpentier would bake and ice the cakes, and prepare the hors d'oeuvres. Ma Lucette would cook a dinner of many dimensions.

Charlo obtained permission to use the school at Mandelie for the reception. Ellit announced that a friend with an electric guitar would be joining the band to play after the ceremony.

Cord and Mounira built their house on the top of the cliff overlooking the pasture, near the spot where Cosmos's hut had been. He built it of the stones that littered the land. Used purpleheart wood inside – hard enough to blunt the jaws of termites. He made it with large windows facing the Atlantic so that the strong breeze from the ocean blew right through the house, taking away flies and mosquitoes. They were close enough to his parents if there were an emergency, but not close enough for Lucette to find out if their beds were made, or how clean Mounira kept her kitchen. The separation forced him to buy a new Austin truck. Red.

Mounira continued to work in the city on weekdays, but moved to Mandelie when she was eight months pregnant. That brought Lucette to their house almost every day.

In the midst of this happiness, Cord saw his father grow tired and distant, as if he had forgotten the place he had set out for so long ago. Cord assumed greater responsibility for running their farms and gardens, and Charlo accepted his decisions with little discussion or objection – even when Cord suggested buying five acres of land with a deposit of white clay near the road to the pasture – for manufacturing bricks.

"Who's going to help you with all of that?" Charlo asked.

"Mounira."

"Mounira? What does Mounira know about making bricks?"

"Not make them. Sell them. I have a friend who knows the business but doesn't have the money or the land. We buy the clay, we have logwood for the ovens. Or we can buy waste motor oil. And the man comes as an employee. Eh?"

Charlo nodded and, for the rest of the day, enjoyed the thought of being a manufacturer of bricks. The next morning, he allowed habit to lead him to the pasture, then to the bananas.

Despite the family's intention, news of Constantine moved from Mandelie to the capital, to the airport and across to New York. Charlo received a letter from Marie-Josette: a simple letter written in a pain too great for eloquence. She gave them the date of her arrival for a two-week visit; wanted to see what she could do about Constantine – and there was something she had to tell them.

Charlo and Cord drove their trucks to the airport. Perhaps their American relative would be arriving with uncountable suitcases and boxes. Lucette and Mounira insisted on going, and Vanius and Maude and Marie-Josette's godfather and Titina and. . .

Marie-Josette retrieved only two suitcases from customs. The uniformed official behind the table looked at the tiredness and surrender in her eyes and did not bother to ask what she had to declare. Told her to take care. She tried to smile her thanks.

They expected her to look more prosperous, fatter, louder. More American. Instead, she looked tired – and her nails were chipped. Her accent had changed – words came through her nose – but she still resembled Charlo, and her mouth twitched before she spoke.

It was two days before those who heard the news of her return allowed the family to talk to her. In the kitchen she insisted on making her own supper of bread and butter, and cocoa – made from a cigar-shaped log of dried cocoa paste. Wanting to avoid the eyes of her family, she concentrated on grating the cocoa; boiling the oily gratings in milk; stirring continuously; and adding a flour and water mixture to thicken the beverage.

"Wait. Let me finish making my chocolate." Then she had to sit.

"Now, tell us about the family. How are the two girls? How's Truce?" Lucette wanted to know how bad the "something" was. They had spoken about it, were waiting for her to tell. But when she did not offer, and wanted to talk instead about Constantine, about how things had changed, they decided to ask.

"We know something is wrong – and it's not about Cons. You're with family now. Who else can you go to? This is your father and your mother. This is your home. No strangers. What is wrong, Marie-Josette?"

"I don't want to go back there," she began.

She had expected it to be cold in New York, and was hoping it would be, so that when she wrote home she could tell them how she shivered, and how they had to light a fire in the apartment Truce had ready, just outside the Air Force base. Imagine that! A fire inside a house. But it was July. Hot. Hotter than home; and without a breeze – just grey air, so hot and heavy that one's sweat did not dry, but ran into one's collars and waistbands.

And yet people rushed – like mourners late for a funeral – no joy at their destination, but hastening to get there before the corpse was buried. Rushing to say things they did not believe; then rushing back to their own coffins, stacked so high in brown and grey-brick mausoleums that it hurt the neck to look up to see where they ended.

"People, people everywhere. All kinds of people: Chinese people, black people, white people; all kinds of clothes: men in long shirts like dresses, women with their faces all covered up so you could only see their eyes, men with plaits on the side of their heads dressed in black suits even in the heat. Car horns blowing. Everybody rushing and pushing. You can't even stop to look in a store window. Nobody looking at you. Nobody smiling. And the tall buildings looking as if they going to fall on you, any time." Marie-Josette paused. Her family shook their heads in disbelief. What a place, what a place.

Even when the sun shone, the sky remained gray and metallic, like the bottom of an old aluminium pan. Marie-Josette had stayed close to Truce, afraid of being pulled into one of the crab-holes leading to the subways; or being swept along one of the sidewalks that pierced the distance. She was convinced that the crowds could envelop and carry her forever around the city and never once acknowledge her presence.

She had stayed awake the entire first night listening to sirens, horns, shouts and trains. Not a single chirp from a cricket or tree frog. Just hard noise. And heat. In the morning, her nightdress was soaked. Later, Truce took her on the train to downtown. Don't say "Good morning" to the ticket seller. No wonder he didn't answer; although his eyebrows jumped at the greeting. Don't stare at the other passengers. Don't look scared. Stop saying 'I'm sorry'. Look at the floor. Read the advertisements. Pretend you're sleeping. Hold my hand; don't let go. Come.

They went to a department store. One million new things: moving stairs, air-conditioning, sweet-smelling air. They bought an electric fan.

Truce let her rearrange the furniture in the apartment. Let her walk down to the street after a week. On the stairs, in the hallways, uninhibited strangers with faces that looked familiar – until they spoke:

"Hi. You the new people in 532?"

"Where you from?"

"Where's that? In Mexico?"

"Been to Mexico once. . . weird food there. Had the shits for days."

"You talk kinda funny."

"Welcome to the US of A."

"See ya later, Señorita."

Don't talk to strangers, Truce had said, but it was impossible not to answer the strangers in their block. They were always so friendly – smiling or speaking before she did, assuming that if she returned a smile she was asking for a chat.

She could not find a church with a familiar liturgy in her neighbourhood. So she went to the white-painted brick one she could hear from two blocks away. She went for a month, fascinated by the screaming, pleading, threatening, leaping, spitting, glistening preacher and congregation. On her first visit, she had expected to leave after an hour, but she had allowed herself to be seated too close to the front and was intimidated by the eternity of stern faces between herself and the door. She didn't want to offend the white-gloved man who had accompanied her to the front. So, for two more hours, she sat and stood and sat and stood in religious consternation as the black turmoil of a pastor ran from one side of the stage to the other; sauntered, slid, hopped skipped and jumped, and flapped his arms so vigorously that he looked like a black-winged angel preparing to leave the earth – and perhaps he would have become airborne if the immense sleeves of his robe had held more starch.

Her sole comfort came from being out of range of the pastor's shower of spit that projected to the four cardinal points and areas between. The choir did not seem to notice the celestial shower, so busy were they with jumping, clapping, shouting, and waving their hands, as if to wipe invisible windshields. The congregation did not seem to mind either, even when the spit was accompanied by droplets of sweat that poured from the pastor like juice from an overripe sapodilla. She suspected the women used the paper fans adorned with cherubs and scriptural texts as umbrellas.

She joined the voices that immediately obeyed when the pastor asked for an "Amen". He pronounced it "A-man".

The pastor implored those who wished to be saved to raise their arms and testify, warning the impure of the eternal consequences of missing that unique opportunity. Marie-Josette hesitated, trying to recall any action in her past that would consign her to eternal damnation. She remembered confessing to the parish priest her entire premarital sexual experience the day before boarding the plane to America, and decided against immediate salvation. Instead, she shouted a vigorous "A-man," and rejoiced that the testifying enabled her escape to the door.

"Mama, Papa," said Marie-Josette, "You never seen such a ta-ra-ra, such a boom-de-yay, people jumping up and down, shoes flying, hats flying, arms and legs everywhere."

After the fourth visit, she fled the "A-mans" and salivary torrents when the preacher made it clear how expensive it would be to get to heaven through the doors of his church. She followed the televised Sunday morning services instead.

"I couldn't take it again," Marie-Josette told them. "These people tried to get me to dance in church. You ever heard of that? People dancing in church? And not just little dancing – big jumping up and screaming, you know."

Truce had left the Air Force when their boy and girl were in high school. Marie-Josette asked for a job in their school cafeteria, but the school board sent her to a different school. The children were relieved.

Truce continued cooking in the corner restaurant he and his best friend had bought fifty-fifty with their retirement money. Just enough business for two and the Haitian lady who cleaned up. The partner did not come to work the day the sheriff served Truce with the foreclosure papers. It was not the sheriff's job to explain. Ask the bank. The bank wanted the money that Truce's partner had borrowed. But the figures in the ledger the partner showed him every Thursday evening? Truce had the books right there. "Cooked," the loans officer said. He did not have the time to look sympathetic – he had to deal with this crap all the time. Did not even say goodbye; pulled open a drawer in his desk and got busy with some papers.

A friend recommended a good lawyer. The lawyer asked for two thousand dollars, filed in court, and forgot the case. Truce got a letter from the court: He was fined one hundred dollars for not providing the documents the court had asked for – the ones he had given the lawyer. When he did find the lawyer's office open, the new occupant told him his lawyer's license had been suspended: "The mother hasn't set foot in court for over a year."

Truce now had more time to sit on the steps at the entrance, to talk to the ex-boxer who collected rent for the landlord. He explained that the ex-partner did not understand the problem, laughed off his demand for repayment: "A Mr. Moneybags like you. What you got to worry about? I ain't got no money, man. All this stuff's my wife's. Even the car. Ask her."

The ex-boxer's fee was six hundred dollars. Truce had five hundred. "OK, five hundred and ten percent of the money I get back. Deal?"

"OK. Deal."

The partner laughed again when the ex-boxer asked for the money.

"Get your sorry ass out of my face."

So the ex-boxer left. Waited across the street until dark. Came back and waited the next night. Waited until the partner left for the corner store. Caught up with him on his way back, between street lights, outside a used-tyre shop. Beat him with a length of one-inch iron pipe until he stopped moving. The doctors told the partner's wife that her husband would never speak or walk again. Truce was arrested and charged as an accessory to assault with a deadly weapon: Two years.

Their son refused to visit Truce in prison, and wouldn't open a school book at home. The daughter's teacher wrote that the girl was skipping classes. Marie-Josette's pleading and tears only irritated them.

One night she went to their bedroom with Truce's belt; locked the door; pulled back the blankets and whipped both of them until she dropped to the floor in tiredness. She had to keep them home for two days because of the welts on their faces.

After that, the two teens stopped looking at television and staying out. They did not say much to her, but their grades improved at school.

When Truce came out of prison, his hair was grey and he was afraid of close spaces, of uniforms – and of other men.

Marie-Josette had not written to her family about those things – for the same reason they had not told her about Constantine.

Charlo looked at Lucette, looked at Marie-Josette. "Come back home," he said.

Lucette nodded.

"All those years abroad? How can we live here? What's Truce going to do?" Marie-Josette asked

"What's Truce doing now?"

"Cleaning offices at night."

"How long do the children have to go in school? And what are they planning to do?"

"Both want to go to college. They have good grades."

"Stay with them until they can manage," Charlo said. "If they want to come, they can come too. But send Truce here. He can work with Cord. Cord wants to build a brick factory. Truce can help him. Cooking food; cooking bricks: same thing."

They had almost forgotten how Marie-Josette looked when she smiled.

When they took her to see Constantine, he remembered her, but not that she was married to Truce, though he was happy that she was married. Marie-Josette sat and held his hand for an hour, and smiled. He smiled back. There was nothing they needed to talk about.

The following week, the family took her back to the airport; Ellit drove with Cord. On the way back, Cord said, "I don't know what's wrong with Pa, but something's killing him."

"Your father's lost his Constantine; things haven't worked out so well for Marie-Josette; and now he's getting tired. What's left for him to do? You can take care of things now. At least Ma Lucette is managing. And things may work out for Marie-Josette and her husband."

"You think I should ask what's troubling him?" Cord asked.

"You do what you want. But I'd leave your father alone. Let him find his own road. You don't know what he's looking for, or when he finds it. . . whatever it is. . . Leave him alone. Don't do anything stupid."

The next time Charlo drove to the city, he withdrew twenty thousand five hundred dollars from his joint account with Lucette. He opened a new account with a credit union with the twenty thousand dollars. He visited his attorney and wrote out a new will that transferred management of his land to Cord. He directed how much should go to Cord and to Marie-Josette after his death; ensured that Lucette and Constantine be well-provided for.

On his return, he drove through Mandelie, and stopped to visit Uselle.

Rafe was chopping firewood. "Eh, Mr. Charlo, long time we haven't seen you. What you doing around here?"

"Come to see what's happening. Wanted to ask Uselle something. Where's she?"

"By the river, washing. Want me to call her?"

Charlo nodded and gave Rafe five dollars. "On your way back, stop at the rum shop. Buy a bottle of gin. We can use some coconut-water to chase it."

He sat on the steps of the shingled house rehearsing what he wanted to say. No subtlety with Uselle, or she would drag it out with questions and ridicule.

"Not more woman trouble?" Uselle said when she arrived.

Charlo shrugged. "There's another kind of trouble?"

"Ismene?" she asked.

"Let's talk," he said.

She put a bench in the shade of a soursop tree near the steps. Lit a cigarette. Listened.

He told her of his visit to Morne Rouge and what Ismene had told him. He had been wretched ever since.

"Why should an old man like me find himself in a situation like that? I have everything: a good family, enough money, and I feel like dog shit. Don't know what to do with myself. Lucette has her prayers; and now Marie-Josette may be coming back. Cord has Mounira; Constantine has his drawings. And me? I have things eating me up inside. What do I do with the rest of my life? If I died tomorrow, you all would forget me two days after the wake. And Lucette would be happy to spend even more time in church. You know, I don't remember the last time I touched her; it's as if she thinks doing that at her age is a sin. Don't even ask about her touching me. If it wasn't for a couple of old, once-a-year, girl friends, I don't know what I'd do."

"If I were you, I know what I would do," Uselle said, "but that's Uselle: a bad example for everybody. I'll tell you one thing, and believe me, nothing you do will make you happy. You have three choices, all bad: If you leave things just like that, you'll be miserable for the rest of you life because you will have to abandon what you want most of all. . . and you'll never know what you missed." She paused to put out her cigarette and light another. "If you leave your family, you will disgrace yourself and shame them – shame all of us – and you'll regret that for the rest of your life, too. Third thing, you can kill yourself; but you're too old for that foolishness. What're you going to do, my friend? And how d'you know you'll be happy at Morne Rouge with a younger woman? If you can't satisfy her and she throws you out, you think you can come back to your wife? Think about that."

"In two weeks," he said, "I'll be fifty-eight. Then I'll be too old to enjoy all the things I've worked so hard for. Every morning, animals. Every day, work, work, work. Then what? They throw your tired backside in a hole. There must be something better for people, Uselle."

"Heaven," she said.

"Don't make jokes."

"Then tell me what it is, friend," Uselle said. "Look at me. Stuck with the most useless man in Mandelie. And what can I do? Who else would touch me? You think any man would come and take me away like Vanius carried Maude away from the rum shop? I tell you, I would offer to carry him instead."

"I am trying to understand what I did for these things to happen to me. Especially to Cons. Cons never hurt anybody. Why him? Why not me? I'm already old and tired."

"I don't know, my friend. At least you still have the others – some people lose everything."

"But Constantine. Our Cons. . ."

"I know, Charlo. I know."

"Can you understand this? I am telling you things I cannot tell my own wife. What a thing."

Rafe returned. Uselle sent him up a coconut tree for nuts. They mixed the gin with coconut-water. Tried to think of other things, and pretended to listen to Rafe discuss his plans for imminent and substantial prosperity.

Twenty minutes later, Charlo rose, handed Uselle an envelope when Rafe was distracted by the entrance of a neighbour's goat into his yard. The envelope contained the five hundred dollars he had not deposited.

"You can always pray," Uselle said.

"I tried, but I didn't hear anything. . . just like when I prayed for Constantine."

Charlo looked into the loneliness that he was sentenced to without the intercession of death. He was aware of his arms, legs, head, and the automatic movements within his chest; but there was no sensation between his legs, as if his sexual organs had been reabsorbed into his body. At that moment he understood that he was condemned to irrelevance until Ismene chose to take him into herself.

He said goodbye to Uselle and Rafe. He hadn't touched his drink.

He drove home slowly, his mouth forming the words of his thoughts: Marriage. Three children. A wedding, then three christenings, three first communions, three confirmations. Birthdays, Christmases and La Rose and La Marguerite festivals. Work: pasture and water the cows, plant the crops, reap and sell – until he'd be too tired, and they'd wait for him to die because he'd be driving them crazy with his senile querulousness. Then they would say nice things at his funeral, cry, drink his family's coffee and rum, then hurry to bury his well-dressed and perfumed corpse before he made the house stink.

Of course, his soul would go to hell forever because he had slept – just once – with his friend's daughter – even if he didn't count Uselle and the other women who came to help occasionally on the estate. For that thing with Ismene – just once. It wasn't as if he had hurt her, or she had hurt him. How could he go and kneel down in front of a priest and say that he was sorry for the best thing he had ever felt in his life? Perhaps the priest would be more understanding if he told him exactly how it felt: how wet she was; how hard he was; how her breath felt in his neck; and how she moved against him; and the sounds she made. As if the priest wouldn't have done the same thing if he had been stuck in the shack down by the bay expecting to die.

Tell me Mr. Priest, how am I going to make myself believe that I didn't enjoy it, and I wouldn't do it if that girl came and lay on my belly again. By the way, we did it twice. Sorry? Sorry for what? I'd be lying if I said I was sorry.

He should have spoken to Ismene before she left their house, instead of behaving like a little boy ashamed after his first piece and avoiding the girl who had done him the favour. He should have told her that she was still welcome in his house; that she was his friend; that he would protect her for the rest of his life; that she didn't have to sleep with him again – just let him know now and then that she liked him. . . and perhaps if the opportunity came again. Who knows? Of course, if she married Cord, things would be different between them, but she would still be his friend.

Instead his silence had made her a prostitute. And everybody would tell him to leave her alone; that she was probably bad from birth. What about the rumours that came with her from Morne Rouge? Nothing true. It was he, Charlo Pardie, husband of the Saint Lucette, and father of three children, who had taken Ismene's virginity.

Someday, before he lost his courage, he would go and see Ismene and say, "I love you, Ismene." It would be easier to say that to her than to Lucette. Imagine saying, "I love you" to Lucette. She'd probably frown and go and do something in the kitchen, thinking that "I love you" was something people said in books, or when a boy wanted to get his finger where a girl did not want.

And why did he have to tell her? They were too married to say these things.

Then he reconstructed his favourite fantasy and let it remain longer than usual. He would turn in the darkness and Ismene would be next to him. His hands would creep over her thighs, and she would open his legs for him. Never saying anything – just opening for him. Every night for the rest of his life.

The hell; he was wrong. The hell; it was a sin. What about his son? It wasn't wrong what had happened to Constantine? It wasn't wrong for Ismene to lose her mother and father? For Bede to die with his face in the mud, without anybody to put a cup of water in his mouth? Look at Cosmos: never hurt anybody in his life – just blew an old saxophone – died in the worst way. For what? Making people dance? And it wasn't wrong for Stanislaus John to die in his wife's bed the same night he went back to her? For the man's heart to stop just when his life was getting better? Before Stanislaus could wake up on a nice Sunday morning, and

185

drink his wife's coffee, and say quietly to himself: "Yes, Constance, I love you."

They were going to tell him that none of these things was as wrong as his wanting to be happy in his old age?

But, your wife, Charlo? What about your wife? they would ask.

And he would answer: Tell me everybody, what is it that I haven't given my wife? What more can I do to make sure she goes to heaven?

He put his head out of the truck window and looked up at the sky. Shouted as loudly as he could: "So tell me, what did I do for these things to happen to me? Who do I go to for compensation. What did I do? What did I do?" Until his voice cracked and his throat burned. And his discontents turned into rage at his life, and everything around him and in his memory.

The wind rustled the leaves of the *gliricidia* trees at the roadside, and a tyrant flycatcher perched on a fence post answered: "Pee-pee-reet, pee-pee-reet."

So, Charlo Pardie plunged into what he decided was his only chance at happiness. Five days later, he awoke early on the morning of his birthday and left Mandelie.

Oh, our Charlo.

CHAPTER 14

The day after he arrived in Morne Rouge, Charlo Pardie took Bede L'Aube's machete and went to his old friend's vegetable plot. He dug out a handfuls of soil, crumbled the dirt in his hand, smelled it, and eyed it slowly as if looking for hidden jewels. He searched the remaining crops for disease, notched the shrubs that needed to be pruned, and marked out in his mind the areas to be ploughed and weeded. He worked until there was just enough light to see him home before dark. When he arrived, Ismene was sitting on the front step.

"I was thinking of sending somebody to look for you," she said.

"A lot of work to do on the land," Charlo said, glad that he was too exhausted to talk, just enough strength to rinse himself off, and to eat. But not too much – his hunger had come and gone.

The next night, Ismene was busy at the oven with Nico. Charlo watched from the sill of the back door. There was no moon, and the only light came from the naked bulb in the oven shed, and from the fireflies signalling their codes around the house. When the last of the loaves was loaded, Ismene came to sit with him. "If we go on like this, we'll see and talk to each other only on Sunday mornings."

"I know. . . but I don't want to sit around and get lazy and fat – with all that bread and cake of yours."

"Charlo . . . you're sorry you came?" Ismene asked.

"No. But I'm trying to understand where I got the courage to do what I did. No, I'm not sorry. You?"

"It was very bad for me before you came. It was very lonely. And I used to go to bed angry every night. I used to ask myself why all these things had to happen to me: I never saw my mother. Then my father died while I was still a child. Then. . . you and me. And look at what I got myself into in the city. . . a prostitute. Charlo, what did I do for these things to happen to me? Before you, I was a virgin. . . and people said all these things about me. You think these things happen only to poor people?"

"You're not poor, Ismene," Charlo said.

"I didn't have much schooling . . . and I come from the country. So, I'm poor."

"I don't know, Ismene. I asked myself the same thing when Cons got sick. I don't know. I just think that life is too busy for little people. . . like you and me. Leaves falling from a tree. Who cares about these little things?"

"I want to stop being afraid, Charlo."

"I'll look after you, Ismene."

Charlo Pardie lived at Morne Rouge with Ismene for three years. For the first year, their love making had been frequent and desperate, trying to recover their first intimacy. Then hard work on the farm and the oven made it occasional. By the end of the second year, it had become the duty of a man and woman living in the same house, eating at the same table, and sleeping on the same bed. Then it became expendable. Occasionally, one felt the bed shake as the other's memory recovered a fantasy for relief. On cold nights, they rested their backs against each other, rubbed each other's pains with liniment, or bathed a cut with tincture of iodine. There had been no arguments, but their silences had grown longer as if they had asked all the important questions, or knew all the answers.

At Christmas, the neighbours came to share the whiskey, rum, gin and ham. Charlo always bought the largest Canadian smoked shoulder he could find in the city. Insisted on soaking the salt away, boiling it, and sticking cloves into it himself. Doing all the preparations outside, so the smells could drift with the wind through the village as a reminder to visit. Ismene baked fruit cakes, so sodden with cherry brandy and rum that one slice could put a child into drunken sleep; sponge cakes encased in white almond-flavoured icing sparkling with silvered sugar spheres; and plaited loaves sweet with raisins and glazed with caramelized sugar.

Even then, they were too busy with the visitors to speak to each other.

When they were finally in bed, she pulled closer to him, took her clothes off, then his, and pulled him over on her. She said nothing. Their only sounds: a quickening of breaths, a gasp, a sigh. He rolled off, and went to pee. When he came back to bed, she was dressed and facing away from him. They went quickly to sleep, tired from baking, washing, carrying, repairing, planting, weeding, selling.

One Sunday, Charlo was sitting near the radio listening to the midday news, and Ismene was ironing. She paused and asked: "Charlo, you regret coming to live with me?"

"Why? What kind of question is that?"

"Well, we're coming just like old friends."

"What's wrong with that?"

"When you first came, you were on me every night; sometimes twice a night. Remember once I used to call you Superman?"

"I'm not getting younger, you know," Charlo said.

"It's not that. When we do it, it's almost as if it's because it's something we have to do. Sometimes it looks like you want to finish fast."

"Sometimes, you do the same thing."

"Sometimes... when I'm tired," she said, then, "That's how it was with your wife?"

He paused for a long while, then turned down the volume of the radio. "It was worse. It was as if Lucette thought doing it was nasty. You could see it in her face. As if I smelled bad. After a while, I couldn't touch her again. She didn't complain."

"But when you had just got married?" Ismene asked.

"From the first, she never liked doing it; just used to lie there without moving. I didn't care, I was getting what I wanted. But always the same way, the same thing. Always, 'Don't put you hand there, don't do that, I'm not doing that.'"

"And what you wanted in your old age was a good, hot screw, with a woman screaming and biting and scratching and cursing." She was grinning at him.

"See the kind of language you went and picked up in town."

"You like it in bed, though. You never complain when I'm screaming and cursing."

"That was before. Now everything is quiet."

"You're the one that's quiet, not me," she said.

189

"Maybe I'm getting too old for you. Sometimes, I don't know if I can finish."

"You're not old, Superman. Still better than a lot of men I know." She stopped. "Sorry."

"Don't worry, Ismene. What's done is done. If I couldn't take it, I wouldn't be here."

He turned back to the radio to hide the jealousy on his face and his resentment of being after all the city men with their big cars and new clothes. When he turned to her, he had forced himself to smile. "Want to go in the bedroom and do it now? If you want, I'm ready to handle you on the floor, here."

"Too early. Somebody could come and knock on the door. Boy, but tonight is going to be a bongo night."

She had provoked a brief moment of arousal, but it was waning. He wanted to return to listening to the news. Ismene was becoming comfortable – like a wife. He had got what he wanted, and what he got wasn't what he had left his wife for. What he had found was reality.

It was reality that looked back at him in the mirror: the white rings around the irises of his eyes, the sagging skin under his chin. And when he looked down: the thinning of his calves and the droop of his belly. He saw Nico lift sacks of flour with an ease that he could no longer fake. And look at Ismene: skin taut and shining like an eel. She looked even younger than she did on her return from the city. Lithe and strong; almost as strong as Nico. Still dancing over the ground when she walked. He no longer had the strength or the want to subdue her in bed. The hunger had been fed. He was tired. He wanted conversation. He wanted to sit and watch her for the rest of his life.

Saturday morning rush at the oven. Enough bread to bake for the weekend. Charlo busy slaughtering a sheep. Heat and sweat at the oven. Tired, tired, tired. After Nico had swept the wood ashes from the oven and was helping Ismene to put the loaves of dough in, he said suddenly: "Ismene, marry me. . . please."

Without looking at him, or hesitating – as if Nico had said the most banal thing – she answered, "I was wondering when you were going to ask me that stupid question."

"You're telling me, no?" he asked.

"I'm telling you that at this minute, while I'm here putting bread into the oven, while I'm hot and tired and covered with flour, while I have another man in my house, and in my bed, I don't want to think about marrying you. But don't go and throw yourself into a *dasheen* swamp again, please."

"So, I can ask you again?"

"At another time. . . when it makes more sense."

"What's wrong with now?" Nico asked.

"You know what I was – before I came back here? You know what I did in town?" Ismene asked.

"Yes, I know everything."

"And you still want to marry me?"

"After what happened to you, there's nothing you still want to know about men. You won't play games with me."

"Why don't you go and find a woman with a better reputation? What will you say when people say you married a prostitute?"

"You think I'm important enough for people to care about the woman I marry?"

"And when we have a fight, the first thing you'll do is throw it in my face."

Nico lifted his eyes over her head, looked past her and the village, past all the years since she had let him touch her. "How can I call my wife a whore?" he asked.

"Please don't say that word again," Ismene said.

"I'm asking you again to marry me. . . or live with me. . . or let me sleep on the floor of your house. We don't have any other place to go to, Ismene, you and me."

"Don't ask me again, Nico. When the time is ready. . . if the time comes, I'll ask you," she said.

"Ask me what, Ismene?"

"I will ask you to marry me, Nico."

Nico sat quickly on a bench to regain control of his breathing. Looking for the smallest sign of a joke in her eyes. She tilted her head to one side as if daring him to find it.

They went back to baking bread. That night at supper, Ismene smiled when she remembered Nico's proposal.

"What happened?" Charlo asked, sopping his fish broth with bread.

"You and your bread and sauce. I think you like that better than the fish itself."

"I think so," Charlo said, "especially when the bread is still hot."

She decided not to tell him about Nico. Whatever happened, happened. She would wait until Charlo made the decision for them.

Cord came on a Saturday evening after the baking was done, and the shop closed; when the night was still hesitant to move in, when the day sounds had grown quieter, but before the crickets and frogs were confident that the daylight had finally left.

Charlo went out to meet him. Ismene remained frozen to her chair, wanting to run out of the house, and to hide among the hibiscus bushes at the back.

"Cord," Charlo said.

"Pa," Cord answered.

"You're well? Mounira? Marie-Josette? Truce? The children . . . your mother?"

"Ma thinks she's not well. She says she only has days to live; the doctor says she has a hundred years. Arthritis in her hips and hands – the usual things. All of us will die before her."

They said nothing for a long time, looked past each other into the darkness. Two boys came to look at Cord's truck.

"Diesel," one said.

"Uh-uh, gasoline," said the other.

"Diesel," Cord said.

"I told you so, I told you so, I told you so."

"You just made a lucky guess . . . and the man was just fooling you, stupid."

The children and their shouts disappeared into the darkness.

Cord spoke first. "Pa, I think you should come home. It's time."

Charlo turned to look at the illuminated curtains of the house. Ismene had answered all the questions he had had about himself. If he stayed, there would be nothing more for them to say. If he went back to Mandelie, there would be the grandchildren to talk to, and the sea to look at, Ellit's violin to listen to, and Maude's

192

jokes to laugh at. And Lucette's teardrop face to look at – for the rest of his life. No more questions to ask, no more things inside him trying to claw their way out of his belly. When he saw Uselle again, he would tell her that he had discovered that it was not possible, or perhaps not necessary to search for happiness. Now and then it would come and sit on your doorstep for a short visit – an hour, or a day – then it had to go see another person.

"You want me to come for you tomorrow?" Cord asked.

"No. . . no. I'll drive." As he walked back to the house, he wished for a moment that his heart would fail, and he would die before anyone could come to help.

Ismene did not look down when he came inside. Her mouth twitched with the smallest smile. "You're going back to Mandelie?" she asked.

"Tomorrow," he answered.

"Yes, I know," she said, then turned away to look at a calendar from a grocery with a photograph of a laughing couple at the store's exit, deliriously happy with their purchases.

He waited for her to say something more; or to look at him. He leaned across the table and forced her to look into his eyes by taking her face in his hands. "I think you want me to go," he said.

She did not give him the comfort of answering, yes. She stared back into his eyes, searching for the precise answer that would please him. Found nothing. Her mouth tightened slightly. That was all.

"Another man?" he asked. "Nico? One of your city friends?" This time, she shook her head. "No. . . nobody."

"You don't want a man living with you?" Charlo asked.

"There's nothing about men I don't know," Ismene answered, "and there's nothing they can give me that I can't give myself."

"What about me?" he asked.

"You've already given me everything a man can give a woman. I don't need anything more. Tomorrow morning, I'll wash your clothes but I won't have time to iron them. . . they'll still be wet . . . especially the pants. I'll be able to do the shirts." After a pause she spoke again: "You're ready to eat?"

That night, he spoke to her for longer than he had ever done before: "Even when I was a child, I don't remember a time when

193

I wasn't working – carrying water, carrying wood for the fire, carrying vegetables; always carrying something for somebody. I started school when I was four years old. Then I had to carry a book and a slate before and after I carried more water and wood. Used to go to bed tired. More work on Saturday. On my knees on Sunday before I had to carry something or take care of the animals. I never asked myself why I was doing these things. I wasn't different. Everybody worked all the time. You know the crops and animals don't have vacations. My hands were so hard, I couldn't even feel a pencil in my hands.

"Same thing when I married and had children. Then on top of the work, I was wiping poop and blood – babies are worse than calves and pigs. No time to ask myself why I was working so hard. If something breaks, you fix it before you can ask yourself if you need it. Ten years, twenty years, thirty, forty, fifty years, sixty. And after that? You think you have a ticket to heaven? When can you find time to think of heaven? Your bones hurt, your feet burn, your eyes cannot see words on a page, you forget the names of your children. Every little cut grows into a sore – and that takes weeks to cure. You're afraid to go to the doctor because he will make you wait three hours to tell you that your body is worse than you feel. And you have to pay him for the bad news. And he wants you to come back so he can give you more bad news from the tests.

Your only consolation is that you'll have a son to take some of the load off your back one day. Then he gets married or goes away, or stays and gives you his family to carry as well.

"Sometimes, you want to hurry up and die because the only time you will get some rest is when you're lying in a coffin of expensive wood – that's nicer and better smelling than you. And for what, Ismene? Who has the courage to stop and think what his life and his hard work are for? Perhaps the old men fighting their pushcarts of shit-buckets at night are smarter than the rest of us; perhaps they are laughing at the truth that they are going to the same place as the governors and bishops, and when they get there, they will not have too much to explain.

"I remember Leotide... arrived one day at Mandelie with only a knife – that was long before you came. Some said he used to

194

work in the sugar-cane valley until he got tired of the same song from the cane leaves. He used to make flower pots from *fougere* stems. That wood is evil: it cuts, scratches, pricks, gets into your eyes, your clothes, bites your fingers; it's like working with broken bottles. Anyway, Leotide spent three weeks on his last pot; carved flowers and trees and animals all around it. Every day, Leotide would find some little cut to make, some little thing to fix. Refused to sell the pot. It was as if he had carved the meaning of his life in that piece of *fougere*.

One morning, we heard Leotide screaming. He was rushing through everybody's yard asking for his pot. Finally, Malvent, who could not understand that something was not his because he wanted it, told Leotide he had taken the pot and was going to keep it. He was willing to pay ten dollars for it – take it or leave it. Leotide walked into Malvent's kitchen and came out with a machete. One blow – whap – and Malvent's arm was jumping around on the ground. . . still holding the pot. Before anyone could move, Malvent's other arm was on the ground. Leotide wiped Malvent's machete clean with a banana leaf and put it back in the kitchen; picked up his pot and went to his house to wait for the police. He'll be in prison for the rest of his life. They let him keep the pot in his cell. . . What does he care? The flower pot is his life, he can look at it, make it a little better any time he wants. Leotide is a lucky man.

"Sometimes, a foolish old man tells himself that he can find happiness in the house of a young woman. So he walks through her door and discovers that she is too busy taking care of her house to slow down for him, and when she remembers to wait for him, he is too tired to dance with her. He starts to spend more time looking for the road that brought him to her house, but his pride has overgrown the road, and he cannot find it. What he wants to do, when she is busy washing clothes and cannot hear him leave the house, is to go and visit the cemetery to choose a nice spot where his grave will have a view of the sea, and hope people won't tie their animals too close where they can pee on his face. That is it."

He wiped the small flecks of foamed spit from the corners of his mouth with the back of his hand.

Ismene sighed loudly, as if she had forgotten to breathe while he was speaking. "That is it," she repeated, and rose to go into the bedroom.

That night, she undressed herself, then undressed him. He waited for her to pull him over her, but she climbed over him instead. As soon as he was inside her, she thrashed against him with such violence that he was convinced she was trying to hurt them both. She bit his lip until he tasted blood; dug her nails into his chest and into his shoulders until he felt the sudden break of the skin; hauled him deep into her, then flung him out again; howled and thrashed and screamed as if she were levelling all the hills and mountains and rocks of their lives; sweated, until she slid and flowed like melted tallow over him.

He was awaiting his death when she finally shuddered and collapsed over him, whimpering like a beaten child. He lay exhausted under her, unable to move, covered in sweat, his lungs burning, begging for air. Then he understood as clearly as if she were shouting it: You are too old for me, Charlo Pardie – you can never own this body lying with you.

When she rolled off him, the sheet and the pillows were on the floor, and the mattress lay diagonally across the bed-frame. There was a salty metallic taste of blood in his mouth: the taste of the beginning and the end of his life.

And what could one stranger say to another when the sun woke them up, when the only requisite was courtesy?

Wait until she takes the bloody sheets off the bed. Give assistance with finding a belt, wiping the dirt off a shoe, returning a long disappeared handkerchief. Take care not to brush against the stranger, or get in her way. Try not to appear too anxious to leave, but goodbye must be adequate like the first cut with a sharp blade; it must not rock back and forth, or drip like cane syrup, and it must not leave room for words of regret – or regrettable words.

When he left in the evening, he did not say goodbye. He bent to speak into her ear. "I am going, Ismene."

Her nod was almost imperceptible.

He drove slowly, to prepare the words he would say to Lucette; and to arrive at Mandelie when it would be too dark for anyone to recognize him. There were no vehicles in the yard of the house when he arrived. He suspected Cord had warned everyone to stay away. The front door was open, sending a yellow javelin of light into the earth. He entered, and heard Lucette in the kitchen. She was wiping invisible crumbs from the table when he looked in.

"I didn't know what time you'd be arriving," she said. "I'll have to warm the soup again. . . I made soup."

"I can wait. . . I'm not too hungry," he said.

They sat at opposite ends of the table. He had forgotten every phrase and construction of words he had rehearsed. After a minute, Lucette began to speak: told him about those who had died, who had married, who had moved away, and who had children. How the weather had been, and how well the brick factory and farm had done. How a cow had twins. That Constantine was visiting more often. She did not bake any longer – Marie-Josette did the baking, now. But perhaps it was time to get one of these electric machines to knead the dough.

Words poured over him like a warm shower, rinsing away everything he could remember since the morning he had walked away from his home, until the furniture and walls around him became a smoke, and the air and the kitchen and the smells of it blended with her voice. He wanted to implore her not to stop before the sun rose, not to abandon him in the tunnel of night to the company of his memories, but he could not find the strength to speak. Occasionally, he smelled her breath; it reminded him of fresh bread.

Lucette marched inexorably through the ranks of Charlo's weakening resistances, oblivious to his occasional attempts to offer a word – an explanation. She offered no compromise. No necessity for anger and reproof – or absolution.

When her voice tired, Lucette moved to the stove to boil the gratings of a raw chocolate stick that she had rolled herself from fermented cocoa beans; she added vanilla pods, nutmeg and cinnamon.

The enemy lay wasted. No need for the slightest displeasure or gloating. No offer of mercy to temper her victory.

Time for her final volley: "Wait until you see Cord's boy. . . Everybody says he looks just like Cons. I think he looks like you.

Yes, just like you. He'll be here bright and early in the morning to see you. That boy. Likes machines. . . like his uncle. Just like Cons. . ."

Even in the dimness, even through her tiredness, she could see his eyes shine with a light she had not seen since the birth of their first son. His face lost its tightness, and the corners of his lips turned up. He struggled to remember loud laughter, long laughter, wrenching, shaking laughter, generous, arms-stretched-out-to-embrace laughter. Good laughter.

She saw his teeth shine in the light of the lamp, and the grasp of his voice took hold of her and the table and the air of the room. Pulled everything in the room to him, caressed them, and shook them.

The words were more in his eyes than in his voice: Thank you, Lucette . . . thank you.

You hear?

EPILOGUE

EPILOGUE

The old man took almost a minute to get off the bus, holding tightly to the door for support. He wore an ancient black suit that was polished by long use, but which he had not touched in over ten years. The shoulders of the jacket were grey with dust.

He walked stiffly up the path to the blue house with white trim, pushing his shoulders back, trying to straighten his back against the pain that the bus trip had aggravated from an ache to a torment.

He paused to look at the oven: it had been well tended, quilted with new lime plaster. The alamanda vines were still vigorous, but the hibiscus hedge was replaced by plants with larger, brighter flowers – bright as painted flowers: yellow flowers with red centres, white flowers with purple centres. Such scandalous, confident flowers.

"I'm coming," the voice said when he knocked at the door.

Charlo Pardie found it difficult to breathe, and was sure she could hear his heart beating outside her door. He wanted desperately to sit down.

When she opened the door, he almost soiled himself. "It's me," he forced himself to say. "How are you?"

She held the door open only wide enough to show her right eye, with its iris orange like the rough pendants of gold from French Guiana worn on Sundays by old widows. Her mouth was still full but her lower lip had begun to droop, just enough for him to notice – because he knew her face so well. She opened the door wider, and the sight of the scar on her cheek made his belly hurt with a pang of pity and love. She looked at him, as if trying to recall a forgotten face, then opened the door wide.

"You have arrived," she said, and before he could answer, "Come inside."

"Nico's home?"

"No. Went to take bread to a shop."

He went slowly to a chair, glad to sit, glad for the chance to see long-lost things again.

"So how are you?" he asked again.

"I'm struggling with my misery," she answered.

He nodded for several seconds. "Life is hard."

They sat looking at each other for minutes without talking, listening to passing voices, beginning questions but not finishing them; not asking about children or grandchildren or companions. Anxiety about the silences grew. Say more words; ask more questions. The information was not important. Ah, something else remembered:

"Not enough rain. . . "

"Hard to get good help with the crops. . ."

"The criminal price of flour. . ."

"Such tiredness in the old muscles. . ."

"I rub the pain away with hot coconut oil. . ."

"Yes. I remember you did that. I'll try it. . ."

"So much traffic on the roads now. . ."

"Children so rude – no manners these days. . ."

"And the politicians? Ah! Don't even begin."

"You're right."

"Twenty years. . ."

"Yes, twenty years."

Then she asked quickly, before she lost the courage, "Why did you come?"

"I did not want to die. . . with you hating me."

"You're asking me to forgive you? Now? After all these years? For what? You did nothing bad to me. You should ask God to forgive you. . . and me. . . both of us."

"God doesn't have time for unimportant things. You think a river cares about the leaves that fall in it?"

"You haven't changed. . ." And she smiled.

He was happy that she smiled. The sad-happy smile that came before the loud, scandalous laugh. She was young again. But the smile died before it became laughter. And they sat for another hour looking out of the window without saying anything. Then he rose reluctantly. "Must go and wait for the bus now."

202

She nodded, "Carry yourself well."

"Stay well," he answered, and rose.

"Tell me, have you been content?" she asked, when he had opened the door.

He turned around. "Surprisingly . . . yes. Yes, I've told myself to be content."

"And you?" he asked.

"Yes. "I've been content, too," she answered.

He looked at the floor and his mouth twitched as if he'd had to stop himself saying something more. He looked up and nodded. It would have done no good to tell her the 'another thing': I wanted you to make me happy again. . . just like the first time – like a sixty-year old adolescent – even if just once in a while. What I needed was a bath of reality. Too late. Just leave things alone. Nothing more to worry about: whether the rains would come in time for planting the vegetable seeds; or whether the flour for her oven would arrive on the next bus.

But if he did not busy himself with these concerns – the concerns of other people – then he would have to listen to the voices of memory in his head reminding him that he had wronged his wife, and had betrayed his children and the girl left in his care. And for these things, he knew he would never stop paying.

She smiled again. "You're sure you won't have a little something to bite on?"

"Ah . . . no. Too much trouble. And it's time for me to go."

She came close and put her arms around his waist, rested her head against his shoulder. "Remember the day you took me from Morne Rouge, and I was sick, and you cut an orange and made me smell it?"

"Yes. . . yes, I remember well."

"That was the happiest day of my life. Even now."

"Thank you, Ti-Ismene," he said. For that moment she was once again the little girl he had comforted.

She stepped back. Looked at his face for the last time. The corners of her eyes crinkled, and she squeezed them shut to ease the burn.

He walked slowly to the road, although his shoulder and waist felt better – perhaps they had hurt from the tension.

Ismene L'Aube stood back from the window, watching him – waiting for the bus, too. She watched as the passengers made room for him. And the bus took Charlo Pardie away, like a river sweeping away another leaf.

Caribbean Modern Classics

Coming in April 2009, the first eight books from Peepal Tree's exciting project to reissue important titles from the 1920s to the 1970s.

Edgar Mittelholzer, *Corentyne Thunder*
ISBN 9781845231118, £8.99

First published in 1941, this vivid family saga was the first modern novel to focus on the lives of immigrants from India in the British Caribbean colonies. Set on the coast of British Guiana, which is evoked with a poetic sense of space, the story spans three generations and revolves around Ramgollal, an old Indian cow-minder on the Corentyne coast who has worked hard for many years to save money and build his herd of cows. He is proud of his children from two marriages, particularly the daughter of his first marriage, who is married to a well-to-do white planter. Their son Geoffry is light-skinned, ambitious, and poised to make a success of his life, and Ramgollal takes much satisfaction in his grandson's accomplishments. When Geoffry seduces and impregnates Kattree, his mother's half sister, however, Ramgollal's world begins to fall apart.

Jan Carew, *Black Midas*
ISBN: 9781845230951; £8.99

Vivid, bawdy, and tempestuous, this classic novel, first published in 1958, is a cautionary epic of greed and class conflict in colonial Guyana. It follows the dreams and delusions of Aron Smart, a youth orphaned early in life, who decides to follow in his father's footsteps as a diamond prospector. He is immensely successful and becomes the legendary 'Shark', in a wild, untamed world of drinkers, get-rich-quick and lose-it-quick prospectors and the whores who haunt the diamond fields. He is determined to use his new wealth to buy his way into the Anglicised middle class, but here he is out of his element in the snobbish colonial world of property and prestige, and, cheated of his fortune, he returns to the interior, to resume mining with a reckless madness, but the beginnings of insight. Though

Shark's Eldoradean quest ends in grief, on the way there is energy, outrageous sensuality and deeply felt engagement with the Guyanese landscape, particularly of the interior.

Jan Carew, *The Wild Coast*
ISBN: 9781845231101; £8.99

In this coming-of-age novel, a young boy learns firsthand about the contradictions that bedevil the people of Guyana, including the legacy of slavery, the clash of cultural traditions, and the sometimes wild, inhospitable terrain. Hector Bradshaw, a sickly child living in Georgetown, finds his life turned upside down when his father decides he would be better off living in the country and sends him away to the remote village of Tarlogie. Once settled there with his kind but old-fashioned guardian, Sister Smart, Hector struggles to made sense of his new community. As time goes by, he is given a dry colonial education, is puzzled by his guardian's fondness for moral precepts, fascinated by the harsh African vision of the old hunter Doorne—and seduced by the sexual education he receives from Elsa. Above all, the boy struggles realise his identity in a world where nature dominates the people's lives—and is so beautiful and so tremendously dangerous.

Wilson Harris, *Heartland*
ISBN: 9781845230968; £7.99

This visionary novel follows the inner journey of Zechariah Stevenson, the son of a wealthy Georgetown businessman, while he works as the watchman at a timber depot deep within the interior. Isolated in the forest and having endured the suspicion of a fraud scandal, the mysterious death of his father, and the disappearance of his mistress, Zechariah begins a journey of self-discovery as he deconstructs previously held certainties about life by losing himself in nature. Aided by ghostly revanants from Harris's earlier novels, Stevenson is forced to confront his sense of responsibility, his notion of masculinity and the very idea of possessing things and people. An immensely sensuous evocation of Guyanese flora and fauna and its potential impact on the imagination, this classic novel, first published in 1964, is a profound plea for an ecological vision of mankind's relationship to nature.

Andrew Salkey, *Escape to an Autumn Pavement*
ISBN:9781845230982; £8.99

A brave and pioneering treatment of sexual identity in Caribbean literature, this novel, first published in 1960, follows the fortunes of Johnnie Sobert, a Jamaican exile who works in London at a club that caters to black American servicemen. In flight from his dominant, possessive mother, he immerses himself in the bohemian Soho scene and adopts a wisecracking persona as a cover for his deep-seated insecurities. Adding to Johnnie's confusion is the fact that when he is not at work, he navigates a completely different life in Hampstead, where he lives in a bedsitter and carries on an unsatis-fying affair with his white landlady, Fiona. These two worlds provide a lively portrait of Britons reacting to the growing presence of blacks and Asians in their neighbourhoods, and Johnnie takes lessons from each place. By the time he finally decides to move in with his gay friend, Dick, he is much better equipped with self-awareness—but he has yet to make a decision about where his desires truly lie.

Denis Williams, *Other Leopards*
ISBN 9781845230678; £8.99

Lionel Froad is a Guyanese who works as a draftsman on an archeological survey in the mythical Jokhara in the horn of Africa. There he hopes to rediscover the self he calls 'Lobo', his alter ego from 'ancestral times', a 'pregnant load' he has carried with him 'waiting to be freed', which he thinks slumbers 'behind the culti-vated mask' of Lionel. But Jokhara brings no magical re-immersion for 'Lionel looking for Lobo'. There are his complex relationships with other members of the team, his love-hate relationship with Hughie, his white boss, and with Catherine, a Welsh girl on the team to whom Lionel finds himself passionately attracted, despite the disapproving inner voice of Lobo and Hughie's paternalistic inter-ference.

With wit and ruthless honesty in its exploration of the themes of identity and belonging, *Other Leopards* is one of the most important Caribbean novels of the past sixty years.

Denis Williams, *The Third Temptation*
ISBN 9781845231163, £7.99

A young man is killed in a traffic accident at a busy intersection of a Welsh seaside resort. Through shifting time sequences and multiple points of view, this brief but intensely detailed novel follows a small group of onlookers whose perceptions, thoughts, and memories— both pertinent and unconnected—are triggered by the tragic scene. The witnessed trauma prompts in one of the characters a deep reflection on the nature of power—the third temptation of Christ. Utilizing the gaudy vulgarity of the resort at the height of the season as a backdrop, this story underscores the power of chance, the ever present threat of misfortune, and the temptations inherent in the exercise of power. This novel, first published in 1968, is a boldly experimental work, a rare tendency in earlier Caribbean fiction.

Neville Dawes, *The Last Enchantment*
ISBN: 9781845231170, £9.99

Newly available after 40 years, this novel is a partly autobiographical love affair with the Jamaican language and landscape. It gives a penetrating look at the politics of the 1950s and 1960s and the search for self in a world divided by race and class. Ramsay Tull is witness to the black racial discontents and the desire for national independence that are threatening the old colonial order; but when a chance comes to study at Oxford University, he becomes immersed in European literary culture and Marxism. On his return to Jamaica, Ramsay becomes actively involved in radical nationalist politics and begins his second journey, away from his middle class origins and back to a true appreciation of the Jamaican people.

Visit our website at peepaltreepress.com for further information about the Caribbean Modern Classics series (Roger Mais, Vic Reid, Garth St Omer and many more to come) and over two hundred other titles.